"Maddy is a s[...]
Howl will probably leave you shocked . . . and dying for the next."   —*Fresh Fiction*

"A roller coaster of emotions . . . An incredible read from start to finish that only further cemented my love for this series, and I highly recommend it."   —*A Book Obsession*

"This series reminds me of the Harry Dresden series by Jim Butcher or Rachel in the Hollows series by Kim Harrison . . . It has enough action, suspense and sarcasm to keep my attention. I look forward to seeing where Christina Henry takes us next."   —*Dark Faerie Tales*

"Action packed. You are sucked in from page one and set on a roller-coaster ride of action till the end."
          —*Paranormal Haven*

BLACK NIGHT

"A riveting adventure of a novel . . . *Black Night* has within its pages the most utterly believable and wonderful depiction I've ever seen of a character forced to face her darkest fears."   —*Errant Dreams Reviews*

"Madeline Black is back and super badass in her second installment . . . If you're looking for a brilliant urban fantasy with page-turning action, witty dialogue and fun characters—this is your book."   —*Rex Robot Reviews*

continued . . .

"The style of this book is just like the first book in the series—playful and light, yet also adventurous and dark . . . The bottom line is that if you enjoy adventure stories, you will enjoy this book, especially if you're a nonstop action junky."
—*SFRevu*

BLACK WINGS

"A fun, fast ride through the gritty streets of Chicago, *Black Wings* has it all: a gutsy heroine just coming into her power, badass bad guys, a sexy supernatural love interest and a scrappy gargoyle sidekick. Highly recommended."
—Nancy Holzner, author of *Darklands*

"An entertaining urban fantasy starring an intriguing heroine . . . The soul-eater-serial-killer mystery adds to an engaging Chicago joyride as courageous Madeline fears this unknown adversary but goes after the lethal beast."
—*Midwest Book Review*

"Fast action, plenty of demons and a hint of mystery surrounding the afterlife make for an entertaining urban fantasy populated by an assortment of interesting characters."
—*Monsters and Critics*

"Henry shows that she is up to the challenge of debuting in a crowded genre. The extensive background of her imaginative world is well integrated with the action-packed plot, and the satisfying conclusion leaves the reader primed for the next installment."
—*Publishers Weekly*

Ace Books by Christina Henry

BLACK WINGS
BLACK NIGHT
BLACK HOWL
BLACK LAMENT
BLACK CITY

BLACK CITY

CHRISTINA HENRY

ACE BOOKS, NEW YORK

THE BERKLEY PUBLISHING GROUP
Published by the Penguin Group
Penguin Group (USA) Inc.
375 Hudson Street, New York, New York 10014, USA

Penguin Group (Canada), 90 Eglinton Avenue East, Suite 700, Toronto, Ontario M4P 2Y3, Canada
(a division of Pearson Penguin Canada Inc.) • Penguin Books Ltd., 80 Strand, London WC2R 0RL,
England • Penguin Ireland, 25 St. Stephen's Green, Dublin 2, Ireland (a division of Penguin
Books Ltd.) • Penguin Group (Australia), 707 Collins Street, Melbourne, Victoria 3008, Australia
(a division of Pearson Australia Group Pty. Ltd.) • Penguin Books India Pvt. Ltd., 11 Community
Centre, Panchsheel Park, New Delhi—110 017, India • Penguin Group (NZ), 67 Apollo Drive,
Rosedale, Auckland 0632, New Zealand (a division of Pearson New Zealand Ltd.) • Penguin Books
(South Africa), Rosebank Office Park, 181 Jan Smuts Avenue, Parktown North 2193, South Africa •
Penguin China, B7 Jiaming Center, 27 East Third Ring Road North, Chaoyang District,
Beijing 100020, China

Penguin Books Ltd., Registered Offices: 80 Strand, London WC2R 0RL, England

This is a work of fiction. Names, characters, places, and incidents either are the product of the author's
imagination or are used fictitiously, and any resemblance to actual persons, living or dead, business
establishments, events, or locales is entirely coincidental. The publisher does not have any control over
and does not assume any responsibility for author or third-party websites or their content.

BLACK CITY

An Ace Book / published by arrangement with the author

PUBLISHING HISTORY
Ace mass-market edition / March 2013

Copyright © 2013 by Tina Raffaele.
Cover art by Kris Keller.

ISBN: 978-0-425-25658-9

ACE
Ace Books are published by The Berkley Publishing Group,
a division of Penguin Group (USA) Inc.,
375 Hudson Street, New York, New York 10014.
ACE and the "A" design are trademarks of Penguin Group (USA) Inc.

PRINTED IN THE UNITED STATES OF AMERICA

10 9 8 7 6 5 4 3 2 1

ALWAYS LEARNING   **PEARSON**

For my sisters three
Marnie, Kimberly and Sherri
With love

ACKNOWLEDGMENTS

As always, tremendous thanks to my editor, Danielle Stockley, who makes my job easier by being amazing at hers.

Many, many thanks to Rosanne Romanello and Brady McReynolds.

Special thanks to Krista McNamara and Chloe Neill for general awesomeness.

A big shout-out to the staff at Einstein Bros. on Southport, especially Cynthia and BJ.

Lots of love to my family, especially Mom and Dad and Chris and Henry.

1

JUDE, SAMIEL AND NATHANIEL STOOD IN FRONT OF the TV, their eyes grave. They cleared a space for me so I could see.

At first I wasn't sure what I was looking at. A reporter's voice came intermittently over the images, but the camera kept jiggling everywhere, and it was hard to see exactly what was going on. People were screaming and running, but I couldn't see what they were screaming at and running from.

Then the camera finally stabilized, and I realized what I was looking at. It was live footage from Daley Plaza, and the camera was shooting the action just in front of the Picasso statue.

There were vampires everywhere, and the sun blazed down on the plaza.

"Gods above and below," I whispered. "Azazel's formula worked."

The angle of the camera shifted and tipped to one side. Blood splattered over the lens. The reporter stopped speaking. The animal growls of vampires and the sickening squelch of flesh being eaten broadcast far too clearly.

"We have to do something," I said.

"You can't fly anymore," Beezle pointed out. "No wings. And you're wearing your pajamas."

A woman's high-pitched wail broke through the sound of feasting.

"I can carry you," Nathaniel said, and I ran for my things.

Jude had already changed into a wolf, discarded his clothes, ran to the door.

I grabbed my sword, pulled my boots over my pajama pants, yanked on my coat and followed Jude. Nathaniel was right behind me, Samiel close on his heels.

Beezle launched from the mantel to my shoulder as I opened the front door. Jude darted down the stairs in front of me.

"Why can't you stay home where I know you'll be safe?" I said to Beezle as he crawled inside my coat.

"Like I would miss this," he said, his voice muffled. "And besides, somebody needs to make sure you don't go dark side."

I ignored his jibe. I'd made some questionable choices lately, to be sure, but when I looked back over them I wasn't sure I could have made different ones. And there were far more important things to worry about right now than my shades of gray.

Jude burst through each of the front doors and bounded onto the porch, my apartment door slamming against the wall as he went through with a burst of speed.

By the time Nathaniel, Samiel and I had clattered down the front steps, Jude was already gone.

Nathaniel scooped me up, carrying me like a child, and opened his wings. Samiel lifted off a moment later. As we rose above the treetops I realized that neither of them was under a cloak of magic.

"That was a little conspicuous," I said. "I wonder what the neighbors will make of two angels taking off from my front lawn."

"Given all the weird shit that occurs in the nexus in and around our house, they probably won't be surprised in the least," Beezle said. "Besides, vampires are eating up all the nice little commuters in the middle of the day. I don't think the regular rules are going to apply from now on."

As we sped downtown as fast as Nathaniel and Samiel could fly, I knew Beezle was right. In a single instant everything had changed. The world that had been hidden from normal people, a world of creatures they'd seen only in their dreams and nightmares, had been split wide-open. Nothing would ever be the same again.

The news report had come from Daley Plaza, the distinctive figure of the Picasso statue looming in the background of the shot. Nathaniel angled a little west from the lake and headed toward the plaza.

As we got closer I could see traffic snarled on the surrounding streets, buses and taxis at a standstill, drivers abandoning their vehicles to run. People crammed on the stairwell to the El, pushing, shoving, stepping on anyone who tripped and fell. The vampires were monsters to be feared, but people didn't exactly show the best face of humanity at times like this.

Then we were over the plaza, and it was worse, far worse, than I'd imagined.

I'd thought that Azazel's potion had to be limited, that there couldn't possibly be that many vamps colluding with him. And even if there were, I'd assumed his death would have cut off the production of the serum that allowed the vamps to walk in sunlight without turning to flames.

After all, Jude, Nathaniel and I had fought several perfectly ordinary vampires at Azazel's mansion only a couple of weeks before.

But there were hundreds, maybe thousands, of vampires on the streets below. They poured from the blue line subway station, emerged from the sewers through manhole covers, an endless seething mass of bloodthirsty insects falling upon any human they could find.

I've never liked vampires, even when they've kept a low profile. I'd always suspected their veneer of civility was just that, and I've never bought into the notion that it's romantic to have your blood drained by a vamp.

This was one occasion when I would have been happy to be proven wrong. It was pretty clear from the carnage going on below us that vampires didn't entertain any romantic notions about humans. To them, we were nothing more than walking, talking bags of meat.

Beezle poked his head out of the lapel of my coat and looked down. "Gods above and below. Where do you even start?" For once there was no sarcasm in his voice.

"We just have to do what we can," I said, and tried to sound confident. "Let's go, Nathaniel."

He brought us down to the platform that the Picasso statue rested upon, which gave us a slightly elevated view of the plaza. On any given day you can see a few brave kids climbing the tilted platform and sliding, whooping and hollering, to the ground below.

Today it was covered with the spattered blood of dozens of victims.

I leapt from the top, swinging my sword to slice the

head from the nearest vampire I could find. When that one was dust, I moved to the next one. I was vaguely aware of Nathaniel and Samiel fighting around me, and of Jude joining the fray, snarling and barking as he tore the vamps' throats out.

I don't know how long we fought. I punched, kicked, hacked, slashed and watched heads roll away, disintegrating into dust as they went. And I kept doing it, over and over and over again.

Still the vampires came.

Still more of them poured from the ground like cicadas emerging from hibernation. And nobody showed up to help us.

The Agency was a short walk from where we fought the tide. I imagined large numbers of Agents were engaged with trying to keep up with the souls pouring from the bodies of the dead, but why not send the rest of the Agents to fight the vampires? The Agency's willfully blind attitude about not getting involved in the actions of other supernatural courts surely couldn't extend to ignoring a massacre under their noses.

Or maybe it could, since the cavalry never arrived.

After several hours of killing vampires, I slipped.

I was tired, hungry and pregnant, and I wasn't completely on my game after a week spent fighting battle after battle.

My boot heel skidded in a pool of blood, and so I was just a little shy of complete decapitation on the vamp I battled. I landed backward, banged the back of my head against the sidewalk, and saw stars for a moment.

My field of vision was filled with the slavering jaws of the vampire I hadn't quite killed, ready to eat my face off. There was no time to think, no time to perform a spell.

Then the vampire was gone, and Nathaniel picked me up from the ground and carried me away.

"What are you doing?" I screamed. "We can't leave. We can't leave those people down there alone."

"We cannot do any more," Nathaniel said grimly. "There are four of us, and thousands of them."

"We can't leave," I said again. I'd never run from a fight in my life.

Nathaniel landed on a nearby roof. Samiel was beside us holding Jude, still in wolf form, in his arms.

"Look," Nathaniel said angrily, holding me by the shoulders so I could see what was below. "The city is overrun. We can't do anything else."

I stared down. It was so much worse from up here, where you could see the pouring mass of vampires undulating through the city streets, into the buildings and buses, leaving empty husks of humanity behind them.

It seemed that the more people who were killed, the more ferocious the vamps became.

"It's a feeding frenzy," I said, sickened. "How can we leave them down there, without anyone to defend them?"

"The police are fighting back," Beezle said, his head popping out of my jacket.

From our vantage point on the roof we could see the teams moving in, hastily mounting barricades. The percussion of gunfire was added to the chorus of screams that echoed in the canyons of the city. My city, overrun by vampires.

"No," I said angrily. "We have to go back. We have to help."

Nathaniel's hands rested on my shoulders and he spun me around to face him. His face was twisted in anger and, to my surprise, fear.

"Just what is it that you think you can do?" he said, giving me a little shake. "Do you not value your life at all?"

I saw Samiel move out of the corner of my eye, obviously intending to defend me from Nathaniel, but I slapped my ex-fiancé's hands away before Samiel could.

"I value my life as much as you do yours," I said. "But I don't value it more than any of them do." I pointed toward the terrified mass of humanity below.

"So you would kill yourself to save one of them?" Nathaniel said.

"I don't think I'm superior to them the way you do," I said coldly.

Nathaniel threw his hands in the air. "Gods above and below, you are the most thickheaded woman I have ever met. Do you really think this is about superiority? Think about your baby. Think about the people who love you. Don't throw yourself away on the impossible."

I stared at him, startled to realize that the fear in his eyes had been for me. He correctly interpreted the look on my face and sighed. "I do not know why you cannot credit me with human emotions, even after all we have been through."

I didn't have anything to say to that. There would always be a part of me—although that part was shrinking almost daily—that would be suspicious of Nathaniel, that didn't trust his veracity.

Samiel tapped me on the shoulder. *This really isn't the time for a heart-to-heart.*

"Yeah," Beezle agreed. "We need to get out of here before the police start firing on us just because we look weird."

"The gargoyle is right," Nathaniel said, lifting me up again. I felt a magical veil settle over us, hiding our appearance from human eyes. "The humans are in a state of panic, unable to distinguish friend from foe."

"That, and Maddy's covered in blood and carrying a sword," Beezle added.

As we flew away I turned my head from the carnage below. I knew Nathaniel was right. I knew that continuing a battle we couldn't win was foolish and pointless. We'd barely made a dent in the endless stream of vampires. But I'd never run away before, and leaving felt less like good sense than defeat.

We continued north toward my house. Sturdier barricades were being assembled by the police farther away from the epicenter of the attack. It looked like the authorities were trying to contain the vampires to the Loop.

The sad truth was the density of commuters and residents downtown would probably keep the vampires busy there for a while. There was no need for the vamps to leave that area as long as there was food, and there was plenty of food to be found.

I could feel the pent-up tension in Nathaniel's arms as he held me, and knew that he longed to have another go at me over my hardheadedness. He held back likely due to the presence of an audience. Of course, if he was waiting for an opportunity to get me alone, he would be waiting forever. There was always someone hanging around my house these days, and Beezle had completely lost all sense of personal boundaries.

We landed on the front lawn, Samiel and Jude beside us. In silent concordance we all trooped back upstairs to my apartment. The television was still on. Jude returned to human form, pulling on his discarded clothing.

I stopped in front of the TV, staring. Nathaniel took my

coat from my shoulders. Beezle flew out of the pocket and went straight to his brooding spot on the mantel.

A sober-voiced anchor spoke over footage shot from a helicopter. I guess they weren't stupid enough to send another cameraman into Daley Plaza.

"We are trying to identify the nature of this threat; however, as unbelievable as it may seem, eyewitness reports have indicated that these creatures are attacking anything in sight, biting and, it seems, feeding on the victims. They are like . . . like some kind of vampires. All we know for certain is that there are hundreds of them, as you can see from our aerial footage of the Loop. The police are attempting to halt the creatures' progress as best they can. A spokesperson for the mayor's office has said that the mayor has contacted the National Guard and that he will be making a statement to the press in approximately thirty minutes. The mayor and his staff have been airlifted out of the danger zone . . ."

"What about everyone else?" I murmured. I'd been there, fighting all morning, and it looked so much worse on TV. The news camera was far enough away that detail was blessedly lost, but the black horde seemed to swell even as I watched, a pulsing, cancerous growth engulfing the heart of Chicago.

I saw dark spots before my eyes. The picture on the screen went blank. A few moments later I opened my eyes to see four anxious faces above me.

"What happened?" I said. Somehow I'd ended up prone on the couch.

"You fainted," Beezle said.

"I did not," I said. I don't know why, but I was embarrassed.

"You did," Beezle said.

"And no wonder, since you have been exerting yourself and have not eaten since yesterday," Nathaniel said.

"You look thinner," Jude added.

"I can't have lost weight since yesterday just because I didn't eat breakfast," I scoffed.

"Who knows what this baby is doing to you?" Beezle said ominously.

I really didn't enjoy it when Beezle implied that Gabriel's baby was trying to kill me from the inside out, so I waved the lot of them away without replying and sat up. Mistake. Everything went wobbly again.

"For the sake of the Morningstar, just rest for a moment," Nathaniel said, pushing me back down.

"Quit manhandling her," Jude growled.

"I will do what I must to get her to take care of herself," Nathaniel snapped.

"You didn't show such a touching concern for Maddy's health when you were trying to kill her in Azazel's mansion during the rebellion," Jude said.

Nathaniel stood to face Jude, his hands curled into fists. "I do not have to explain myself to you, wolf."

"Not this again," I muttered, then louder: "Enough, both of you. I don't need you talking about me like I'm not here. If you want to be helpful, you'll go and get me something to eat."

"I wouldn't mind a little something myself," Beezle said.

"You don't need it," everyone in the room replied, including Samiel, who signed the words.

"If you're going to be that way about it," Beezle grumped.

"We are," I said.

Samiel went into the kitchen. Nathaniel and Jude continued bristling at each other.

"Why is my life filled with men?" I said to no one in particular.

"Beats me," Beezle said. "It's not your charming personality—that's for sure."

I gave him a sour look.

"I don't even have to try," Beezle said. "The punch line was right there."

"Stand down," I said to Nathaniel and Jude.

They both turned to look at me, and it was only then that it really registered that they were both covered in blood. And so was I. I was abruptly aware of the gore drying on my face, of my red-stained hands. It was a sad commentary on my life that I was so frequently covered in blood that I wouldn't notice its presence even when I was soaked in it.

Samiel reentered the living room carrying a sandwich. The thought of eating it while covered in the ichor of dozens of vampires made my stomach turn.

"Help me up," I said.

Nathaniel rushed to help me but I gave him a pointed look. "I asked for Samiel."

My brother-in-law put the sandwich on the coffee table as Nathaniel backed away with a frozen look. I knew there was a reckoning coming with Nathaniel. Sooner or later I'd have to decide whether he was an ally or an enemy. I couldn't keep him floating in the netherworld between forever.

Don't touch that sandwich, Samiel signed to Beezle.

"I know how to get my own food," Beezle said loftily.

Don't touch that sandwich, Samiel repeated.

He came around to take my arm as I stood. Now that the adrenaline of the fight had worn off, my legs had turned to mush.

"Bathroom," I said, and Samiel helped me limp along while the other three silently watched us go.

Samiel helped me as far as the tub, then looked at me expectantly, his face red.

"Yes, you do need to help me get my clothes off," I said.

"I'm sorry. Chloe would be better for something like this."

Samiel's face went tight at the mention of Chloe. *The Agents we saved from Azazel were taken to Northwestern. I overheard Sokolov's goons talking about it.*

Sokolov. The lapdog of the Agency administration who seemed to have devoted his life to making mine miserable. Just thinking about him made my fists curl.

I knew what Samiel was worried about. Northwestern Memorial Hospital was downtown, just off Michigan Avenue. But it was several blocks north and west of Daley Plaza.

"Don't worry," I said, and I was glad Samiel could only read lips. I didn't sound very convincing. "The barriers were being set up south of the river. The hospital is well north of there."

You know and I know that if the vamps get inside the hospital, it will be a bloodbath, Samiel signed.

"Chloe's tough," I said.

She's also recovering from major trauma.

"All right. All right. We'll go get her," I said. "Just let me clean up first."

Thank you, Samiel signed, his face relieved.

We managed to get me through the bathing process with a minimum of embarrassment on both sides, and Samiel helped me dress. As I pulled a tank top over my head he touched the long scabs on my back where my wings used to be.

Do you miss them? he signed.

I put a sweater over the tank top and nodded. "I never thought about how much I relied on them before they were gone."

I wonder if you'll ever get them back.

"I don't think so," I said. "They were part of my Agent's powers, and I'm never going back to the Agency."

But you're Lucifer's granddaughter.

"Much diluted by thousands of intervening generations."

Samiel shrugged. *You've had other latent powers appear.*

"I suppose," I said doubtfully, looking at the missing two fingers of my left hand. Lucifer had assured me some time ago that the digits would grow back, and they never had. So I wasn't putting a lot of stock in the idea that I might regrow my wings.

Samiel left the room for a few minutes. When he returned I'd managed to get my socks on. He carried a plate with a sandwich.

"That doesn't look like the same sandwich," I observed.

Can you guess what happened to the other one? Samiel signed. *Now, eat up. I swear you are looking thinner by the minute.*

I'd thought they were all exaggerating about my appearance, but I'd noticed my jeans were looser than they were yesterday. This was probably a worrisome development, but given all the other worrisome developments in my life, losing a little weight ranked low on the priority list.

I stuffed the sandwich in my mouth. I didn't realize just how ravenous I was until I took the first bite.

"There's one thing I want to do before we go to the hospital," I said after chewing the last bit of sandwich. "Call J.B."

He won't be able to help us, Samiel signed. *He's on thin ice with the Agency as it is.*

I had a flash of J.B. spread-eagled on a table, tortured by Sokolov and his goons. "Yeah, you could say that. But he'll be able to confirm the location of the hospitalized Agents for us."

I'll get your phone, Samiel said, and went out again.

I could hear raised voices coming from the living room, but I didn't have the energy or inclination to intervene in yet another argument. Jude and Nathaniel probably needed to have it out once and for all anyway. I just hoped they didn't destroy the living room in the process. My house had been trashed enough in the last month or so.

Samiel returned and handed me the phone. I saw that there were four missed calls, all from J.B.

I dialed his number and waited for him to pick up. There was barely half a ring before he barked into the receiver. "What's the point of having a phone if you never pick it up?"

"So sorry. I was busy battling the vampire menace taking over the city," I said dryly.

"I know where you were," J.B. said. "I saw you, and so did everyone else in Chicago with a television set. You and Jude and Nathaniel and Samiel."

"We were on the news," I said, dread filling me. This was not good.

"Goddamn right you were on the news. And you'd better be more careful from now on. Half the reporters have decided you've been sent from heaven to save humanity from the plague of vampires, and the other half have declared you should be shot in the street with all the other monsters," J.B. said. "I've got to go. It's total chaos here. The whole Agency is in lockdown mode."

"Wait," I said. "Can you tell me if Chloe and the other Agents we saved from Azazel are still at Northwestern?"

"Yeah, the Agency hasn't had time to move them with everything else going on. We can't even come close to keeping up with the new souls. The board is diverting Agents from other regions to help. Wait—why do you want to know about Chloe?" J.B. asked warily.

"Samiel wants her with us," I said shortly. "Why doesn't the Agency put together an army to fight the vamps instead of struggling to clean up the mess?"

"You know the answer to that," J.B. said.

"If the Agency doesn't get off their ass and do something, there won't be any souls left to collect in this city."

"You don't have to tell me that," he said. "But I'm not exactly a trustworthy figure around here anymore. No one in upper management is going to listen to me."

"You spend too much time with me."

"That's the way I like it," he said. "I'll call you later. My mother is outside the window doing her best banshee impression."

"I thought you had devised some spell to keep Amarantha away from you," I said.

J.B.'s mother had been a faerie queen of her own court before I'd killed her. Unlike most creatures, she had chosen not the Door but an existence as a ghost. I think she did it just to piss off me and J.B.

"The spell will keep her out of the Agency and out of my home, but it won't stop her from hanging around outside and driving me crazy. Try not to burn down the hospital."

He hung up before I could respond.

"Why does everyone think I'm going to destroy a building as soon as I walk into it?" I asked Samiel.

Your track record speaks for itself.

"But those were accidents," I protested.

Most people don't have those kinds of accidents more than once.

"Most people don't have supernatural enemies trying to kill them every second of the day, either," I said, standing up cautiously.

The shower and the food had gone a long way toward making me feel human. I felt better equipped to fight another horde of vampires, although with any luck I wouldn't have to.

The barricades were north of the bridges that crossed the Chicago River. I didn't know how long city authorities would be able to contain the vamps in that area once the monsters ran through their food supply.

Of course, they would likely be evacuating most of the Loop and Michigan Avenue soon. And if they moved the patients at the hospital, we would have a lot of trouble finding Chloe.

"She's probably safer away from mc, anyway," I muttered. The sad fact of my life was that the low mortality rate of my companions was more luck than anything else. Since Gabriel had died I'd been braced for impact, waiting for the next, inevitable loss.

What was that? Samiel signed. *You have to look at me when you're talking or else I can't read your lips.*

"Nothing," I said. "Let's go get Chloe."

2

NATHANIEL HAD PREDICTABLY ARGUED AGAINST RE-
moving Chloe from the hospital.

"She's safe enough there, and it's an unnecessary risk
for you," he'd said.

But Jude had come down firmly on my side, and that
meant Nathaniel was outnumbered. A couple of weeks earlier all of the werewolf cubs of Jude's pack had been kidnapped and their memories stolen as part of a plot of
Azazel's. Even though Jude thought Chloe was weird and
unpredictable, he'd felt indebted to her since she'd found a
way to restore the werewolf cubs' memories.

"You can stay here if you prefer," Jude sneered, the
implications of Nathaniel's cowardice clear.

Nathaniel's jaw tightened. "As if I would leave Madeline's safety to you."

I could have pointed out that "Madeline's safety" was

not reliant on either of them, as I had saved my own self plenty of times, but I did not want to get embroiled in another of the stupid arguments that went around our group with annoying regularity. So I just said, "Let's go," and we did.

Nathaniel carried me, and Samiel carried Jude in wolf form. Beezle, surprisingly, had opted to stay home.

"I need a nap," he said.

I suspected that what he really wanted was time to brood over what he thought were negative changes in my personality, so I let him stay. I didn't want to argue with Beezle about every decision I made.

Nathaniel hid all of us under a veil. I knew how to do this, but it was difficult for me to hold such a delicate spell over four people for a prolonged period of time. And Nathaniel had pointed out that secrecy was vital now that we'd been exposed on television.

As we flew above the city I could see the streets below were jammed with fleeing citizens. People tossed hastily packed suitcases into cars, collected their offspring from schools and hightailed it out of town. It looked like a scene from an end-of-the-world movie.

Lake Shore Drive was bumper to bumper, cars and buses moving only by centimeters. Several hundred people who either lacked personal transportation or decided to abandon their cars streamed in crowds up the bike path that ran along the lakefront. Everyone was heading north. No one wanted to go through the Loop, even if you could stay outside the barricaded edges.

The mass panic, the sheer numbers of vampires . . . The problem seemed overwhelming for one ex-Agent of death and her merry band of misfits.

"Where the hell is Lucifer?" I asked. "He could do something about this."

"He could," Nathaniel agreed. "If it suited him to do so."

"If he could find some personal advantage, you mean," I said bitterly. "He won't intervene unless the deck is stacked in his favor."

"You must stop attributing Lucifer with humanity," Nathaniel said. "He is not human. He is not even a mere angel. He is more powerful than any of us can comprehend, and the problems of humans are small things to him."

"Yeah, that's what everyone keeps saying. But he's scared of Puck," I said thoughtfully.

"The faerie who assisted you in Titania and Oberon's court? The one who came into the house through the jewel?" Nathaniel asked, surprise evident in his voice.

"He's no faerie. I don't know what he is, but he definitely isn't a faerie."

"Whatever he is, I don't think you should embroil yourself any further into matters of the faerie court."

"I haven't 'embroiled' myself in anything," I said. "The faeries are the ones who came looking for me."

Nathaniel acknowledged this with a nod. "Still, curiosity about Puck's origins is probably not wise."

"I know what happened to the cat," I said.

"What cat?" Nathaniel asked.

"You know, curiosity killed the . . . Never mind. Anyway, I've got a feeling Puck's not going to leave me alone."

Nathaniel shook his head. "What is it about you, Madeline? I have never met another creature with such a knack for attracting trouble."

"When I figure it out, I'll let you know," I said. "I'm really starting to see the attraction of a quiet life."

"You will never have a quiet life," Nathaniel said. "Even if all your other troubles magically disappeared, you would still be Lucifer's granddaughter. You are the last direct descendant of Evangeline. He will never let you go."

Especially now, I thought. Especially now that I was going to have Gabriel's child. Lucifer would never let such a prize slip through his fingers. Gabriel had been half-angel and half-nephilim, Lucifer's immediate grandson. I was also related to Lucifer, although more distantly. The Morningstar was not able to resist the call of his own blood-lines, particularly when combined in such an interesting way.

Northwestern Memorial Hospital was a giant network of buildings just east of Michigan Avenue and south of the Water Tower. We'd decided the easiest way to find Chloe would be to check the computer in any one of the many reception areas throughout the complex. I'd devised a semi-sneaky plan for distracting anyone at the desk.

We hadn't anticipated that the hospital would be completely locked down. Security guards were posted at every entrance. All doors and windows were closed tight.

The four of us stood on the sidewalk, staring through the glass doors. A few hospital personnel rushed back and forth. The guards at the doors appeared ready to snap.

"Perhaps we can get in from an upper floor?" Nathaniel said.

I shaded my eyes in the bright sunlight and peered up the face of the building. Movement caught my eye—something blue and gelatinous-looking darting between the windows, attached to the building like Spider-Man.

"What is that?" I asked, pointing.

"Gods above and below," Nathaniel swore. "That is a pix demon. They are scavengers. They feed off the sick, the dying. And where there is one, there are always more. Like rats. They do not usually come out during the day, however."

"Must be trying to take advantage of the chaos," I said.

"They will not be the only ones," Nathaniel said.

I shuddered. Wasn't it bad enough that vampires were running loose during the day? Did I also have to worry about other, unseen menaces crouching on the outskirts, waiting for things to *really* fall apart before they pounced? How was I supposed to keep my baby safe when all these thrice-bedamned *things* were invading my city?

The pix demon slipped inside a window that looked like it might be cracked open half a centimeter.

"We can't let that demon run rampant inside the hospital," I said.

Nathaniel scooped me up and we flew to the pix's point of entry, Samiel and Jude following. Urgency now trumped subtlety, so I blasted the window apart with nightfire and hoped that the falling shards of glass wouldn't hit anyone below. Cold winter wind blasted into the room.

The creature crouched over a young woman lying prone in bed. Her eyes were wide and staring. The IV hooked up to her arm dripped fluid into a body that didn't need it anymore. The heart rate monitor flatlined, sounding an urgent alarm that no one answered.

The demon looked up as we entered, its face covered in the flesh and blood of the dead girl. It hissed, displaying sharp predator teeth. I blasted it with nightfire before Nathaniel had finished setting me on my feet, but the monster had bounded from the room already.

"Damn it all," I swore, and chased it into the hall, the other three following close behind.

The hallway was empty.

"Those things are fast," I said.

"Yes, and it is doubtless feeding on another victim," Nathaniel said. "The fact that its own life is in peril will not override its instinct to eat."

"Split up and check the rooms," I said, already moving down the hall.

Jude barked behind me, and I didn't need to speak wolf to know what he said.

"I know; we shouldn't separate. Nobody leaves this floor, all right? Check the rooms and then meet up by the stairwell."

We searched the floor, which seemed to be empty of nurses and doctors as well as pix demons. All the patients on the floor were soundly asleep. Everyone gathered near the stairwell and looked expectantly at me.

"Is it more likely to go up or down?" I asked Nathaniel.

"Down, I would think," he said. "They usually prefer dark places."

I stared at the vents in the wall. "Like air ducts?"

"You are not checking the air ducts," Nathaniel said. "If you were caught in an enclosed space with more than one of those creatures, they would tear you apart like a pack of piranhas."

Yeah, I'm drawing a line there, too, Samiel signed.

"I wasn't suggesting I go into the air ducts," I said, although I'd been thinking that very thing. "I'm just saying that maybe it's using the air ducts to travel through the building. There would be a lot more screaming if it were running loose in the halls, don't you think? Especially since everyone is already on edge because of the vampires."

"I suppose we could monitor the air ducts, but that seems inefficient," Nathaniel said.

"Yeah, it's so much more efficient to find the pix when it's already gnawing on someone's guts," I said.

"It is simpler to find it by the suffering of its victims, yes," Nathaniel acknowledged.

"Don't you care that someone has to die to make things easier for you?" I said angrily.

"I am merely pointing out that this hospital is a warren of hallways and alcoves, and it is not in the least productive for us to hare up and down corridors in search of this demon," Nathaniel said. "I thought we were here to find Chloe."

I took a deep breath because it would not be productive for me to punch him in the face. Sometimes he surprised me with his humanity, but it was times like this I remembered Nathaniel was not human at all. He came from a world where death was meaningless, and the death of an innocent even more so.

"We are here to find Chloe," I said evenly. "But it's not okay for us to let the patients get eaten by a demon when we're the only ones who can stop it."

I'd been vaguely aware of Jude sniffing up and down the hallway as I argued with Nathaniel. He seemed frustrated, and I suspected that he couldn't get a fix on the demon's scent.

"Too many people have passed through here," I said to Jude, and he barked in acknowledgment.

"And there is too much sickness in the air," Nathaniel added.

Jude barked again, shorter this time, as if he were only reluctantly acknowledging that Nathaniel might be correct about anything.

"Samiel, why don't you see if you can get into the computer on this floor and find out where Chloe is," I said. "I don't know where all the staff is, but we might as well use their absence to our advantage."

Samiel went down the hall to the empty reception area. Nathaniel gave me a look. "And the pix demon?"

"We keep looking. I don't care if it takes all day."

"It has probably already found another victim."

"Then we stop it from getting another one."

"What is the point?" Nathaniel said. "What do you think will happen to everyone in this building when the vampires cross the river? Isn't that why you came for Chloe, why you were so eager to save your friend?"

"Samiel wants Chloe with him," I said, trying to ignore the nagging guilt that I'd been suppressing since we'd undertaken this task.

"And it's all right to leave everyone else to their fate," Nathaniel said. "When the hospital is overrun by vampires and all of the helpless, ill and elderly are devoured in their beds, at least the person *you* care about will be home safe."

I did slap him then, my temper running over before I had the chance to stop it. "What would you have me do? I can't save them all. I don't even know how to try."

"You cannot," Nathaniel said, grabbing my hand before I hauled off and hit him again. "And you know that I will stay with you, no matter what foolish enterprise you are engaged in. But do not deceive yourself. If you stop the pix demon, you are not saving innocents. You are merely prolonging the final moment of their death."

I stared at him, knowing what he said was true, but everything I was inside fought against it.

"I can't stand by," I said, yanking my hand away. "I have to use my gifts to help those who have none."

"So you can make yourself feel better? So you can sleep at night?" Nathaniel asked. "So when you close your eyes you can see the grateful face of the person you rescued at the last moment from a demon, never wondering what became of them after you disappeared into a swirl of smoke?"

"When I close my eyes I see Azazel's sword cutting out

Gabriel's heart. I see Gabriel falling into the snow, surrounded by his own blood," I said, my voice hard. "Don't presume that you know me, or what drives me. If I save someone from a monster only to have them get hit by a bus fifteen minutes later, then at least I did the right thing when I had the opportunity. I wouldn't walk by a pix demon eating someone just because a vampire might be right behind."

"Even if it means you risk your life for no purpose?" Nathaniel asked.

"You're not human. You wouldn't understand."

"I have seen plenty of humanity. The vast majority would not help their fellow neighbor unless forced to do so at gunpoint," Nathaniel said.

Our argument was interrupted by Samiel's return. *She's two floors below here.*

I rubbed my forehead, practicality warring with unfinished business. "Samiel, you and Jude go get Chloe and then get out of the building. Nathaniel and I will track down the pix."

Samiel looked doubtful. *Every time we split up something bad happens.*

"I need to know that the three of you are safe," I said.
What about my need to know that you're safe?

"I'll be fine," I said. "I've survived worse than a pix."
You died once.

"And I came back," I said, giving him a half smile.
I wouldn't count on that happening a second time.

Jude barked in agreement.

"Please, just get Chloe out and get home. Trust that I can take care of myself."

Samiel looked at me for a long moment. Finally, he nodded. *I'll text you when we're home.*

"Okay," I said. The world went wobbly for a second, and

I realized my eyes were filling. I swallowed hard, willing the tears away. If Samiel thought I was worried, he wouldn't leave. But I'd had a strange feeling for a moment, the feeling that one of us was not going to make it home.

Jude nudged my leg with his nose. I kneeled down so I could look him in the eyes. I could see his reluctance as clearly as if he'd shouted it. Jude fancied himself my protector, and he'd never completely trusted Nathaniel.

"Take care of Samiel and Chloe," I whispered, and put my arms around his neck, burying my face in his fur. "I *will* be home soon."

He rubbed his nose across my cheek, and then the two of them disappeared into the stairwell. I knelt on the floor, staring after them, hoping I hadn't made a mistake. Hoping I hadn't sent them to their deaths.

"You cannot be responsible for everyone's lives," Nathaniel said quietly from behind me.

I stood and faced him. "That's what love is. When you love someone you're responsible for them, and they you. Until you understand that, I'll never believe you when you say you care about me."

"I do understand it," he said. "But you are the only one that has ever made me feel this way."

He seemed bewildered when he said this, like the feeling was some foreign disease that had invaded his body. I was all too aware of the fact that we were alone, and that he was not Gabriel.

"Let's kill that demon so we can go home," I said abruptly. "Beezle will probably have eaten everything in the pantry by now."

Nathaniel didn't say anything else as we silently agreed that further discussion on this topic was just going to make us both uncomfortable.

We took the stairway to the next level, peering cautiously around the fire door. There was a little more activity here— a nurse moving from room to room, patients being pushed along the corridor by an orderly—but it wasn't the panicked rushing of folks who'd just seen a vision from their night-mares. I looked at Nathaniel, and he shook his head.

We skipped the next floor since Jude and Samiel were there, and presumably any monsters would be dispatched by them.

Nathaniel had dropped the cloak that covered us when we entered the hospital. I understood why. It required a lot of energy to maintain a veil *and* stay on your guard against demonic attacks. It was doubly hard to keep four people covered.

The thing was, Nathaniel's wings were such an essential part of his appearance that I didn't often think about them. Plus I was little preoccupied with finding the pix demon and not thinking too hard on what Nathaniel had said about my motivations.

So when we came face-to-face with a security guard on the next floor, I wasn't thinking about the vampires, or the fact that all the humans were on edge. I wasn't thinking that Nathaniel would look extremely strange to a normal.

We pushed through the door, and it was just unfortunate luck that the security guard stood there. And that his weapon was in his hand, and that he was ready to go off at the least provocation.

I was in front of Nathaniel, and the guard was a few feet in front of me. He turned as soon as he heard activity behind him, and while he was definitely tense, he might not have fired if he hadn't seen Nathaniel's wings.

"What the hell is that thing?" he shouted, and pulled the trigger. His hand was shaking, so his aim probably wasn't as good as it normally would be. Likely it was the first time he had ever fired his weapon on the job.

Which was why the bullet hit me instead of Nathaniel. And why Nathaniel blasted the guard with nightfire as I fell to the ground, the bullet tearing through the soft flesh just under the joint of my shoulder, just above my heart. I screamed, not because it hurt but because it was too late for the guard. Nathaniel had killed him before my eyes.

I could feel the burning path where the bullet had torn through me, the wet stickiness of blood flowing from an open wound.

"Madeline," Nathaniel said, already turning to me, falling to his knees beside me, the guard forgotten.

"What the hell did you do that for?" I shouted. Rather, I wanted to shout, but my voice barely rose above my normal speaking tone.

Inside me, my baby gave a little flutter, but nothing more. I guess a little physical distress was old news at this point.

The guard was prone on the ground, a smoking hole where his chest used to be. Farther down the hall behind him, a male doctor in a white lab coat stood frozen in place, his eyes wide.

Nathaniel scrabbled at my coat, pulled it away from my shoulder so that he could see the blood-soaked mess beneath. My sweater and shirt stuck to the open wound. He put his hand over the hole where the bullet had entered.

The warmth of the sun lit my blood, flowed from his hand and through the heart of me, healing the bullet wound as if it had never been. I sat up, still a little woozy. Blood loss is blood loss, whether your wound heals immediately or not. It takes a while to get your strength back if you've got anything bigger than a shaving cut.

The doctor watched us now with speculation instead of fear. Nathaniel had exposed his powers by healing me.

"What did you kill the guard for?" I hissed as Nathaniel helped me to my feet. I don't think he yet realized we had an audience.

"He shot you," Nathaniel said, frowning.

"He was scared to death. He didn't know what he was doing."

"He shot you," Nathaniel repeated.

I put my hands to my face for a moment. "In point of fact, he was trying to shoot you and got me by accident."

"That hardly recommends him," Nathaniel said.

"Couldn't you have stunned him instead of killing him?"

"I was not contemplating all the angles of the situation," Nathaniel said, anger in his voice. "I saw someone threatening you and I eliminated the threat. I do not know why we are discussing this in any case. The man is dead. What is done is done."

"We're discussing this," I said through gritted teeth, "because I don't want you to do it again."

"Duly noted," Nathaniel said, and then he turned his body so that I was behind him. I stood on tiptoe and peered over his shoulder so I could see what was going on.

The doctor approached us, his hands held high to show that he was no threat. He stared at Nathaniel in fascination. That fascination was almost as frightening as terror. The doctor looked like he wanted to whisk Nathaniel away and get the angel under a microscope as soon as possible.

"Do not approach any further," Nathaniel said, the old arrogance in his voice.

The doctor stopped walking, dropped his hands to his side. "Who . . . who are you?"

"That's not what you want to know," I said, moving a

little so that the doctor could see me. My voice was hard. Nathaniel wasn't my favorite person, but I didn't want anybody getting ideas about turning him into a lab rat. "You want to know *what* he is."

"Yes," the doctor said, barely giving me a glance.

"It's none of your damned business," I said, and stunned him right between the eyes. The doctor crumpled to the floor.

"I did not detect any threat from him," Nathaniel said.

"I did," I said grimly. "Come on, let's check this floor for the pix before someone finds us standing over two bodies."

"No," Nathaniel said. "Let us wait."

"Why? Do you want to pick a fight with another security guard?"

"You want to capture the demon, yes?"

"Of course."

"The smell of the newly dead is irresistible to a pix," Nathaniel said, gesturing to the guard's body.

"Don't tell me you killed the guard to attract the pix," I said, disgusted.

"I told you, I killed the guard because he shot you," Nathaniel said impatiently. "Think of this as an added bonus, as you would say."

"That right there is the difference between you and me," I said. "I can't think of anyone's death in terms of a 'bonus.'"

"The world is changing," Nathaniel said. "You may find soon that our perspectives are not so far apart."

He dropped a cloak over the two of us, and we settled back to wait.

We didn't have to wait long. A set of long fingers curled over the flaps of the air vents, and a moment later a vent popped free. The pix's gelatinous blue body slithered from the air ducts.

"Told you they were in the air ducts," I murmured.

Nathaniel moved his hand to shush me, but the pix hadn't noticed us in the least. Every part of the demon focused on the body on the floor, every bit of it straining for what it wanted.

There were no marks on the demon from the nightfire blast I'd shot at it earlier. That combined with the ease with which it had leapt away from my magic told me that no simple spell would take this thing down.

The pix bounded atop the guard, making little clicking noises that sounded like glee. It buried its face in the guard's chest, and I heard a slurping sound.

Nathaniel tensed beside me, a sign that he was readying a spell. I decided to follow his lead since he knew more about the pix than I did. Then the doctor stirred, and the pix lifted its head.

Nathaniel let loose his magic just as the pix leapt toward the doctor. The spell caught the demon behind its back leg, far off the kill shot that Nathaniel had no doubt intended. The blast was enough to knock the creature off its course, but now it was alerted to our presence.

It jumped for the ceiling, skittering along upside down like a bug, seemingly unhampered by its injury. Nathaniel's spell had taken a big chunk of flesh out of the pix's leg, and little drops of a jelly-like substance dripped from the wound.

I swore aloud, blasting electricity at the nasty thing. As with Nathaniel, my spell caught only a little of the demon. The electricity also didn't slow it down a bit, even though I could smell barbecued demon in the air.

I ran down the hall after the demon, which was wickedly quick. The doctor reached out and grabbed my ankle as I went by.

The sudden halt in my momentum made me stumble, and my second blast went wild, spraying electricity into the wall. Smoke rose in the air, setting off the hallway sprinklers. The pix disappeared at the other end of the hall.

"Dammit, dammit, dammit!" I said, stomping down on the doctor's fingers with my other boot. The doc howled and released my ankle, and I took off down the hall after the pix, Nathaniel close behind me.

"I thought we were not harming innocents?" he murmured.

"Just stay focused on the task at hand," I snapped.

Nathaniel chuckled quietly.

The demon, of course, was gone when we reached the end of the hallway. The sprinklers had obliterated any trail of goo that the pix might have left behind.

I stopped in front of a bank of elevators, staring at Nathaniel with a mixture of annoyance and hopelessness, water pouring over us.

"This is so freaking irritating," I said. "Why can I take down a Grigori, a shapeshifter, and a nephilim on my own, but you and I together can't defeat one scavenger demon?"

"The difference is that the others wanted to defeat you, so they stood and fought. The pix wants to survive, so it is not foolish enough to face two creatures that it knows very well are more powerful than it is."

"Don't try to be logical," I said. "I'm ready to say to hell with it and go home."

"You are?" Nathaniel asked, tilting his head curiously.

"Well, no," I admitted. "At this point I just want to kill the stupid thing out of spite."

Then we heard a sound like a muffled explosion, and the building trembled beneath our feet.

"What was that?" I asked, my eyes wide.

We ran to the windows, but what we could see of the streets below did not appear any different than it had been when we arrived earlier.

"Perhaps there is a television we can check," Nathaniel said.

"There will definitely be one in a patient's room," I said.

We peeked into a room and found it empty. I wondered why more patients hadn't come rushing to their doors when they heard the ruckus in the hallway. I supposed it meant that most of them were unable to get out of bed without assistance, and that probably meant almost everyone on the floor was elderly, terminally ill, or both. The thought made me very grim. If the vampires got into the building, these people had no chance at all.

It was also more than a little strange that the hospital staff hadn't rushed to the floor. Strange, and probably ominous. It meant there was something going on that was more pressing than a smoke alarm on a patient floor.

Nathaniel found a remote and turned the television on. A daytime talk show was running, the host interviewing the starlet of the moment. He flipped through the channels—cartoons, reality TV, sports highlights.

It seemed wrong that the rest of the world would go on as normal when it felt like we were in the middle of an apocalypse. But most programming was broadcast out of New York, and the stations wouldn't interrupt their regular schedule even if the world was coming to an end.

"Find a twenty-four-hour news network," I said. "Or a local channel. They probably can't get enough of this story."

The twenty-four-hour networks would be making hay out of this for weeks. There's nothing a news channel likes better than a major tragedy and a big pile of bodies to go with it.

Nathaniel continued cycling through the channels. "Why do humans need so many useless programs?"

"That's a question I've been asking for years," I said. "You should ask Beezle. This is his favorite time of day, programming-wise."

"Yes, I am familiar with the gargoyle's junk TV obsession," Nathaniel said dryly.

"What did he make you watch?"

"*American Idol*. I was unwilling to actually gouge my eyes out, but I strongly considered it many times."

I snorted. "You got off easy. You should see some of the other garbage he watches."

"No, thank you," he replied, and then we both went silent as he finally found a channel with the words BREAKING NEWS in the top corner.

As earlier, the shot was an aerial view of the Loop. Any smart reporters were staying away from on-the-ground coverage. This shot was better taken from above, in any case.

It showed the Michigan Avenue bridge that ran over the Chicago River from East Wacker. The vampire horde, that ravenous seething mass, had pushed up to the river at all fronts. The Chicago River wrapped through the Loop in a lazy L curve from Lake Michigan and roughly followed the shape of Wacker Drive. The city authorities had set up sandbag walls on the northern and western sides of all the bridges. As an added precaution, the bridges had been raised.

There was a female news anchor giving commentary, but I didn't hear a word she said. Obviously the hope was to contain the vampires, but I wondered what was being done on the south side of the Loop. There was no natural geological feature at that end to keep the monsters in.

It didn't matter in any case. As we watched, the vampires drove a handful of human survivors before them. The people were screaming, desperate, and when they reached the bridges they howled for the police and soldiers on the other side to help them.

Instead, the vampires surged from behind, overtaking them. And the soldiers fired into the crowd. I turned my head away.

"They have no choice," Nathaniel said. "Those people are all dead in any case, whether at the teeth of vampires or the bullets of humans."

"That doesn't make it any easier for me to watch the government kill its own citizens," I said.

"You cannot save them," he said.

"Yeah, I know," I said.

"No," he said, and turned me to face him. "I need you to understand this. You *cannot* save them, or most of the other people in the city, either. This is a hemorrhaging wound and you cannot staunch the bleeding."

I looked into his eyes, pale as winter, so very unlike Gabriel's.

"I can't stand by. I have to do something," I said.

"Why not? Why do you need to sacrifice yourself in some Quixotic quest to save humanity?" He pointed to the TV. "This is what you want to preserve? Reality TV? Big Macs?"

"It doesn't matter if you hold us in contempt. It doesn't matter if we eat junky food and watch junky TV. It doesn't matter if we're desperate, selfish or vain. It doesn't matter if we're loving, giving and modest. It doesn't matter if we're not perfect. Anyway, I've yet to meet an angel who is."

"You are talking as if you are one of them," he said. "You are not. You are more than they are."

"No, I'm not," I said. "I'm human. And I'm not going to stand by and watch my own kind be wiped from the planet."

Nathaniel turned back to the spectacle on the television screen. "You may not have a choice."

3

THE NEWS HAD RETURNED FROM A COMMERCIAL break. Now the footage showed the surging vampires leaping over the raised bridges and assaulting the fortified roadblocks. The positions were quickly overwhelmed.

Suddenly there was a massive explosion behind the sandbagged wall set up on Michigan Avenue. It wasn't clear who had set the explosives but there was a tremendous ball of fire where the National Guard used to be.

Flame whooshed through the crowd of vampires, and the eerie piercing wail that rose up was the sound of the death throes of monsters. The vamps that hadn't yet leapt over the bridge paused for a moment as their brethren turned to ash.

"Those soldiers sacrificed themselves for the greater good," I said. "How can I do any less?"

"Their sacrifice is meaningless," Nathaniel snapped.

"There are many more vampires than can be halted by a small explosion."

"But they tried."

"Is that what it is to be human? To try? To push, like Sisyphus, ever more fruitlessly at the boulder that will simply roll down the hill and over you again?"

"That is part of being human," I said. "To struggle, to succeed."

"What if you never succeed?"

"You still try. You have to."

"I will never understand humans," Nathaniel said. "It makes no sense to repeat the same behavior over and over when you know the outcome."

"But you don't know the outcome," I replied. "It's why people play the same lottery numbers week after week, year after year. They're hoping their luck will change."

"There is no such thing as luck. Only chance."

"Most people would have said that there's no such thing as vampires, either, and yet here we are," I said, gesturing to the television.

"That is only because they did not know any better," Nathaniel said.

"Who's to say that you don't know any better, either? I know luck has saved my life plenty of times."

"You were saved by your own skills, your own wits, which are more prodigious than you give yourself credit for."

"Don't let Beezle hear you say that. He thinks I just stumble around setting things on fire."

"Well, you do that as well," Nathaniel allowed. "But stumbling around setting things on fire seems to be a key component of your skill set."

I would have laughed, except that at that moment the pix demon crashed through the ceiling and landed on my head.

Its gelatinous body molded itself to my shoulders and head so that I couldn't see. Clawed fingers raked up the side of my throat and blood spurted from the wounds.

I reached up and grabbed the monster's ankles and blasted electricity through my palms. The demon growled but held on tight.

"Nathaniel," I gurgled. I could feel the torn flaps of skin on my neck, could feel the hot flow of blood running under my shirt.

There were sounds of a struggle, and the smell of ozone filled the air.

"More," Nathaniel grunted, and I knew I'd have to save myself. I was bleeding out too fast for Nathaniel to help.

Nightfire didn't seem to bother the pix much, nor electricity. Which left the most destructive tool in my limited arsenal.

Everything burns.

I pushed my power through my blood, through my heart-stone, where it was lit by the heat of the sun. That spell poured through my palms and through the skin of the pix demon. It screeched and released its grip on me, falling to the floor and writhing as it burned from the inside out.

I wasn't that great at the healing spell, having performed it only once, so I slapped my burning hand on my own neck to cauterize the wound.

This time I screeched, because the pain was agonizing. Sometimes I really wonder about my ability to think things through to their logical conclusion. It hurt like nothing I'd ever felt before, and the wound probably looked horrific, but after a moment there was no more flowing blood. I lurched around to see Nathaniel battling three demons.

I stumbled forward, dizzy and still in pain, and latched on to the neck of the nearest pix. My burning hands blasted magic through its skin. Smoke poured from its mouth. The pix tried to break away from my grip but I held fast, pouring fire inside until the air filled with the stench of burning.

Nathaniel was fighting with two other demons. The bodies of three others lay at his feet, their heads missing. He slashed out with his sword, keeping them at arm's length, but his blasts of nightfire didn't seem to do much more than annoy them.

I could fix that.

I was tired and woozy from blood loss, but I had enough magic left for one last push. I grabbed the nearest pix demon's head and sent fire through my palms. Freed of the necessity of fending off two attackers at once, Nathaniel stepped forward and beheaded the final creature just as I dropped the smoking body of the other to the floor.

We stood, both panting from exertion, and looked around at the mess. The beheaded demons had some gloppy blue stuff pouring from their severed necks. The pix that I had barbecued were still smoking slightly.

And still no one on the floor had come running at the sound of the struggle. No patients gaped in the doorway; no security personnel wondered what we were doing. There was something wrong here. Something bigger than the pix, or even the invading vampires.

Nathaniel moved toward me, and put his hand on my neck. The healing light of the sun flowed through the cauterized wound. "What did you do to yourself?" he murmured.

"It was a field dressing," I said.

He kept his hand where it was for a moment, staring at the place where his fingers brushed my skin. "You made a mess of this. There will be another scar."

I touched his wrist, pulled his hand away. "What's another scar?"

He stared at me for a moment. It was so hard for me to know what he was thinking, to read his eyes. Gabriel had been so open to me.

I took a deep breath, because every time I thought of Gabriel I saw him falling in the snow, surrounded by pooling blood.

"There's something wrong in this hospital," I said. "We've been raising a ruckus all over the place and there have only been a couple of people moving around."

"The doctor, the security guard," Nathaniel said. "You are right. This is a large facility. There should be more activity."

"There should be staff running around, if nothing else. And the only patient we've seen was being eaten by the pix," I said. "Let's check some of the other rooms and see what's going on."

I stepped carefully over the pile of demon bodies. They were decomposing quickly into a mass of goo that looked a lot like blue gelatin.

There was nobody in the hallway, no sounds at all. Now that I was aware of it, the silence seemed heavy with menace.

Nathaniel poked his head into the patient room across the hall and I crowded behind him. There was an elderly woman sleeping in the bed, seemingly peacefully. Her chest rose and fell with each breath. We looked at each other and shrugged.

I led the way to the next room, where we found another patient in an identical state of slumber. Then we went into the next room. And so on, until we'd checked the whole floor and discovered that every patient was sleeping as soundly as Beauty after she'd pricked her finger on the spindle.

Along the way we found several nurses, doctors and orderlies, lying peacefully on the floor.

"Someone put a spell on the building," I said.

Nathaniel nodded. "But it did not affect everyone. A large spell like this would have to be extremely powerful to catch every individual in its net."

"It's pretty powerful regardless," I said. "But who could have done it?"

Nathaniel shook his head. "There are several individuals that have the ability to do this. Certain faeries, for example. Or any of the Grigori."

"But what motivation would any of the Grigori have for doing this?"

"Perhaps someone else is working with the vampires in the wake of Azazel's death," Nathaniel said grimly.

I'd been so preoccupied with the strangeness of the spell that I hadn't thought through the implications. "Everyone here has been prepped like a lamb for the slaughter. Whoever did this made the hospital a cafeteria for vampires."

Nathaniel nodded. "Once the horde gets here, none of these people will survive."

I had faced some impossible odds since I discovered I was Azazel's daughter. I'd fought some of the worst monsters imaginable. But I had never felt so helpless in the face of a threat before.

"What can we do?" I said.

Nathaniel shook his head. "There is nothing we can do."

"That's unacceptable," I said angrily.

"We cannot undo the spell without knowing who cast it, or even what exactly they cast. If we tried to pull apart the magic without knowing its provenance, we could kill everyone by accident."

"We can't leave these people unprotected," I said, thinking hard. "What if we cast a protective spell over the sleeping spell? Like a shield, or a veil?"

"You are talking about magic that requires a tremendous amount of force. We would have to combine our abilities, and even then I am not certain we would be able to do it."

"We have to try," I said. "I can't leave them like this."

"Even if we succeeded, we would likely use up our magic for some time. We would be left vulnerable to attack."

"You have a sword. I have a sword. They don't," I said, pointing at the slumbering patient.

Nathaniel looked doubtful. "Lord Lucifer would not condone any course of action that might lead you to harm."

"Lucifer can stick it," I said. "I'm not kneeling to anyone. I don't know why we keep having this discussion over and over."

"I have been alive for hundreds of years, and in all of that time I have had a master. First my father, then Azazel. And always Lord Lucifer ruled over all."

"I've only been alive for a few decades, but I have never had a master. And I'm not about to start now."

"You would not yield to Azazel, either," Nathaniel murmured. "It angered him so."

"Yeah, well, you know what I did to Azazel," I said.

"You would not be able to do such a thing to Lord Lucifer, and I advise you not to even think of it," Nathaniel said seriously.

"I won't go after Lucifer if he doesn't give me a reason to," I said.

But I hoped he wouldn't give me a reason, because despite my bravado even I knew that it was very, very stupid to go one-on-one with Lucifer. I'd felt his power and it was a thing of tremendous force. I also knew that he had shown me only the smallest fraction of it.

"Sometimes I wonder if you are trying to commit suicide," Nathaniel said.

"Sometimes I wonder that myself," I said.

"I am not joking," Nathaniel said.

"Neither am I."

There was a long pause after this, as I contemplated the truth of my statement and Nathaniel watched me with his frozen blue gaze. I didn't want my baby to die. I wanted to protect him. But sometimes, especially when a fight didn't seem to be going my way, a fleeting thought would say, *If you just let go, you can be with Gabriel. You and the baby.*

"We're off topic," I said, wanting to transition away from the awkward moment. "I want to protect the hospital."

Nathaniel rubbed his forehead. "I must consider how to do this."

While Nathaniel came up with a plan, I thought deep thoughts about who could have cast the sleeping spell in the first place and, more important, why.

My first thought was that Titania was in league with the vampires. Amarantha had been colluding with Azazel before she died, so there was a very real possibly that the queen of Faerie had picked up where her subordinate had left off. And when I was in Titania and Oberon's court I'd thought that they were deliberately trying to harm me in order to provoke Lucifer.

At the time it seemed insane for them to try to tick off the Morningstar, but if they were working with this army of vampires, perhaps they thought they had an advantage.

My second thought was that one of the Grigori had taken up Azazel's personal mission. Certainly any of the Grigori would be powerful enough to cast the sleeping spell, and presumably they would also be able to control the army of vampires.

"But who's the contact?" I murmured.

"Pardon?" Nathaniel said, frowning. He looked like he

was trying to do intense mathematical calculations in his head.

"I was just thinking. There has to be a vampire overlord or whatever, right? They've got a pretty rigid court system, as far as I know."

"They do," Nathaniel acknowledged. "And their heads of court are kings and queens, like the Faerie."

"So they have little courts that are overseen by one big court?"

Nathaniel nodded. "You are thinking that the vampire king had to know about this prior to the attack."

"If he's got a good grip on his kingdom, then he should definitely have known about this. Is his court in Chicago?"

Nathaniel shook his head. "No. He is based in New York."

"Isn't it interesting?" I mused. "Lucifer's court is in Los Angeles. The vampire king's court is on the opposite coast. The high court of Faerie is in some dimension all its own. And yet all this trouble is here at my door."

"Lord Lucifer has made it very clear through both word and deed that he would like you to be his heir."

"So you're saying that as long as Lucifer keeps going around talking me up, the other courts will swipe at me?"

Nathaniel's eyes were troubled. "You would be safer if you would accept Lord Lucifer's offer."

"I don't want to be his heir," I said. "More important, I don't want my child to be his heir."

"I do not know if you can resist for much longer. Your life is becoming more dangerous by the moment. And Lord Lucifer has a way of boxing you in before you realize the walls are there."

Emotion flickered across his face.

And what did he do to you? I wondered.

"Look, let's just get these people as safe as we can so we

can go home. I need to figure out some way to eliminate these vampires."

"I believe that we can put some form of protection over the hospital," Nathaniel said. "But in order to do it correctly we will need to leave the building, which will put us at risk."

"Why will we need to leave?"

"Because the conditions of the enchantment will prevent creatures of supernatural origin from entering. If we are inside when the magic is settled, we would be forcibly ejected by the spell."

"But what about the Agents that are still in the hospital? Samiel and Jude got Chloe out—at least I hope they did," I said, fumbling for my cell phone so I could see whether Samiel had sent me a text. I patted all of my pockets and came up empty. "For the love of the Morningstar. I lost it again."

"The Agents will be protected," Nathaniel said. "Their magic is different from a supernatural creature's."

"How?"

"Agents are human," Nathaniel said simply. "They may have magical abilities, but at the core of it they are human. Their essence is not born of the otherworld, but this one."

"But the spell will keep out vampires and pix demons and all that?"

Nathaniel nodded. "If it works correctly. If we can project enough power. This is a very large hospital, and I am presuming that you are not simply interested in protecting this building."

I shook my head. "Of course not. Why would we protect the helpless patients in this building and ignore the others? I wonder if the whole complex is under the sleeping spell."

"We are not going to check," Nathaniel said.

"So what are we going to do?"

Nathaniel looked uncertain for a moment, like he knew I wouldn't like what he was going to say. "We have to combine our powers."

"Okay . . ."

"We will need to mingle our blood in order to most effectively achieve this."

"Are we talking about an I'm-your-blood-brother paper cut here, or a gaping wound? Because I've had enough gaping wounds today, thank you."

"The cut itself will be relatively small," Nathaniel assured me. "But combining our magic will feel . . . intimate."

Now I was the uncertain one. "You mean, I'll feel you inside me? And you'll be able to feel me?"

Nathaniel nodded. "I understand if such a thing is reprehensible to you."

Reprehensible? Not exactly. More like a betrayal. Because there was only one man I'd ever been intimate with, and mingling anything with Nathaniel felt a lot like I was spitting on Gabriel's grave.

But if I didn't do this, then everyone in this hospital was nothing but a buffet for the vampire horde.

I held out my hand to Nathaniel.

4

NATHANIEL TOOK MY HAND IN HIS. HIS SKIN WAS SO much warmer than mine. Angels are born of the sun, and the light of the sun beats within them. I had the heartstone of an angel, but my light would always be tempered by my humanity. I would never really be one of them.

He turned my hand over, drew his sword. "It will only hurt for a moment."

"I've had worse than a slice from a sharp blade," I said.

All the monsters I'd fought flickered in my memory for a moment, and then Nathaniel cut my palm open with the sword. I flinched, because it's natural to flinch when you see your flesh rent open, but I didn't make a noise.

Nathaniel repeated the same action on his own palm. He held the bloodied hand up for me to match. I pressed my wound against his and felt the tingling of magic, still banked.

He pulled me close, wrapped his other arm around my waist. I was hyperaware of all the places where our bodies touched, of the warmth of his breath on my hair. The air crackled with energy.

"Hold tight," he murmured.

The glass of a nearby window exploded outward. Nathaniel shot through the opening and into the sky. We hovered above the roofs of the giant complex that composed the hospital.

Nathaniel leaned close to my ear. "I want you to push your power up and out, into the place where our blood touches. I will direct the spell. Now."

I closed my eyes, found the place inside me where my ability lay quietly waiting for me, and I woke it up. I didn't try to control or direct it anywhere except toward Nathaniel. The power roared forth, an unrestrained howl. As the heart of my magic met Nathaniel's, my eyes flew open and met his.

Magic scorched the air.

Bitter wind cut through our clothes but I barely felt it. All I could feel was Nathaniel. It was like he was running wild in my blood, burning me from the inside out.

I knew his power, and his heart. I felt his struggle to direct the spell, to corral this wild surge that neither of us had expected.

I felt the confusion that roiled inside him, the passion for me that he had proclaimed but that I had always denied.

I don't know what I revealed to him, but he looked as shocked as I felt.

We were locked together by magic and surprise, by a spell that had gone out of control almost as soon as it had been cast. The power poured forth from us, its strength almost beyond comprehension. It settled beneath us, draping all the innocents below in a protective veil. I knew that no vampire or demon would be able to harm the sleeping inmates of the hospital.

Our magic mingled and swirled, and when he put his mouth on mine it didn't seem like a choice but an inevitability.

Part of me wanted to pull away. Part of me thought that it was far too soon for me to kiss some man who was not Gabriel.

The rest of me welcomed the heat, the burn, the wild play of magic in my blood, his mouth ravenous and devouring, our bodies pressed so tight that there was no air between us.

I don't know what would have happened if someone hadn't started shooting at us.

Nathaniel tore his mouth away, and the shock of his retreat brought the flow of magic to a grinding halt. I could still feel the remnants of him inside me.

A bullet whizzed past, close enough for me to feel the disrupted current of air that trailed behind it. I tried to look around, to see who was shooting, but Nathaniel held me tight and flew upward.

I was still full-body pressed against him, and this is not the best position for flying. I released his bloodied hand and put my arms around his neck and my legs around his waist. This made other, more intimate parts of us press together. I tried not to think about what was touching and focused instead on the fact that our lives were in danger. But the lingering remnants of the spell remained, and I could tell that Nathaniel was having trouble concentrating on the situation at hand as well.

"Do not move around," he said through gritted teeth. "And keep a tight hold. I am going to have to let go in order to blast them with nightfire."

"Who is it?" I said, still trying to crane around and see over Nathaniel's shoulder at the creatures chasing us.

"Bryson," Nathaniel said. "And at least two other Agents with weapons."

"Bryson," I repeated. How had he found me? Was he chasing me at Sokolov's request or for his own reasons?

The super Agent hated me, and with good reason. I'd captured him spying on my property and Nathaniel had tortured him at my behest. But why was Bryson chasing after me and trying to kill me now? Didn't the Agency care that the city was under siege?

Nathaniel spun in the air, blasted nightfire at the Agents, then turned back to fly away from them. I heard one of the Agents cry out. I really wished I had my wings back. I was useless like this.

Nathaniel dipped and swerved, careening around buildings and into alleys in an attempt to shake off the Agents. But the staccato rhythm of gunfire chased us as we headed south. All I could see from my position was Nathaniel's strained face. I kept my grip tight and tried not to distract him while he was trying to save our lives.

And then the unbelievable, the unthinkable, happened. I couldn't see Bryson and his cohorts behind us. I was concentrating too hard on keeping a close grip on Nathaniel. But the sound of the gunfire changed, and I've seen enough movies to know what an automatic weapon sounds like.

Nathaniel cried out in pain, a sound I'd never heard from him before. I glimpsed Bryson's malicious, triumphant face. Then I heard the horrible sound of tearing flesh, felt the hot stickiness of Nathaniel's blood on my hands.

It happened so fast that I hardly knew what was occurring until we were falling out of the sky. The shock of it caused my grip to loosen and then I was alone, in the air.

"Madeline!" Nathaniel cried. His hands reached for me, missed. I glimpsed the terror on his face as I plummeted toward the earth.

This was how it was going to end. I was going to be smashed on the ground like a bug. Nathaniel fell toward me, spinning this way and that, a gruesome rain of scarlet spraying from his body. I saw his left wing flap as he tried to right himself, saw him reach for me.

Our fingertips brushed together, slipped apart. Then he grabbed my wrist, his face strained, the muscles of his neck bulging with effort as he struggled to halt our descent.

That was when I noticed his right wing hung at an unnatural angle, and that it wasn't moving.

Nathaniel managed to slow us down enough that our brains wouldn't splatter all over the sidewalk, but we were still going to hit the ground with more force than the human body could take.

Inside my belly, a tiny pair of wings fluttered in distress.

Nathaniel jerked my hand, grabbed my waist with his arm and managed to turn over in midair. We were locked together like a pair of lovers, lying prone as we fell. Nathaniel's face was grim.

A second later we crashed to the ground. Nathaniel's body cradled me, protected me from the worst of it, but I still felt the impact reverberate in my skull. I saw stars for a moment. When my vision cleared, Nathaniel's eyes were closed. He was paler than death.

I touched his cheek. "Nathaniel?"

He opened his eyes, and they were full of pain. His voice rasped out, "I need you to move off me, very slowly."

I slid carefully to one side. I could tell that Nathaniel was trying not to cry out again. In the process of moving I noticed a twinge in my shoulder. I sat up on the concrete and put my fingers to the hole in my coat. They came away bloody.

"Bryson hit you," Nathaniel said. He watched me from his position on the ground. He hadn't moved a centimeter since we landed.

"I think the bullet just skimmed me. I didn't feel it," I said, watching Nathaniel in growing dread. "Nathaniel, did you break your back?"

"Yes," he said, and he sounded so strained. "I am attempting to mend it. But my powers are quite depleted at the moment, as, I imagine, are yours."

It seemed like it had happened hours before, not minutes. The mention of the protective spell we'd put over the hospital—and what had come after—made me blush.

"Nathaniel," I began, but he shook his head at me.

"If you have any magic to give now, you must use it to get away," he said. "I do not know what became of the Agents or why they halted their pursuit. They may return to complete the task they have begun. But more important, there are vampires are approaching."

"How do you know?" I asked, glancing around.

We were on the sidewalk in front of McCormick Place, next to the traffic circle and between the south and west wings of the complex. It looked like a ghost town. There was no traffic on King Drive—no taxis, no buses, no bikes. Nobody roamed through the pedestrian bridge that connected the two buildings. Everywhere was the detritus of people abandoning the area in haste. It was like we were the last two souls on the planet.

"I can hear them," Nathaniel said. He'd closed his eyes again. "Madeline, you must go."

"And leave you here to die?" I said.

"I will have fulfilled my pact with Lord Lucifer. I have protected you from harm, and now I can die with honor."

"Are you out of your effing mind?" I said, grabbing his hand. "I am not going to leave you here."

I tried pushing the healing spell into him, but my magic flickered and sputtered instead of pouring forth in a steady stream.

"Do not waste your energy on me," Nathaniel said. "You must go. You must protect your child."

"I won't leave you," I repeated.

"Madeline, you do not love me. I know this. I felt it inside you when our powers merged."

"I don't have to love you to know that it's wrong to leave you," I said fiercely. "I only have a little power left, and so do you. But we can put what we have together. Maybe we won't be able to heal your wing, but we can at least repair your back so that you can walk."

"Why will you not leave me?" Nathaniel said.

"I can't," I said. Everything I'd ever felt for Nathaniel—the hate and the anger, the sometimes friendship, and, yes, the lust I'd barely admitted to myself—roiled inside me. It would be easier to leave him, to let him fulfill the destiny that he thought Lucifer had written for him. But I couldn't. Nathaniel had saved my life more than once. And I didn't know yet just what he was to me.

"Madeline," he began again, but I stopped his mouth with a kiss.

This wasn't the kiss of before, full of passion and power. This was a connection born of desperation, of a need that I did not fully understand. Into that place where our bodies joined, I poured the remnants of my magic. My power touched Nathaniel's, and his light was so depleted, so fluttery and small. For the first time, I felt really afraid. I could feel him slipping away.

"Stay with me," I said against his lips. "Stay with me."

Tears were slipping down my cheeks, falling on his face, and it wasn't just Nathaniel's face but Gabriel's, Gabriel's frozen body in the snow. Nathaniel's life wavered, a candle flame flickering in the draft.

"Stay with me," I said again, and summoned all the strength, all the will, that I had remaining. I pushed that will inside Nathaniel, let my power twine around his.

The guttering flame grew brighter. It wasn't the blazing heart that it had been before, but I knew at that moment I wouldn't lose him.

Our magic flowed together through his body, found the broken vertebrac and reknit them—slowly, laboriously. There would be nothing left to mend his broken wing, but he would be able to walk and—I hoped—run.

After a long while I lifted my head and opened my eyes. Nathaniel studied me in silence.

"What?" I asked.

He looked contemplative. "I think I begin to understand you."

"It doesn't appear that understanding me has brought you any joy," I said, pushing away from him and standing up. I offered my hand. "Do you think you can stand?"

Nathaniel ignored my hand. He sat up slowly before coming to his feet. His face was white as chalk.

Once he stood I could see the damage to his wing more clearly. It was sickening.

It appeared that Bryson had deliberately shot several times into the place where the root of the wing grew into Nathaniel's back. Muscle and cartilage lay exposed, and the wing looked like it might snap off at any moment.

I reached toward his wing with my left hand, and that was when I noticed it.

"Nathaniel," I said, and my voice was barely a whisper.

"What is it? They approach. We must move . . ." He trailed off as I held up my left hand and wiggled my fingers. All *five* of my fingers.

He grabbed my hand, inspecting it, then looked up at me in wonder. "How?"

"I have no idea," I said. "This morning the last two were missing, just like they have been since Samiel cut them off. Now they're back. There's been so much other stuff going on I didn't have time to notice the spontaneous regeneration of my digits."

"Perhaps when we combined our powers the first time," Nathaniel said speculatively. "The force was significantly greater than I expected. Perhaps this regrowth is a side effect."

"Maybe," I said. "Or maybe the fingers just grew back the way Lucifer always said they would."

Nathaniel cocked his head to the side like a dog, like he was listening hard. "Unfortunately, we do not have time to contemplate this miracle. The vampires approach quickly."

"You can't run far with your wing like that. We've got to find some way to tape it up before we move any further." I pointed at the glass doors of the convention center. "Let's see if there's a first aid kit somewhere in there."

Nathaniel looked doubtful. "If we are trapped in there, we will be rats in a maze."

"I've already survived a maze," I said. "And we don't really have a choice. If your wing breaks off, I doubt that it can be fixed. Do you want to be grounded for the rest of your life?"

I could tell that he wanted to argue further but the thought of being flightless halted him.

"Very well," he said. "Let us move quickly. If we are fortunate, the vampires will be unable to distinguish our scent from that of other humans so recently near."

As we hurried toward the doors something occurred to me. "But we don't smell like humans."

"I know," Nathaniel said, and grabbed the handle of one of the doors. It opened easily. Whoever had left the building last hadn't bothered to lock up.

I remembered the vampire I'd met in an alley the previous November, whose eyes had flared at the prospect of taking my blood because I was a descendant of Lucifer. I wondered how easy it would be for the vampires to find us.

We entered the cavernous hall. Stairs and escalators were before us. To our right was an auditorium and signs for bathrooms at the bottom of a short flight of steps. Advertisements for upcoming events open to the public were piled on a ledge directly to our right.

"There has to be an aid station here," I said. "We just need to find a map and get there so we can tape you up."

"And then return outside as quickly as possible. I do not like the idea of being closed in this building with vampires."

After some searching we found a map of the building and located the aid station. McCormick Place is a sprawling complex that comprises several buildings. We were in the South building. The first aid center was on level 2.5, next to a FedEx office.

"Level 2.5?" I said as we hurried up the long flight of stairs to the upper floor. It was slower going than our usual hurry. Nathaniel really struggled. Even though we'd healed some of his wounds, the blood loss and exertion were taking their toll on him.

He paused on the stairs, panting. "You ask the question in a way that expects an answer from me. I have no possible explanation for any of the strange things that humans do."

"If Beezle were here, he would have something snappy to say," I said, putting my arm around him to help him to the top of the stairs.

"If Beezle were here, he would have stopped at the nearest pastry shop for a snack during the attack by the Agents," Nathaniel said.

"That was pretty good," I said. "A little more practice and you'll be up to sparring with my gargoyle in no time."

"I cannot wait."

His face was so serious as he said this that I burst out laughing. He smiled at me, a little half smile of satisfaction, and it almost stopped my breath. Nathaniel never smiled. He scowled; he frowned; he contemplated life in great seriousness. But he didn't smile, and I don't think I'd ever heard him laugh. Seeing him smile was like looking on the face of a different person.

We limped along until we found the mid-level concourse that housed the aid station. A large orange first aid sign hung above a glass door. I yanked on the handle and found it locked.

"Wait here for a second," I said, letting Nathaniel go.

He leaned against the wall, his pale eyes rimmed by circles of black, his blond hair sweaty and hanging in his face.

I put my hand on the door and spoke the words. "I am the Hound of the Hunt, and no walls shall hide my quarry."

The wall became fluid beneath my touch, and I slipped

through it. I had a moment to wonder when Lucifer was going to make me pay for this ability. So far it had been pretty useful to me but he hadn't called upon me to use it.

I unlocked the door and Nathaniel stumbled inside. I indicated that he should sit on the handy cot while I rummaged around for the necessary supplies. I returned to him with an armload of tape, gauze, disinfectant and painkiller.

"Take off your shirt and coat," I said.

"I have always wished you would say that, but I was hoping it would be under different circumstances," he muttered.

"Wow, two jokes in one day," I said. "Someone call Guinness."

"Why would you call a beer company to tell them that I had said something humorous?" He looked genuinely puzzled.

I laughed. "I guess angels don't worry too much about world records."

"The only records that matter for the fallen are Lord Lucifer's," Nathaniel said.

I touched the lapel of his coat. "I've got to see how bad the damage is."

He nodded, and we carefully pulled the coat down his arm on the uninjured side. Nathaniel paused, his face contorted in pain.

"Perhaps you should cut it off," he said.

"But we have nothing else to cover you. And it's January out there," I said. "We're not going to be able to take the El home, you know?"

"I only need to wear clothing as a concession to humans. The cold does not bother me," he said.

"If you say so," I said doubtfully.

"I would prefer to endure the cold than the excruciating pain of attempting to carefully remove the coat."

"Okay," I said, sitting on the cot beside him. "Turn toward the wall."

Nathaniel turned so his back faced me. The torn right wing was gruesome. I delicately cut from the hem of his coat up the middle of his back, through the space between his wings, and then pulled the two flaps of cloth away.

His white dress shirt was stuck to the middle of his back. He'd bled profusely, and then the blood had dried. In some places there were scabs that would be torn open as soon as I removed the shirt.

"Nathaniel," I said.

"I know. Do it quickly."

I made the cut with the scissors from the tail of the shirt through the collar. I grabbed the two pieces of the shirt at the top, bit my lip, and pulled.

Nathaniel only grunted as his skin was torn away. He drew the sleeves over his arms and off his wrists, dropping the remains of his shirt on the floor.

I wiped my eyes with the back of my hand, took a deep breath and opened the bottle of disinfectant. "This isn't going to get any better."

"Do not weep for me," he said quietly, then hissed as I poured the solution into his wounds. "After all the pain I have caused, I deserve whatever harm may befall me."

I paused. "What happened to, 'I was under orders, I didn't have a choice, and I didn't mean any of it anyway'?"

"I kissed you," he said simply. "When our magic entwined, I saw your heart. And I finally understood how you saw me, and why you held me in such contempt."

I applied gauze to the worst of the open wounds. There

were several bullet holes in addition to the broken wing. "That's probably the first time a kiss from me has ever had such a transformative effect," I muttered. "And I never held you in contempt."

"You did," Nathaniel said. "Your feelings for me were stronger than dislike from the beginning."

I thought back to the first moment I'd seen Nathaniel in my father's court, golden and glorious and full of disdain.

"You looked like an arrogant jerk. And it doesn't make a woman think well of you when you say, 'Hello, we just met, we're getting married.'"

"I was doing as—"

"Azazel told you, I know. Nathaniel, what happened to the bullets? Are they inside you? I don't want to patch up these holes now only to have to cut the bullets out later."

"My body rejected the bullets as part of the healing process," he said.

"Like Wolverine," I said, cleaning and covering the bullet holes.

"Whom?"

"I could explain, but you probably still wouldn't get it," I said. "Nathaniel, just what exactly did you do for my father?"

There was a long pause, and I wondered whether he would answer. I finished bandaging the bullet wounds and then contemplated my final task. I had thus far avoided looking too much at the mess that was his wing. I'd have to find some way to immobilize it until we could get him healed the angelic way.

"I am not certain that my status will improve with you if you know precisely what I did for Azazel," Nathaniel said carefully.

"I know that you didn't do anything good," I said.

I carefully touched the top part of the wing root, the part that had torn away. "I've got to move this closer to your back. I'm going to put it more or less in its proper place and tape it there."

I cut several long strips of tape to have at the ready.

Nathaniel nodded. I shifted the wing toward his spine. The exposed muscle and arteries squelched. I turned my head away, gagging.

"This is not a task for a pregnant woman," Nathaniel said.

His body had stiffened as I moved the wing into place, and his fists were clenched so hard that the veins in his arms bulged.

"The only person available is a pregnant woman," I said, breathing in through my nose and out through my mouth until the nausea passed. "If you want to talk about things a pregnant woman should or should not be doing—I probably shouldn't be fighting demons or killing vampires, either. But there's no choice. There's no one in this city besides me who both cares enough and has the ability to fight."

I packed gauze around the wings as best I could and then started tacking on tape to hold it in place. Once I'd managed to fix the wing into the position I wanted it, I took a roll of tape and wound it diagonally from Nathaniel's shoulder, over his back, under his rib and back up his chest to his shoulder again so that the tape looked like a sling. I repeated the action a few times until I was pretty sure the wing would stay in place.

"Done," I said finally.

Nathaniel tried to stand, trembled, and sat down on the cot again. "Now that you have mended me, you must get home. I am too weak to travel at this moment."

"Do we have to have this discussion again?" I said. "I'm not going."

"Madeline, I must sleep," he said. "My power can be restored if I can simply rest. But it is too risky for you to stay. If the vampires discover us here, we are, as you might say, sitting ducks."

"And what will you be if you're found here alone and sleeping? We've been here for a while and haven't been discovered. If the vampires were approaching as quickly as you thought they were, then surely they would have passed by the place where we landed already."

"It seems very unsafe to make such an assumption," Nathaniel said, or rather, mumbled. He was so tired that his words slurred together. His eyelids were almost closed, and all I could see was a slit of pale blue rimmed by white.

"Go to sleep," I said, pushing him down. "I'll keep watch."

He was too exhausted to argue any further. His eyes were closed and he was breathing deeply a moment later.

5

I WATCHED NATHANIEL FOR A MOMENT, MY THOUGHTS troubled.

I'd never expected what had happened when we put the veil over the hospital. I'd never considered the possibility that I'd be kissing Nathaniel at all, much less kissing him like I wanted that kiss to go somewhere.

That might have been the aspect of the situation that bothered me the most. In that moment I had wanted Nathaniel so much I had forgotten about Gabriel entirely. I put my hand to my stomach, to the place where Gabriel's child fluttered safe and sound inside me.

Gabriel had been mine for such a brief time that it seemed like a dream, the dream of another woman in another life. Every day I woke up to a new reality, a new threat, a new enemy. It had not been long since Gabriel died, but it felt like eons had passed.

I brushed Nathaniel's sweaty hair out of his face. He was so deeply asleep that he didn't even shift. I pulled my hand away, almost as disturbed by this newfound tenderness toward Nathaniel as I was by the lust I'd felt.

I moved away from him and noticed a phone hanging on the wall. I eagerly picked up the handset, thinking to call in the cavalry, and found the line dead. Beezle had probably worn out his little thumbs trying to text my cell phone. I just prayed to the Morningstar that he hadn't called J.B. My former boss tended to lose his mind when I was incommunicado.

Thinking of J.B. made me feel almost as guilty as thinking about Gabriel. J.B. had offered to marry me, to make Gabriel's son his own. J.B. had told me that he loved me, and I'd told him I would always love Gabriel.

Which I would. But then I'd kissed Nathaniel, and everything had gotten mixed up in my head. Things were further complicated by the fact that whenever Nathaniel was kind to me, I saw Gabriel. Were my feelings for Nathaniel real, or was I projecting Gabriel on him?

My baby moved around in my belly, and then my stomach growled. As usual, I was in the middle of a crisis with nothing to eat.

Nathaniel slept soundly and the concourse was silent outside. I hunted around the aid station until I found a couple of energy bars that someone had stashed on a shelf. They had the approximate taste and consistency of chalk but I was too hungry to care.

After I'd eaten I drew my sword and stood by the door. I passed the time by making a mental list of all the things I was going to eat when the vampire apocalypse was over and the restaurants reopened.

A hamburger with blue cheese and mushrooms and a

giant pile of waffle fries. Ann Sather cinnamon rolls. Pizza with peppers and mushrooms and onions and hot wings on the side. Toasted ravioli. Onion rings. Beezle would be in hog heaven. If I ate any kind of junk food, he interpreted that as default permission to gorge himself silly.

The concourse got darker and darker as the afternoon passed. I wondered whether safety lights would automatically switch on at a certain time, or whether the convention center remained unlit when not in use. Out of curiosity I flicked the switch on the wall and realized the point was moot. The electricity didn't seem to be working.

Was the whole city out, or just this part of it? It was bad enough to contemplate vampires running loose in the daytime. The thought of a lightless night crawling with monsters was too horrible to think about.

The day passed, and night fell, and Nathaniel slept on. I was half dozing on my feet, my shoulder leaning against the wall, when I saw something moving outside on the concourse. It was too dark and too far away for me to see clearly, but I could see enough to tell that it didn't move like any human.

I glanced back at Nathaniel. My first instinct was to investigate and possibly destroy without disturbing him. But if there was more than one creature or it was a protracted engagement, then we might end up separated. Nathaniel could die, sleeping and defenseless, while I was off playing Sherlock.

So I backed slowly away from the door, praying my movement would not be detected by whatever was out there. I knelt at Nathaniel's side and put my mouth close to his ear.

"Nathaniel," I whispered.

His eyes opened immediately. "You have let me sleep too long. There is something near."

"Yes," I said quietly.

He sat up with much more vigor than he'd had before his nap and picked up his sword. In the darkness I noticed a phenomenon I had observed once before. Nathaniel was surrounded by a faint aura, a glow that I did not have because I was not a full-blood angel. He moved toward the door without making a sound.

"Wait," I said. "Can you hide your halo? Otherwise whatever is out there will see you as easily as they would a firefly."

Nathaniel paused for a moment. "It is likely that whatever is out there will be able to scent us, but you are correct. We should not advertise our presence. Do you feel that your power has returned to its former strength?"

I shook my head. "I've probably got enough for a couple of nightfire blasts, but that's about it. I need sleep and a lot more food before I'll be back to normal."

Nathaniel nodded as if he'd expected this. "I will veil both of us; then we can investigate."

I felt the spell drop over me, and a moment later Nathaniel winked out of sight. The glass door to the aid station opened, and I eased out. The door closed behind me.

I had no idea where Nathaniel was because of the veil, and the darkness was almost total. It belatedly occurred to me that this was a very stupid idea. I'd been worried about getting separated, and now we were.

I slid as quietly as I could along the floor. Nathaniel could move as soundlessly as air when he chose, but I am not the ninja type. I gripped my sword in front of me, the blade raised high, ready to slash at anything that came near.

I had only a second to swing when the monster came out of the darkness. There was a skittering noise, and then the gaping maw of the vampire appeared, grainy and blurred in the heavy darkness. I didn't stop to think. I just let muscle memory do its job and take the vampire's head off as it had so many times before.

The whole episode lasted less than a minute, but my nerves were strung so tight that I stood there panting for a moment. Nathaniel spoke from behind me.

"There are more in the building. I can hear them investigating."

"How many? Can you tell?" I whispered.

"It seems like an exploratory party. Perhaps twenty. If they find anything of note, they will report back to the horde."

"Do you think they know this one is dead?" I asked.

"Vampires generally cannot sense the death of one of their own unless there is a blood bond, such as that between a maker and his child. But we must assume that all of these vampires consumed Azazel's serum, and we do not know what kind of effect that may have."

"Let's just try to get out of here as quickly as we can," I said. "And stay near me. I don't want to lose you."

The aid station wasn't far from the stairs at the entryway, so after a few moments of groping our way through the darkness we were back at the top of the escalators. I looked down the stairs.

It was full dark, but we didn't need light to detect the mass of vampires on the street outside. Through the glass doors and high windows, we could see the horde moving almost as one giant animal, a tremendous shape writing in the darkness. We backed away from the stairs.

"I don't think we want to go that way," I said.

"Where are the other exits?" Nathaniel asked.

"There's another pedestrian walkway going over to the lakeside center," I said. "Or we can try to get into the Metra tunnel and follow the tracks for a while, but the tracks terminate at Randolph and we'd be right in the epicenter of the horde. Plus, the tunnel goes away pretty quickly and we'd be out in the open."

"It does not seem wise to put ourselves in a position where we might be trapped in a tunnel," Nathaniel said.

"We have to take the same chance either way. If we go into the pedestrian bridge, we'll have several feet where we have no way to escape if there are vamps ahead and behind. If we go into the Metra tunnel, we'll be underground until it comes out of McCormick Place."

"And then we will be exposed."

I didn't need to see Nathaniel's face to know that he was brooding. I didn't particularly like our choices—or our chances—either.

I had no wings. Nathaniel's wing was broken. My magic was burned out for the time being, and we had no way to call for help. Most annoyingly, I could sense that Lucifer was somewhere out of touch again. The snake tattoo on my right palm had been very quiet for some time now. I wondered, as always, where Lucifer went on these occasions. Puck had said that the Morningstar was going somewhere he should not. What secrets of the universe were closed off to a being as powerful as Lucifer?

"It seems wisest to move toward the lake," Nathaniel said finally, his quiet voice breaking my reverie. "The vampires appear to be avoiding the shoreline."

"Why?" I said. "Is there any truth to that old chestnut about vampires and running water?"

"Obviously not, since they crossed the bridge over the Chicago River with ease," he said. "But they do not like the lake, it seems. I observed that none of them came close to it as we flew over the city."

Nathaniel's hand found mine in the darkness, and I let him hold it. I didn't want to get separated.

The convention center seemed so large and empty as we crossed through it, a relic from a time that had passed and might never return. How could the world go on as it had been before everyone knew that vampires existed? How long would it be before other things-that-went-bump-in-the-night decided not to hide their existence anymore?

We paused as we reached the pedestrian tunnel that crossed to the lakeside center. The passage yawned into the darkness. Nathaniel squeezed my hand.

"I cannot sense the vampires any longer," he said. "They may have rejoined the horde."

He dropped the veil. It was a waste of energy if we didn't need it.

"I can't believe the death of one of their own would go unnoticed," I said as we stepped into the tunnel.

The bridge crossed over Lake Shore Drive and was lined with windows. The flurry of activity that we had seen that morning had long since ended. Cars sat lined up bumper to bumper. Their occupants had either been eaten by the vampires or fled successfully on foot.

My palms were sweaty. The air inside the tunnel was stale and hot despite the cold outside. I was afraid, and it was a terrible shock to realize this. I'd faced many enemies, and been many times outnumbered. I'd defeated plenty of powerful foes, much to their shock and mine.

But I didn't have my wings anymore, and my magic was quiet. I had a child to protect. I'd never felt more vulnerable. The dark had become a place of lurking nightmares, and I wasn't sure I could overcome them.

We reached the lakeside center without incident. But my dread only intensified. My luck was not that good. I'd never been able to hide from the monster in the closet. My monster always came out to try to eat my head.

"You must calm yourself," Nathaniel said softly. "I can feel your blood pulsing through your hand. If I can detect it, then the vampires will be able to as well. They are bred to detect weakness, to feed upon distress."

"I know," I said, and my voice didn't sound like my own. I could hear the strain and the panic. I was panicking. I never panicked.

"You are not yourself," Nathaniel said, and scooped me up like a baby in his arms.

"You c-c-can't," I said. "How will you fight if you're holding me?"

"Shh," Nathaniel said. "I do not sense any threat nearby, but you will draw one to us if you continue to behave thus."

"I don't know what's wrong with me," I whispered. I could feel my heartstone inside my chest, pulsing hot, but my skin was cold.

"I suspect that you are exhausted and, if you will forgive me for saying so, in the grip of your hormones," he said. He moved swiftly through the dark, descending to street level.

"You think this is happening because I'm pregnant? Is it normal for pregnant women to have panic attacks?"

"Is it normal for a part-human to carry the child of a creature that was half-nephilim? Is it normal for a pregnant woman to run all over the city fighting demons and vampires and then spend hours watching over me when she ought to be sleeping?" He sounded angry with himself for spending so much time resting.

We emerged from the lakeside center by a small walkway that connected to the lakefront path. There was a bike rack with a rusty bike frame attached to it just in front of the doors. Both of the bike's wheels were missing.

To the north of us was the museum campus. I could see the dome of the Adler Planetarium on its jetty protruding into the lake, and the distinctive bowl of the Soldier Field. The Field Museum and the Shedd Aquarium lay beyond, and farther past was the beautiful skyline of my city.

To the right the lake crashed against the shore, plates of ice shifting and breaking. The wind whipped frosted caps of waves in the moonlight, and more stars than I'd ever been able to view above Chicago.

The lights were out as far as the eye could see. The city had been swallowed by the night. In the distance I could hear the occasional scream, the staccato pop of gunfire. Overlaying that noise was a steady, high-pitched hum, like the buzz of cicadas—the sound of the vampire horde moving through the city.

Nathaniel paused. I could tell that he was assessing the possibility of a vampire attack. My panic had eased once we got outside, and with its diminishment came embarrassment.

"You can put me down now," I said.

Nathaniel shifted his gaze to my face. My cheeks heated under his assessing look. After a minute he placed me on my feet. He was wearing only his black dress pants and boots, and the sheath for his sword was slung over his shoulder. The cold did not seem to disturb him in the least.

"We must try to escape the horde," Nathaniel said apologetically. "I know you are tired."

I shook my head. "You're right. We have to get home somehow and meet up with the others. We're not going to get there unless we walk."

We fell into step beside each other on the path. I figured we were ten or eleven miles from my house. At the pace I was trudging it would take at least four hours to get home.

Nathaniel was on high alert, but we walked for several minutes without encountering anyone or anything.

The vampires did seem to be avoiding the lake. I wondered why. As far as I knew, nothing more dangerous than sturgeon lived there. As far as I knew.

I looked at the dark surface of the lake, which suddenly seemed like it had some unknown menace lurking in its depths. I shook my head. I had enough menace in my life without imagining more. If there was a monster in the lake, then it could stay there, and so much the better if it worked as an anti-vampire repellant.

We passed under the overpass next to the Shedd Aquarium. The path curved around the building before turning north again. Water broke against the rocks below the safety wall. Nathaniel paused beneath the overpass.

"There is someone on the path ahead," he whispered, drawing his sword.

I couldn't make out the person—or creature. It must be keeping to the shadows.

"Is it human?" I said very softly.

"No," he replied. "Stay back."

The moon shifted behind the clouds.

One second Nathaniel was beside me, and the next he was gone. I didn't even see him move.

The clouds drifted past the moon. I saw Nathaniel silhouetted in the lunar light. He stood over an unmoving form, his sword at his side. The tip of the blade faced the ground. There was a dark stain sliding down the metallic surface. He turned his head to look over his shoulder at me, and his expression was full of savage glee. He did not look like himself. He looked like . . . someone. I couldn't put my finger on it. Someone I had seen recently, had spoken to . . .

"You may approach," he said, and the smoky tendrils of memory slipped away before I could grasp them.

I came to Nathaniel's side and looked down at the creature he'd beheaded. It was a sort of humanoid/snake combo.

"That thing looks like Amarantha and Violet after Lucifer cursed them," I said.

"It is one of Focalor's foot soldiers," Nathaniel said.

"Focalor, huh?" I said, nudging the body with the toe of my boot. "I'd almost forgotten about him with everything else going on. Do you think he's behind the vampire attacks?"

"He was one of Azazel's conspirators in the uprising against Lucifer. But I am not certain that Azazel would have trusted Focalor with his plans for the serum and the vampires. I always sensed that Azazel was not entirely forthcoming with Focalor."

"Then why are Focalor's flunkies hanging around Chicago?" I asked.

Nathaniel shrugged. "Focalor knows how to take advantage of a bad situation. And he is not the only one."

"The pix demons," I said.

Nathaniel nodded. "And others like them. There will be many creatures that see this city as a fruit ripe for the plucking. Soon it will become a battleground."

In my mind's eye I saw my fair city decimated by violence, the humans dead or gone, demons tearing one another to shreds in the streets as they fought to give their master a jewel for their crowns.

If that happened, I, too, would be dead, and my child with me, for none of those masters could possibly allow me to live. I would always be a threat, especially with the shadow of Lucifer standing behind me.

Lucifer would drop the magical equivalent of a nuclear bomb on the city if I was dead, and that would be the end of any war. The Chicago I knew would cease to exist either way.

"Every time I think I've thought through all the implications, I realize how stupid I've been," I said tiredly.

"You are not stupid," Nathaniel said.

"I must be. Why else would I think I could stop this?" I jabbed my hand in the direction of the skyline. "I've got enemies galore but hardly any allies to speak of. I put myself at a disadvantage by giving up my Agent's powers so I could make a point to Sokolov."

"You are still the granddaughter of Lucifer, as you yourself told Sokolov."

"As far as I can tell, being the granddaughter of Lucifer has brought me nothing but grief," I said, my lips pressed together as I stared off in the distance. "And, Nathaniel . . . he's backing me into a cage. I can feel it. Slowly, inexorably. I twist and I turn, I growl and I claw, but Lucifer is the lion tamer and he holds the whip. Soon I'll realize I've gone too far backward and the cage door will close."

Nathaniel said nothing. Nathaniel, whatever he felt for me, would never go against Lucifer voluntarily. He had done so once at Azazel's behest, but I was sure that he would not put his existence on the line for me to squirm away from the Morningstar. He seemed unable to do so himself.

"What did Lucifer do to you?" I asked, giving voice to the question I'd wondered earlier.

He was silent for a long time. I wasn't sure whether he was going to answer me .

"Lord Lucifer excels at letting you think that your choices are your own when they are actually his," Nathaniel said finally.

"I know," I said, thinking of my marriage, the relationship that was forbidden until Lucifer had decided otherwise.

At the time I'd thought it was a reward. Once Gabriel died and I'd realized I was pregnant, I discovered that Lucifer had manipulated us so that he would get the grandchild he wanted. "What did you want so badly that Lucifer gave it to you?"

"Power," Nathaniel said. "I wanted to be respected, to have the status I felt that I deserved as the son of a Grigori. It is only now that I see that I desired power because Lucifer taught me to do so, because he manipulated me into wanting it. To betraying . . ."

He trailed off, ruminating on the past.

"Betraying who?" I asked quietly.

It seemed like he was drowning in his memories, and that he was having a hard time swimming back to the surface.

"My mother," he said.

"Your mother? What did she ever do to Lucifer?" I asked.

"She chose my father," Nathaniel said simply. "Lucifer wanted her, and when Lucifer desires something, he gets it. My mother, Cassiel, would not have him. She already loved Zerachiel. Lucifer seemed to withdraw from the field with grace. When I was born, he took a special interest in me, favoring me over the other children of the Grigori. He was like a beloved uncle, always ready with a game or a prize. He told me I was special, that I would sit beside his throne one day. Cassiel and Zerachiel took Lucifer's interest to mean that they were forgiven. It was not so.

"When I was old enough, he promised me that if I would help him with some small tasks here and there, I could come to his court as an apprentice to Azazel, his own right hand. It was heady stuff for a young man. Azazel held much power in Lucifer's realm. As his apprentice I would be ranked above many of the fallen who were much older and more experienced than I.

"The tasks seemed simple enough at first. I was asked to carry messages, and I did, full of my own importance. Then I was asked my opinion on events I witnessed in my father's court. Soon I was eavesdropping on private conversations, lurking in places where I might be well positioned to hear, and reporting, always, back to Lord Lucifer.

"Then, one day, I fell asleep in the garden under the gazebo. The flowers and grass were tall there, and I was well hidden by the foliage. I had simply been enjoying the sun and drifted off. When I awoke, I heard voices arguing. They were trying to be circumspect, but they were loud enough for me to hear that one of them was my mother. The other was a man I did not know. They were speaking of Lord Lucifer. I did not hear all of the words. But I heard Cassiel say 'treason.'

"I remained where I was until their conversation was concluded. All I could think of was that I had uncovered a plot of treason, and Lord Lucifer would reward me well for such a discovery. I rushed to report what little I had heard to the Morningstar. I did not consider that my mother would be caught in the net. I was thinking only of the other man, the one she had argued with. I thought Lord Lucifer would ask my mother whom she was speaking to so that he could find the real conspirator. I thought that she was trying to dissuade the man.

"Of course, I was young and foolish. Lord Lucifer considered them both as plotters, and when my mother was taken for questioning and tortured, she admitted as such. But she would never tell Lord Lucifer who the other man was.

"She was executed in the Morningstar's court. When my mother was beheaded I was standing at the right hand of Azazel, who stood at the right hand of Lucifer."

He fell silent again. My heart ached for the boy he had been, for the weight that he had carried over the years. He had watched his mother killed because she had committed treason against Lucifer, because he had revealed her.

He must have thought his life was over when Azazel had ordered him to participate in a rebellion against their highest lord. I wondered, not for the first time, why Lucifer had allowed Nathaniel to live. Then I realized how much Lucifer enjoyed serving his revenge ice-cold.

"Cassiel picked Zerachiel over Lucifer, and then he waited years and years, until you were born and old enough to be used as a tool for vengeance?" I asked.

"Yes," Nathaniel said. "It is why I tell you over and over not to cross him."

"And you still declare your fealty to him?"

"I have no choice. I must have a master. It is the way of my kind. And as Lucifer is the most powerful of us all, it is safer to be under his wing than in his sights."

"You aren't under his wing," I said. "Lucifer plays the long game."

Nathaniel's life would come to a sudden end one day for his participation in Azazel's plot. I knew that with the certainty of the sun rising, and I was sure that Nathaniel knew it, too. Yet he kept protecting me, kept putting his life at risk, kept trying to restore his honor even though he was a dead man walking. I realized I could love that kind of man, and that was a disconcerting thought.

"Let us keep walking," Nathaniel finally said. "There may be other creatures lurking and it is unwise for us to linger so long in an exposed area."

As we walked it was hard to get my mind off the tale that Nathaniel had just told. It made me see him in an entirely different light, one in which his selfish behavior and his icy demeanor were just a shield to protect himself. Nathaniel was brooding, locked in his own thoughts.

We continued on the path around the aquarium without further incident. I wondered what would become of all the animals inside with no keepers to care for them.

Beezle liked to go to the aquarium sometimes—safely hidden in my pocket, of course. He enjoyed the seahorses, of all things, and the otters. He also liked the popcorn stand on the lower level, because he could eat popcorn and watch the dolphins swimming.

No one would be taking care of the dolphins now, or the sharks or the starfish. Some of them might be dead already with the power out and the filters on the tanks silent. Whatever wasn't dead would be soon.

It was another problem I could not fix, another tragedy I couldn't prevent. And then I was crying again, crying so hard I could hardly see in front of me. It was almost foolish to weep over animals when so many people had died in one day, but I couldn't help it. I was sick of death. In my life I'd seen more of it than I ever wanted.

Nathaniel stopped, touched my shoulder. I turned toward him. He did not offer platitudes. He did not embrace me. He wiped the tears from my cheeks with his hands, his face troubled. His hands lingered on my face, cupped it as he studied me. The silence between us stretched thin. I realized I held my breath, and my tears had stopped.

"You do not love me," Nathaniel said. His voice was steady.

I thought of Gabriel. "No."

"You do not need love for this," he said, and then his mouth was on mine, savage and unrelenting, taking my breath away.

6

I FELT THE FLARE OF HEAT BETWEEN US, THE POWER that flowed from him now that he had been restored by sleep. I clung to him, unsure about what I needed but knowing that this was what I wanted.

Nathaniel offered me no comfort. He did not treat me gently. I didn't want gentle. I wanted his power and his ferocity. I wanted him to be everything Gabriel wasn't so that I could forget how much it hurt, just for a little while.

He pulled his mouth away, his breath harsh, and looked into my eyes. "You do not need to love me. But you do need to choose me."

I started to speak, but he put his thumb over my mouth.

"If you choose me because you want comfort, I will not object. If you choose me because you want to forget, I do not object. If it is simply a matter of lust, I do not object. But I want you to look at me and know who I am. I want you to choose me, not fall into my arms in secret and pretend I am somebody else."

I nodded. He was right. However complicated our relationship was, he didn't deserve to be a cipher for Gabriel. Gabriel's memory was worth more than that to me.

"I'm not ready to make that choice," I said, moving reluctantly away from him.

He released me, his hands brushing over my throat, my shoulders, before pulling away.

"Do not wait too long, or you may find your choices taken from you."

"What does that mean?" I asked as we began walking north again. Nothing stirred this close to the lake except for us. It was like Nathaniel and I were the last two people on earth.

"I am aware that you do not make yourself a priority; nor would you wish to contemplate matters of court politics when there is a larger crisis at hand," he began.

"I'm sure you've heard what I think of fallen politics even when there's *not* an apocalypse going down."

Nathaniel nodded, acknowledging the truth of this statement. "However, you cannot think that Lord Lucifer will let you go long without a consort, especially in your current condition."

The bars of the cage were closing around me. "Are you saying I'd better choose a partner soon or Lucifer will choose one for me? Are you offering to sacrifice yourself?"

"You could do far worse than I. J.B. is also an acceptable choice."

I raised an eyebrow at him. "Most guys don't like to talk up the competition when they're trying to get a girl."

Nathaniel shrugged. "J.B. is steadfast. He is both magically powerful and politically well connected. If you married him, you would be somewhat protected from Titania's wrath."

"I notice you only say 'somewhat' protected," I said.

"You diminished Oberon in front of his queen and the highest court in the faerie kingdom. Whatever the terms of your trial by combat, Titania will not be able to let such an insult stand. But if you marry the king of a lower court, she will not be able to kill you outright. And there are more ways to protect your child from her if you are wed."

"You're not making a real strong case for yourself, pal."

"Very well," Nathaniel said, drawing himself up. "I am the only son of Zerachiel of the Grigori and Cassiel, an angel of the host. I served as the right hand of Azazel for over two thousand years, and I have pledged my fealty to Lord Lucifer, your grandfather. If you were to wed me, you can be assured that I would devote myself to you and the protection of your child."

I shook my head at him. "You still don't get it. Politics and status don't matter to me."

"They should. But that is not all I have to offer," he said, and then his hand was beneath my coat.

I stood still, mesmerized by his eyes, by his touch. "I thought we weren't doing this anymore," I said, but I didn't pull away.

"I did not say that. I said I wanted you to choose. I will use whatever weapon I have to make you choose me." He smiled, and his smile was so wicked that I almost damned myself then and there just so I could find out what was behind that look.

He pulled his hand away slowly, and I could think again.

"Keep walking," I said raggedly, and he chuckled beneath his breath.

How could my feelings for one person change so quickly?

It wasn't that long ago that I wanted to kill Nathaniel, and I wouldn't have shed a single tear if I had. But since we'd joined our powers to create the protective veil over the hospital, it was like I couldn't stay away from him. What had that spell done to us? In some ways the blending of our magic had felt more intimate than sex, and sex bound people together whether they wanted to be or not. Or . . .

I looked at Nathaniel through the corners of my eyes. He seemed calm and self-contained, as usual. Could he have cast a spell on me while we were joined? Could I be drawn to him now because of something artificial he'd planted inside me?

But you saw inside his heart, a little voice in my head argued.

That doesn't mean anything, I argued back. *He's thousands of years old, and much more practiced in duplicity than you are.*

But his duplicity is a front. He's just playing the game that Lucifer taught him.

But what if that whole story was just another manipulation to make me believe in him? I was giving myself a headache trying to see all of the angles.

And then there was the matter of his changeability, his moral fluidity. I never could get a fix on Nathaniel from the start. It always seemed that he was adjusting to the situation, that he would be whatever he thought he should be at the moment. Just like a . . .

I looked at him more sharply now, realizing who it was he'd reminded me of as he stood over Focalor's soldier in the moonlight.

Puck.

"Nathaniel, who did you say your father was?" I asked,

like I couldn't remember, like he hadn't just told me his whole family history.

"Zerachiel of the Grigori," Nathaniel said. "But I thought you said you did not care for politics."

"Are you certain he's your father?" I persisted.

"Have you not seen him at the court? I am the mirror image of my father," Nathaniel said with a touch of irritation.

"Do you have any brothers or sisters?"

"No. Why the abrupt interest in my family?" he asked.

"Just curious," I said, my eyes searching his face for confirmation of my suspicions.

I couldn't tell him what I thought without proof. There was one more thing I needed to ask, though.

"Does Zerachiel have children among the nephilim?" I asked.

"No," he said, and there was a real haughtiness to his voice, almost like the old Nathaniel. "My father alone was able to exercise self-restraint in the face of his lust. He knew it was not natural for angels to procreate with human women. It was one of the things Cassiel loved about him. She hated the nephilim children of the other Grigori."

"I don't think so," I muttered, deciding now wasn't the time to be offended on behalf of human women.

From what I knew of angels, they would take any opportunity to spread their seed far and wide, and they had no trouble doing so. Azazel had at least two other children besides me—Antares and an unnamed nephilim. He may have had more.

On the heels of that disconcerting thought came the further disconcerting thought that another half sibling might show up on my doorstep and try to kill me.

Stay focused. No need to borrow trouble.

Lucifer had more children than he could count, especially since it seemed he'd screw anything that stood still long enough. Heck, even Gabriel had gotten me pregnant on the first try.

What were the chances that Zerachiel had managed to make only one child in thousands of years?

Pretty damn slim, I thought.

It was Titania and Oberon all over again. Puck had come to Titania in the guise of Oberon to preserve the myth that she was not cuckolding her husband. But genes had a tendency to tell. Titania's son, Bendith, had Puck's brilliant blue eyes. There could be no doubt who Bendith's father was, no matter what Titania and Oberon said.

Puck could have come to Nathaniel's mother in the guise of Zerachiel, as he had done to Titania in the form of Oberon. Somehow he'd manipulated the conception so thoroughly that not a trace of Puck's physical traits had shown up in Nathaniel. But his true nature was still there, underneath the skin, waiting to be unlocked.

Could Nathaniel really be Puck's child? If he was, then Puck had done a good job of not betraying the relationship in Titania's court. He'd acted like he was meeting Nathaniel for the first time.

Of course, if Lucifer found out—or even suspected— that Puck had a child inside Lucifer's organization, then Nathaniel's life wouldn't be worth squat.

Maybe all of this was in my head, anyway. I had no proof of my suspicions, and nothing to go on except Nathaniel's expression in the moonlight.

But maybe, just maybe, that was why Nathaniel's mother had been killed. Maybe she hadn't been plotting against Lucifer, but had simply borne a child that had not been her husband's. There were plenty of examples in human history of queens whose lives had been forfeit because they had betrayed their kings. The sanctity of the bloodline must always be preserved. That was treason enough if Lucifer was looking for a reason to take revenge on Cassiel.

But Lucifer couldn't have suspected that Puck was the father of her child.

And he moved differently, I thought. When he'd killed Focalor's creature, Nathaniel had moved more quickly than he ever had before. And he could suddenly hear the vampires moving all over the city, a skill I was only just realizing was notable. It wasn't precisely a smoking gun, but a lot of circumstantial evidence was there.

None of these abilities had manifested before I'd kissed Nathaniel. Had I somehow unlocked powers he was not even aware of? And would that make him more recognizable to Lucifer as Puck's child? Had I inadvertently put his life in greater danger?

"You seem very troubled," Nathaniel said. "The frown on your face would terrify a demon."

I made a concerted effort to unfurrow my brow. "Just worried about the vampire problem."

"And about the situation between you and I," he said.

"Yeah," I said, because it was sort of true, and because I didn't want him to ask any more questions. I might betray myself.

Somehow we'd managed to walk almost to Navy Pier without my noticing or without encountering any monsters. We approached the double-decker bridge that connected the lakefront path to its continuation north of the bridge. The upper deck of the bridge was Lake Shore Drive.

There was a slight grade here, and we both paused, assessing the situation. The path took a soft turn at the strut that supported the bridge, and the lack of streetlight made the blind turn ominous.

"Can you hear anything up there?" I asked very quietly.

"No," he said. "However, that does not mean something isn't there."

"It doesn't feel right," I said, and Nathaniel nodded. "But I can't tell if it's because the whole city doesn't feel right, or because something specifically is wrong up there."

"We have no other way of getting home," Nathaniel said. "We cannot fly. If we go west, we will walk right into the thick of the vampire horde."

I looked dubiously at the river below. "Swim in the very cold water?"

Nathaniel shook his head. "I think it would be very unwise to get into the water at this time. I have noticed the lake is changing."

I'd been too wrapped up in my thoughts to notice anything special about the lake. Now I observed that a light, phosphorescent fog rose above the surface as far as the eye could see.

"That can't be good," I said.

"Something is awakening. Something ancient," Nathaniel said, and it was almost as if he were in a trance. "I can feel it in the back of my mind."

"And is this ability to feel primeval creatures in your mind a new thing?" I asked casually.

Nathaniel frowned and looked at me. "I have never sensed its presence before."

Great. More new powers. "Handy that you can now," I said quickly, before he thought too deeply about why. "So we don't want to jump in the river, as I'm assuming whatever's in the lake would not be impeded by the locks."

"The creature gives an impression of great size."

"That would be 'no,' then. The bridge it is." I drew my sword, and Nathaniel followed suit.

We approached the bridge slowly. As the girders rose above us, it was hard not to feel like we were being enclosed in a cave. Lower Wacker was to our left, and connected both Lake Shore Drive and Wacker Drive via ramps that were just south of us.

Lake Shore Drive was silent above, a cemetery of abandoned cars. Strangely, there was only one vehicle on our level—a yellow cab. It looked like the driver had simply stopped in the middle of the street and jumped out.

There was a dark stain in the road beside the open door of the car. It might not have been blood. It might have been an oil stain. A really big oil stain.

The wind picked up and blew my hair in front of my eyes, and that distracted me for a second. I touched my hair, which Chloe had neatened into a pixie cut for me only last week. Now my curls brushed against my jawline.

"Nathaniel, my hair grew back," I said, and looked down at the missing fingers that had so recently reemerged. The scabs on my back itched.

"Hmmm?" Nathaniel said. He was scanning the area for threats, which was probably the smart thing to do.

"My hair grew back. And my fingers grew back." *And you have powers that you never had before.* My conviction that something had fundamentally changed inside both of us during the spell was getting stronger by the moment.

Nathaniel stopped and focused on me. His eyes widened as he took in my new hairstyle. "Your wings . . ."

"I thought of that, too," I said. "But so far my back is just itchy."

We were about halfway across the bridge. A metal fence separated us from the river below. I couldn't see anything lurking in the shadows ahead, or above.

I wasn't really thinking about the possibility of something coming up from below. So when the vampire struck, neither Nathaniel nor I was prepared.

7

THE VAMPIRE'S ARMS CURVED OVER THE FENCE AND took me off my feet before I had half a chance to think. Before I knew it the vamp had bound me tight to its side with a fiercely strong grip and nestled me against its cold body. I couldn't move my arms. The world stank of blood and meat, and the vampire chittered wildly, sounding like an insect.

It was skittering upside down on the underside of the lower deck of the bridge. I faced downward, but I couldn't see anything except the blood-soaked jaws of the vampire. My head and stomach whirled. Nausea was an inevitability. I was already exhausted, but I had nothing in my stomach to throw up. I was plastered to the side of a vampire, gagging on my own bile.

I'd dropped my sword on the bridge—I'd heard it clatter on the pavement—and my magic was still burned out and useless.

Then there was a tremendous roar of rage, and the whole bridge shook. The vampire paused, the way spiders will when they know they're about to get crushed under somebody's heel. I could see nothing, but there was a sound of cracking pavement, and chunks of street smashed into me.

There was the ozone smell of nightfire. The vampire screamed, started to fall. I was falling, too, and then Nathaniel's hand was somehow wrapped in my coat, holding me fast while the vampire descended into the river below. He pulled through the hole he'd smashed and rolled me into his arms.

"That was close," I said, my voice muffled. My face was pressed against his bare chest.

He didn't say anything. He just held me tight. It might have been pleasant under another circumstance, but I couldn't move my arms and it was a little difficult to breathe.

"Nathaniel," I said. "Nathaniel! I need oxygen."

He finally released me, and I took several deep lungfuls of air.

"I should have been more cautious," he said. "I am sorry."

"Are you apologizing for not predicting the unpredictable?" I said. "I wasn't looking for the vampire under the bridge, either. Although I probably should have been, given that I encounter monsters with abnormal frequency."

"I feel like a fool," Nathaniel said. "I had only just declared myself to you. I'd pronounced that I would protect you and your child, and a monster stole you from beneath my nose."

"Don't beat yourself up about it. It happens to me all the time. You know what's weird, though? Why didn't the vampire just eat me right away?"

"Perhaps it had gorged itself earlier and was planning on saving you for another meal," Nathaniel said.

I shook my head. "I don't think so. Don't you think it would have at least drained me a little so I would be more compliant? It seemed it wanted to take me somewhere."

"To its master, perhaps?" Nathaniel asked.

"That would be logical. If it was fetching me for a higher-ranking vampire, then it probably wouldn't want to offend its boss by taking my blood."

"Which then begs the question of why the vampire wanted you specifically."

"Yeah. That's not really a question I'd enjoy answering. I'm sure I won't like the result, whatever it is." I looked around. "Where's my sword?"

"There," Nathaniel said, pointing back toward the place where the vampire had grabbed me. "I could not lift it. It would not allow me to touch it."

"But you gave me that sword," I said. "It belonged to your father."

"The sword seems to have given itself to you completely."

Or maybe the sword of Lucifer recognized the blood of the Morningstar's sworn enemy, but I wasn't going to say that. Not yet, anyway. Not until I was 100 percent sure— but I was getting there. I wondered how Nathaniel would react if I was right. It might unhinge him. He put a lot of stock in the quality of his bloodline.

I fetched the sword, and then jogged back to Nathaniel. "Let's get home."

There was the distinct click of a safety being released behind us.

"You've got to be kidding me," I said.

We turned around slowly to face Bryson's furious glare. He held a semiautomatic pistol, and it was pointed at me.

"What is your problem?" I asked. "Has it escaped your attention that the city has been overrun by vampires?"

"Sokolov wants you brought in. So you will be brought in," Bryson said. "He's had enough of your defiance."

"Does he know you tried to shoot us out of the sky earlier?" I asked, thinking of Nathaniel's shredded wing, our terrifying fall through the air. "Or am I wanted dead or alive?"

Bryson smiled briefly. "I am supposed to bring you in alive. But if there were an unfortunate accident, I believe Sokolov would understand."

I was suddenly angry, so angry that I didn't know what to do with all that energy. I was sick to death of being hounded by the shortsighted Agency when there were more important problems at hand.

My magic leapt to the fore, and my power pulsed through the night.

Nathaniel put his hand on my shoulder. "Ease down, unless you wish to destroy the bridge while we are still on it."

The darkness was filled with light, and it was coming from me.

"Hear this, Bryson," I said, and my voice was different. There was a power and a promise in it. "If you attempt to take, threaten or harm me or my friends again, then I will destroy you so utterly that the world will not even recall that you ever existed."

I could crush him like a bug. His gun was a toy, a meaningless thing that he used to feel powerful. I blasted his hand with nightfire and the weapon clattered to the ground.

I stalked toward him, and Bryson, super-soldier of the Agency, backed away from me.

"You have been broken by one of my kind before," I said. "But obviously not enough. The pain you felt then will be nothing compared to what horrors you will suffer at my hands."

I could do it. I knew I could. I could make him hurt. The power was in me. There was a dark shadow in my heart, and it urged me onward.

"Madeline!" Nathaniel said behind me, and his hand roughly pulled me back. "Madeline! You are not yourself. Think."

He gave me a little shake, and I nearly blasted him before his urgent tone got through to me. The darkness receded as suddenly as it had emerged.

"What . . . what was that about?" I gasped. I looked to my left. Bryson had fled. Which was good. I didn't think I could live with myself if I'd done all the horrible things I'd been contemplating.

"You must be careful," Nathaniel said. "As more of Lucifer's power is revealed in you, so, too, is his darkness."

I had felt hints of this before, a sinister undertone to the magic that was emerging slowly inside me. But I'd always thought I was in control of it, that my own personality would overcome any darker impulses. Now I wasn't so sure.

I tipped my head forward to Nathaniel's shoulder for a moment, weary beyond belief. Now that the burst of power had receded, my whole being just wanted to lie down and rest. But I wouldn't be able to rest until we were home.

"Let's go," I said, lifting my head. Nathaniel nodded.

It took us most of the night. My weariness was extreme, and while the vampires avoided the path along the lake, there were plenty of other things that did not—demons, mostly, roaming for stragglers.

We avoided the creatures if we could, always mindful of the fact that neither of us could fly. When we could not avoid conflict Nathaniel's newfound strength and speed tended to keep the encounters short. As we got farther away from the Loop, we felt safer cutting west and then north again on the city streets. As the day approached, we were on Clark, the distinctive curve of Wrigley Field's façade before us.

The streets were so quiet. Many people had obviously fled, and any who had stayed behind were safely tucked inside their apartments and condos, cowering behind furniture stacked against doors.

In their hands would be Mace and hair spray and fire extinguishers and guns, for those who believed in that sort of thing. Others would be on their knees, hands folded and eyes shut tight, calling the name of their chosen savior.

All around us was the debris of a fallen world—a smashed cell phone, a Starbucks cup, a dropped scarf, a suitcase that had broken open and spilled its contents all over the street.

Inside the case were the things its owner had considered important—a wedding photo in a silver frame, the glass shattered; wool socks rolled in multicolored balls; lacy underwear; designer jeans; a stack of Fiber One bars; a jewelry roll that had already been stripped of anything valuable; a deck of cards.

Farther down the street was a stuffed dinosaur, trampled in some mad stampede. The sight of it made me painfully sad. The child who'd dropped that stuffed toy would be crying, confused and scared, and now lacked even the simple, basic comfort of their favorite friend. Wherever that child was, the night would be a little darker, a little colder, without their dinosaur. Everyone knows dinosaurs keep the monsters away.

The bars on Clark Street advertised drink specials, live bands, half-priced hamburgers. The flags above the storefronts fluttered pathetically in the wind, the logos of the Cubs and the Blackhawks, the Bulls and the Bears. The red stars of the Chicago city flag looked like bloodstained hands lined up in a row.

Yesterday all of these things had seemed desperately important—whether or not the Hawks beat the Wings, or your friend was late to the bar. Today everyone was just trying to hold on, to not have to witness their family being devoured by vampires.

All of the edifices of humanity—the roads and the cars, the fast-food joints and the parking meters, the smartphones and the bicycles, lazy days at the ballpark, afternoons grilling while the kids scoot up and down the sidewalk, boutiques and thrift stores, Italian ice and Italian beef, cheering for a touchdown in a bar with a mouthful of nachos and beer sloshing over the table, complaining about the traffic, complaining about the taxes, complaining about the mayor and the garbage pickup and the noisy college kids having a party, library books and comic books, kissing in the kitchen or on the front porch or in the shadow of a tower—all of these things had been swept away. Maybe someday there would be a new normal. But for now everything that had made Chicago was gone.

"Madeline," Nathaniel said. His hand was at my elbow. "Madeline, we are nearly home."

I realized I stood in the middle of Clark Street with the dinosaur clutched to my chest.

"Madeline," Nathaniel said again, and put his arm around my shoulder, made me move my feet.

"How can anything be the same again?" I said.

"This is what happens during war," Nathaniel said, and his voice was gentle, so like Gabriel's that my heart ached.

"The war is here because of me. These people suffered because of me, because Azazel hated me so much that he needed to send the monster to my doorstep."

"If it was not Chicago, it would have been some other city, some other innocents. And you would have felt just as responsible, because Azazel is your father."

I squeezed the stuffed dinosaur in my hands. "You're right. I would have. But that knowledge doesn't make this any easier. He destroyed my home, the city I loved."

I'm not sure how we got home. The last mile or so was a blur. I remember ringing the doorbell—my keys had gone missing somewhere in the night—and Samiel opening the door, his face white and drawn with worry. I fell into his arms, and then everything was black.

When I opened my eyes again I was in my own bed. The sun streamed through the windows, and Beezle sat on the pillow next to me, watching me sleep.

"Do you know that your hair has grown about four inches while you slept?"

I sat up and rubbed my eyes, and the stuffed dinosaur rolled onto my lap.

"You were clutching that filthy thing for two days," Beezle said. "No one could pry it out of your hands. I wiped it down with antibacterial gel as best I could so that you wouldn't get botulism all over your sheets."

"I was asleep for two days?" I asked.

"Yes. And have I mentioned your unusual hair growth, and the fact that Nathaniel's essence is different from what it was when he left?"

I went still. I hoped Beezle hadn't blabbed about the change in Nathaniel.

"You mentioned my hair. Twice. So it grew back. What's the big deal?"

Beezle narrowed his eyes at me. "What happened between you two while you were out there?"

"I'm sure Nathaniel told you all about it," I said with studied nonchalance.

"I'm sure you've noticed that Nathaniel is somewhat taciturn," Beezle said. "He's not what you'd call a gripping storyteller."

"What's to tell? We put a veil over the hospital to protect the people inside. We were chased by Bryson and a bunch of his goons. They shot us out of the sky and we had to walk home, dodging monsters along the way."

"And nothing else happened?"

I gave Beezle my best big brown eyes and tried not to blink too much. I'd read somewhere that blinking was a sign of lying. "Nope. Nothing else."

The door opened and Nathaniel came in. It was like all the air had just been squeezed from the room.

Beezle turned his head slowly from me to Nathaniel and back again. Then he addressed me. "You are a crappy liar. Don't think you'll be able to hide . . . whatever this is . . . from the others."

And he flew out of the room, grumbling under his breath.

Nathaniel closed the door behind him. He looked clean and rested, and he was dressed more casually than I'd ever seen him in a gray sweater and blue jeans.

It was hard for me to look at him now that the crisis was over. What had happened between us seemed like a moment out of time, a thing that had happened once but couldn't happen again. I could only imagine what Samiel would think if Nathaniel and I became involved. I'd just buried Samiel's brother, and I was carrying his brother's child.

Even as I thought all of this, Nathaniel sat down on the bed beside me. He took my hand in his, and the space between us crackled with electricity. I had serious doubts about my self-restraint. Something was compelling me toward Nathaniel, despite all reason, despite our history, despite the fact that a part of me sensed it was dangerous for both of us to go any further. Was I turning into a woman who wanted the wrong man for all the wrong reasons? Would my baser instincts really prevail?

"You are well?" Nathaniel asked. "Your powers are restored?"

I did a quick internal check and found that everything was as it should be. My baby fluttered its wings reassuringly.

"Yes. And you?" I said. "Is your wing healed?"

Nathaniel turned so that I could see that his wing had been restored. "Samiel helped me repair it."

"That's good," I said, then decided I might as well forge right ahead before I lost my nerve. "Nathaniel, what happened between the two of us . . ."

He put his hand on my lips. "What I said to you still stands. I want you to choose me. I do not wish to be a dirty secret."

"I understand," I said, although part of me wanted to keep him as just that, if only so I could satisfy the unreasoning lust that had appeared when I'd kissed him the first time. "I just want you to know that I'm not ready to make that choice."

Nathaniel rubbed his thumb over my mouth. "Then I

will have to convince you," he said, and replaced his hand with his lips.

As soon as he kissed me it was like I was falling again, falling into a mad abyss where I didn't care about anything except Nathaniel, Nathaniel's touch, Nathaniel's heat. I could sense the same madness on him, as his mouth became more insistent, more demanding. His hands moved over me, and it seemed I moved inevitably toward him, that there was only one way this could end.

He pulled away, rested his forehead against mine. "Madeline. I cannot control myself around you."

"I know," I said, moving reluctantly away and rising from the bed. "Whatever this is, it seems to get stronger the more we . . . do stuff."

The corners of his mouth quirked upward at my phrasing, but he sobered quickly. "I cannot tell if this is the normal course of intense attraction, or if there is another factor at work here."

"Do you think someone put us under a love spell?" I was pretty much grasping at straws here.

"To what end? Who would benefit from our joining?"

"Maybe someone who wants me to be distracted."

Nathaniel shook his head. "It does not have the sense of a love spell. Everything goes back to the moment when our powers combined. It was as if your magic unlocked something inside me. Since that moment I have felt stronger, more powerful. I have abilities I did not have before. And I sense something more, something untapped beneath the surface."

He was coming into the legacy of his bloodline. I understood how he felt. I'd gone through this when Lucifer's powers had manifested inside me, and I think the full magnitude of that magic still had not fully presented itself.

"Maybe we should quit the touching and the kissing for a while until we figure out what's going on," I said, and I felt a pang of loss. My words were sensible, but my body craved him. It was a little frightening.

"That seems wise," Nathaniel agreed. "But it will be difficult."

"We have to try," I said.

"When I slept, I dreamed of you," Nathaniel said. "I dreamed that you rose above the city on silver wings, and all below you fell to their knees in wonder and awe. The power of the universe burned within you, and as that power flowed, you shone brighter and brighter. As the light of your sun touched the faces of the vampires below, they were destroyed utterly. Even the ash of their remains was vaporized by your light."

He'd said all of this as if he were in a trance. As he spoke a chill washed over me. I felt the cold hand of destiny draw a finger down my spine.

"Do you think it was a prophecy?" I asked quietly. I didn't like prophecies. Most of my life had been ruled by prophecies, the deaths foreseen at the Agency. I liked to feel as though I was the mistress of my own fate.

"I believe you have the ability within you to end this war. That is what my dream revealed to me."

"I don't have powers like that," I said. "I don't even have wings anymore."

"The potential is inside you. It just needs to be revealed."

I rubbed my forehead tiredly. "I don't know how to reveal it. Maybe Lucifer would know if he'd answer my damned phone calls."

I gave the snake tattoo on my right palm an angry glare. It lay quiescent and unmoving, the way it did when Lucifer was out of touch.

There was a brief knock at the bedroom door and Jude came in. I took a moment to be grateful that the wolf hadn't walked in while Nathaniel and I were embracing. Jude did not trust Nathaniel at all.

"You need to come out here," Jude said. "There's something on the television that you need to see."

I followed Jude into the hallway and Nathaniel fell in behind me. Chloe, Samiel and Beezle waited in the living room. Beezle sat on the coffee table holding the remote. Samiel sat on the couch with Chloe in his lap. Beezle followed the direction of my gaze.

"Sickening, aren't they?" he said. "Ever since she got out of the hospital they can't keep their hands off each other."

"Jealous, little gargoyle?" Chloe asked, resting her head on Samiel's shoulder. She had dark circles under her eyes, and she didn't look completely recovered from her ordeal in Azazel's mansion. Her vivid purple hair was pushed away from her face with a headband that had little skulls printed all over it.

Beezle scrunched up his face. "Absolutely not. I just think there's a little too much PDA going on around here. Human procreation is so gross."

I'm not human, Samiel signed.

"Close enough," Beezle said.

"How do gargoyles procreate?" Chloe asked.

"Nope, I'm drawing the line there," I said before Beezle could respond. "I do not want to hear how you make baby gargoyles."

"It's quite a fascinating process, actually," Beezle said.

I stuck my fingers in my ears. "Nope, not listening, la-la-la-la-la."

"I thought you wanted her to see something on television," Jude growled.

"I do," Beezle said. "But there's a commercial on. It will come up in a minute. The news anchor said the footage would be up after the break."

"Footage of what?" I asked, a pit forming in my stomach. This couldn't be anything good, and I'd had enough of bad news.

"Just wait," Beezle said. "Although you wouldn't have to wait if you'd gotten that DVR like I said you should."

"You mean the DVR we can't afford? You're lucky we have cable."

"If we had a DVR, I could have paused the program until you got your butt out of bed."

"Oh, I'm sorry. I spent a day and a night running for my life while pregnant. For some strange reason I was exhausted."

"Not exhausted enough," Beezle muttered, and I understood from his tone that he was referring to the changes in me and Nathaniel.

Luckily, the news program came back on before we could pursue that line of conversation in the presence of an audience. Of course, a reckoning in front of my gang of misfits was probably as inevitable as what would happen between Nathaniel and me. Even now I was aware of him in a low-level way, a presence in the back of my mind.

The anchor—one of those plastic newscasters who look like they've been pressed in an attractive-but-not-in-a-threatening-way mold—was recapping the events of two days ago, even showing the same clip of the vampires in Daley Plaza that had sent us down there in such a hurry.

"Why did I get out of bed for this?" I asked.

"Just wait," Beezle said.

My stomach rumbled audibly. Samiel patted Chloe's shoulder and she slid off his lap onto the couch.

I'll make you some breakfast. I've already seen it.

"I'm feeling a little peckish myself," Beezle said.

"You already ate enough waffles to sink the *Titanic*," Jude said.

"That was a long time ago," Beezle whined.

"It was a half an hour ago," Jude said through his teeth.

"Quiet," Chloe said. "It's coming on."

I missed the anchor's lead-in to the clip, but I didn't need it. The meaning was clear enough.

A dark-haired, green-eyed vampire sat at the head of a long wooden table. Behind him was a wall of gray stone with no identifying characteristics. The vampire looked young, but that didn't mean anything. He could have been turned hundreds of years before. The camera stayed close to the vampire so that the viewer could not see the rest of the room.

"Greetings, citizens of Chicago," the vampire said, and there was a smugness in his silky voice that made me want to punch him in the face. "I am Therion, lord of the Fifth Court of the United States, headquartered here in your fair city. You may have noted the presence of my brethren."

He smiled when he said this, and showed his fangs. "We have always lived among you, keeping to the shadows. However, recent advances in medical science, shall we say, have allowed us to now walk with you under the sun."

"Medical advances, my ass. The blood of Agents," Chloe said angrily. "That piece of garbage Azazel practically drained us dry in the name of his experiments."

Therion continued speaking on the screen. "I understand if you think we, ahem, seemed aggressive when first we emerged. Many of us have not seen the sun for several centuries. It made us somewhat unrestrained."

He smiled again, and I said, "I want to hit that guy just on principle. He's too smug to live."

Jude growled his assent. "I hate vampires anyway. It's no skin off my back to kill as many of 'em as I can get."

Therion's voice broke into our discussion. "However, we do not wish to live as monsters. We want to demonstrate that we can be reasonable. If you meet our demands, we will withdraw from the city and the citizenry may safely return. Then we can draw up a plan for a peaceful coexistence between vampires and humans."

"He's lying," I said. "If we give them what they want, they'll have no motivation to withdraw. Why would they cede the city when they've already taken it?"

Nobody answered me. Everyone knew the answer to that question.

Therion spread his hands wide, and the camera panned backward, revealing the rest of the room. It was a cavernous stone hall, set with flickering torches. All around the room hung cages, and inside the cages were Agents. My heart stopped when I recognized them.

"Oh, my god. J.B.," I said, and fell to my knees. "J.B."

I crawled closer to the screen, searching the blur of faces for one face, the one person I needed to see. Therion spoke on, but nothing he said registered until I heard my name.

". . . Madeline Black, this message is for you. If you willingly give yourself in exchange, then all of these *innocents*," Therion said, and the way he emphasized "innocents" let me know that the choice of Agents for this display was no accident, "will go free. If not, then I will slaughter all of them three days hence, at the hour of noon, and then my horde will move out of Chicago. Human authorities will not be able to stop us. We will spread like a cancer over this country, and every person will succumb. But if Madeline Black will voluntarily turn herself in at a Vampire

Authority station before three days have passed, then all of these people will go free, and we will withdraw. This is Madeline Black."

Therion gestured, and an image appeared over the screen. It was a still image of me fighting the vampires in Daley Plaza. The photo had caught me in action, sword mid-swing, my other hand behind me, my overcoat billowing, my boots covered in blood.

I touched my hair, which now brushed the tops of my shoulders. In the picture it was still cropped close to my head.

"If you see this woman, or know her, I urge you to turn her in at your closest Vampire Authority station. Madeline Black, if you are listening, know that you can save millions of lives if you would simply come forward."

The camera focused on Therion's face again, the humans in cages disappearing from the screen. "I'll be waiting."

The picture went dark.

8

THE BROADCAST CUT BACK TO THE ANCHOR.

"No!" I slammed my hand against the TV screen. "No! I didn't see him. I couldn't find him."

The news anchor started talking again. The still photo of me was up in the corner of the picture. Underneath the photo, in bright yellow letters, were the words, "Who is Madeline Black?"

"Shut the TV off," Jude said.

"Maybe they'll show the message again," I said, my eyes glued to the screen, willing the newscaster to show me that precious few seconds again so that I could see whether J.B. was there, whether J.B. had been captured.

"Shut it off," Jude repeated.

I felt his hands on my shoulders, prying me away from the screen. "J.B.," I said.

Jude turned me to face him. "You don't know that he's there."

"I can't leave any of them there, but especially not him," I said.

"You cannot be considering acquiescing to Therion's demands," Nathaniel said. "You said yourself that if the vampires had what they wanted, then they would have no motivation to withdraw."

"That was before I found out they were holding Agents hostage," I said. "And what in the name of the Morningstar is a Vampire Authority station?"

Samiel reentered the room carrying a plate with scrambled eggs, bacon and toast. I sat on the couch next to Chloe, who looked at my plate and then at Samiel. She blinked her eyes once.

I'll make more, he signed, and went back to the kitchen.

"So, yeah, Vampire Authority station," Chloe said. "A lot has changed while you were passed out."

"Like what?" I said through a mouthful of eggs. "Has Therion established some kind of fascist vampire state?"

"Actually, you're not far off," Chloe said. "The day you came home, all of the vampires suddenly stopped rampaging all over the place."

"Half of them disappeared off the streets altogether, and the other half started marching in the streets in military order," Jude said. "Then they went building to building collecting human stragglers and rounding them up for containment."

"Containment?" I said, scraping my fork against my plate and realizing I'd already inhaled everything on it.

"Camps," Jude said. "They've got hundreds of people penned up just west of the Loop in the parking lots around the United Center."

"On the second day the flyers appeared," Chloe said. She grabbed a piece of paper from the end table and handed it to me.

It would have been comical if we weren't in such deadly circumstance. The vamps had adopted the CTA's "If you see something, say something" motto. It was emblazoned in large letters at the top of the page. Underneath the motto it read, "The time has come to restore civil order to this city. If you believe that you have seen a crime being committed, we urge you to report to your nearest Vampire Authority station. The personnel at these stations are there for you. The stations are conveniently located approximately every half mile throughout the city."

At the bottom in bold letters it read, "TOGETHER WE CAN RESTORE ORDER TO CHICAGO."

"I notice that they have neglected to mention they were the ones to disrupt the peace in the first place," I said, tossing the flyer to the side in disgust. "Do you know if people are buying this bullshit?"

"I think some of them are," Jude said. "People are scared. They don't understand what's going on. If they think that turning looters in will save their families, then they will do it."

"Stupid," I said. "They need to get off the grid, not draw attention to themselves."

"Then today there was this message," Chloe said, gesturing to the TV. "The major networks have been broadcasting it every hour or so. Along with plenty of speculation about who you are and why the vampires are so interested in you."

"They can speculate. I hope they enjoy themselves," I said, thinking. "They laid the groundwork for that message pretty neatly. Everyone in Chicago is going to be looking for me to turn me in, especially if they think the vamps will leave once they have me."

I had a lot of problems to solve, but one that was more pressing than the others. "I need to get in touch with J.B. Are the phones working?"

"No," Beezle said. "The electricity only came back on yesterday. The vamps must have turned the power back on just to make sure Therion's message was broadcast."

"I need to know if the vampires have him or not," I said.

"Why? You're only going to do something foolish to save those Agents from Therion anyway," Beezle said. "What difference does it make if J.B.'s there or not?"

"Because I need to know if he's safe," I said.

"I don't think anybody is safe anymore. The rules have changed," Beezle said.

"This is not really the time for a philosophical discussion," I said.

"I'll go," Jude said. "I can check his home and the Agency and find out if he's been taken or not."

"No," I said. "We don't need anyone else roaming the city out of communication."

"Yeah," Beezle said, looking pointedly at me. "When members of the group get separated, bad things happen."

I knew what he was referring to, and was careful not to look at Nathaniel. I wasn't going to rise to Beezle's baiting.

"I can move through the streets as a wolf much more quickly and quietly than the rest of you," Jude argued. "If I find J.B., I'll bring him back here. If I don't, then I'll see if I can discover what happened to him."

"I don't like it," I said. "If something happened to you, we'd have no way of knowing. If you want to go get J.B., then I'm going with you."

"No, you're not," said everyone in the room.

"I'd like to see any of you stop me," I said.

"Shall we put it to the test?" Nathaniel asked. "Perhaps one of us would be unable to restrain you, but I think all of us could. You've been through an ordeal. You're not to go haring off on another mission."

"I don't know if you've looked at yourself in the mirror today, but you look like death warmed over," Chloe said.

"And you would only be an encumbrance," Jude said brutally. "You can't run as fast as I can. You can't fly."

"I can blast a truckload of vampires from here to eternity," I snapped.

"Nobody is going to let you out that door," Beezle said. "Besides, you need to stay home and figure out how to defeat the vampires so I can get takeout again."

"If the city is restored, I doubt that most people will consider delivery of hot wings to be a priority," I said.

"But the sooner the vampires are gone, the sooner food delivery can resume."

I put my knuckles to my forehead and rubbed the place between my eyes where a headache was forming. Samiel came out of the hallway carrying several dishes of food. He loaded them up on the dining room table and went back into the kitchen again.

Beezle and Chloe sprang from their seats and settled in at the table before the rest of us could move an inch. Samiel reentered with a plate of bacon. He did not appear to be in the least surprised to see Chloe and Beezle shoveling food on their plates like they hadn't eaten for twenty years.

I figured it was easier to just make enough for everybody, Samiel signed. *Plus, I never know how much she's going to eat.*

"Where did all the food come from?" I asked. "I know my kitchen is not that well stocked."

"Sam and me went to Costco when we got back from the hospital," Jude said.

"It was open?" I asked in amazement.

"No, it was locked up tight. But we broke in and got some stuff we needed," Jude said, then saw the look on my face. "We left money by the register; don't worry. And we made sure that no one else would be able to get in and loot the place."

"I don't even want to know," I said.

Samiel was watching Chloe, who was hunched over her plate. *I don't know where she puts it, really.*

"It takes a lot of food to fuel this brain, pal," Chloe said.

She'd never looked up, so I have no idea how she knew what Samiel had said. From Samiel's wide eyes I could tell he didn't know how she did it, either.

Jude and Nathaniel had joined the others at the table. They were both filling their plates rapidly, although with slightly more decorum than the other two.

"Come on, eat," Beezle said. "I think you lost another ten pounds on your little adventure. Plus, you've got the brain trust here—such as it is. You can pool your thoughts on the defeat of Therion the Smug."

I sat at the head of the table, pulled a plate over and started loading up before the food disappeared. "The first order of the day is to find out where J.B. is."

"I told you I could do that," Jude said.

"And I told you I'm not sold on that plan," I said.

"If you would think logically instead of emotionally, you would see that what he's saying makes sense," Chloe said.

"If you weren't a chick, I'd punch you in the face for that. What, you think that just because I'm pregnant I'm all emotional?"

"I didn't say that," Chloe said mildly. "I just said you were thinking emotionally. And if you hit me in the face, I'd hit you right back. Not that that it would do me any good, really. People who hit you tend to die screaming in little pieces."

All the men at the table watched this exchange with the uncomfortable expressions of males who do not want to get in between two women. Even Beezle kept his head down and his mouth shut, although that may have been because he'd put about six slices of bacon in his craw.

"I wouldn't kill you just because you punched me," I said, insulted. "I'm not a monster."

"Are you sure about that?" Chloe said. "Because you seem to be a 'smash first, ask questions later' kind of person."

"Not everyone who has fought me has come to their mortal end."

"Oh, yeah? Name one."

"I have fought with Madeline and I'm not dead," Nathaniel said.

"From what I understand, that's not for lack of trying."

Samiel rapped the table with his knuckles. *She didn't kill me even though I cut half of her hand off.*

His eyes automatically slid to the digits in question. I saw them register surprise. *Your hand . . .*

"Just got around to that, did you?" Beezle muttered.

"When did that happen?" Jude asked. "And how?"

"It happened sometime after we put the veil over the hospital. As for how, I have no idea. They were just suddenly there again."

Jude looked from Nathaniel to me with suspicion. "Just what was involved with this spell, anyway? Because you've smelled different ever since you got back," he said, addressing Nathaniel.

I took a moment to be grateful for the fact that Jude had never met Puck; otherwise he would have made the connection immediately.

"Can we refocus, please?" I said loudly. "Whether or not I am a monster can be debated at a different time, as can the consequences of the protective spell."

Although I hoped to never talk about the circumstances of the spell with anyone. It would do none of them good to know that I had tried to climb inside Nathaniel in midair.

Jude pushed back from the table, his plate cleaned. "I will look for J.B. and return within a day."

"We didn't settle that," I said.

"There is no point in going around in circles only to come to the same conclusion," Jude said steadily.

"Wade will kill me if anything happens to you."

"Wade knows well the risk I have taken in staying here."

"I wouldn't be too happy, either."

"Madeline Black, I have been alive since the time of the Romans. I can handle a few vampires."

"Everything can die," I said softly, and we all knew who I was thinking about.

"But I won't," Jude said.

You can't make that promise. I took a deep breath, tried to think with my brain instead of my heart.

"Okay," I said, hoping I wasn't making a decision I would regret. "Okay. But don't bother checking his condo. I can guarantee that J.B.'s been sleeping at the office since all this started."

"That may have protected him, then," Nathaniel said. "Does not the Agency have wards to keep out vampires?"

"Yes," I said. "But if he was out on a soul pickup, or if he decided to fight the vamps against orders . . ."

"Or if the vampires brought in a witch to break the wards," Beezle said.

"A witch," I said, looking at Nathaniel. "A witch could have put all the patients in the hospital under that sleeping spell."

"Another player?" Chloe said. "How big is this game?"

"It's not a game."

"It is to Therion," Chloe said. "And probably to Lucifer, too."

She was right, but it really went against the grain for me to admit anyone was right but me.

"I'll be back within a day," Jude promised, and he transformed into a wolf, his clothing falling to the floor.

I walked him to the front door, opened it, and followed him downstairs to do the same for the external doors. We emerged into the cold on the front porch.

It had snowed again in the last couple of days. The streets were unplowed, the sidewalks unshoveled. Jude nudged the palm of my hand with his nose.

I looked down at him steadily. "You come back in one piece, you understand?"

Jude barked once. He took off running. A moment later all that was left of him was fresh paw prints in the snow. I stayed there for a minute, shivering in the cold. Then I went back upstairs, now wondering whether I would lose two friends to this folly.

Beezle and Chloe had demolished pretty much every morsel on the table, and my plate was missing.

I put yours in the kitchen, Samiel signed. *It seemed safer. I'll get it.*

He rose, clearing the empty plates away. Nathaniel helped Samiel carry the empty dishes, and I realized that

Nathaniel really had changed. The old Nathaniel would never have done "the work of a servant."

Had he been changing all along, or was this another side effect of the spell? Or—and this was much more disturbing—was he just trying to be what he thought I wanted?

Samiel returned with my plate, the food covered by another dish so it would stay warm. Chloe looked expectantly at me as I uncovered the meal.

"Forget it," I said.

She looked slightly disappointed, but not surprised.

Beezle had already retired to his favorite pillow on the couch. He sprawled on his back in a sunbeam, his belly at least two times its normal size. His eyes were closed.

"You look like you swallowed a basketball," I said.

Beezle belched in response.

There was nothing to do except wait. And wonder.

So that was what we did. Chloe convinced me to play UNO with her, and Beezle and Samiel joined in. Nathaniel watched us like he was observing alien life on another planet.

Chloe and Beezle were both loud, demonstrative players. More than once the play of a certain card was punctuated by a noisy "Ha!" or "Beat that!"

I tried to keep my mind on the game, to not mentally follow Jude through the streets of Chicago. I tried not to think about what the Agents might have suffered already in Therion's tender care.

Most of all, I tried not to think about J.B. standing on a street corner telling me he loved me.

After a while, Chloe and Beezle needed more food to fuel their antics, and Samiel produced another feast. We turned on the news for a bit but they had nothing new to say, and the sight of Therion's face made me want to smash things, so we shut it off.

Beezle popped *JAWS* into the DVD player in concession to my extreme anxiety. For some reason that movie always makes me feel better, like comfort food for my brain. There's probably something wrong with me at the proton level if a movie about a town being terrorized by a great white shark is comforting.

We had just gotten to the point where Quint was telling the story of the U.S.S. *Indianapolis* when I heard the howl of a wolf.

"Jude," I said, and bolted for the door. Samiel beat me there, clattering down the steps to let Jude in. I stood at the top of the stairs, my heart in my mouth.

Jude sprinted inside. J.B. was not with him.

"Oh, god," I said, covering my face. Therion had him.

Nathaniel put his arm around me and drew me inside. Jude had already changed back into a man.

"It's not what you think," Jude said as soon as he saw me. "Therion doesn't have him. Titania does."

9

"TITANIA?" I SAID. "WHY?"

"It took me a little time to put the pieces together; otherwise I would have been back sooner," Jude said, pulling on his clothes as he spoke. "But I managed to eavesdrop on that little shit Sokolov."

"How did you get inside the Agency?" I asked. "J.B. told me three days ago that the place was on lockdown. Shouldn't the wards have kept you out?"

"The wards recognized me as a friend. I was cleared when the cubs were there, remember?" Jude said. "And I know how to keep to the shadows. Those security guards in the lobby never even saw me run past."

"So what did Sokolov say?"

"He was complaining that Titania had overreached her authority by taking J.B. from the Agency, even if he was a king of a faerie court. And the person he was talking to asked why it was so damned important for Titania to take J.B. when there was a crisis going on. Sokolov said it was to punish you."

My heart stilled. "She's going to use J.B. against me in repayment for Oberon."

Jude nodded. "They came for J.B. just after the vampire invasion started."

"She's had him for three days? For the love of the Morningstar. He could be dead by now."

"No," Beezle said. "She wants to hurt you. If she's going to kill him, then you can bet she wants to make you watch. But I bet he wishes he was dead."

Nathaniel nodded. "Faeries are well versed in methods of torture."

"Not helping," I said shortly.

"You're not going to like this, either," Jude said. "There was blood all over J.B.'s office. He put up a fight."

"How much of the blood was his?" I whispered.

"Enough." Jude's face was grim.

"Well. I'm not going to wait for an invitation from Titania. We've got to go and get J.B. out of there now."

"Whoa, whoa, whoa," Chloe said. "What about the vampires, and Therion's threat? You've only got two more days to solve that problem or else the vampires are going to invade the rest of the country. Are you really going to let hundreds of innocent people die so you can rescue one man?"

"Who says I'm going to let them die?" I said. "First I get J.B. Then Therion will pay."

"And how are you going to defeat the vampires?" Chloe said.

"I don't know yet," I said. "But once I know J.B. is safe, then I can figure something out."

"What—once all the Avengers are assembled, a solution will magically appear?"

"I will not leave J.B. in the hands of that bitch," I said through gritted teeth.

"Watch out. She's using the B-word."

"Keep arguing with me and I'll be using the C-word. I thought you were on my side."

"I am," Chloe said. "But you're following your heart again instead of your brain. The bigger problem here is the vampire invasion, not Titania's gripe with you."

"She never uses her brain," Beezle said.

"Oh, great, another country heard from," I said. "I'm doing things the way I've always done them."

"Well, the way you do things is inefficient and illogical," Chloe said.

"It works for me," I said.

"Fine, fine," Chloe said, throwing up her hands. "Let's break out J.B. I have nothing better to do. How do you propose we get there?"

Nathaniel looked at me. "Lord Lucifer brought you there the last time, through the old ways."

"And Lucifer is out of touch. But I know someone else who will take us there. For a price."

"Madeline, no. You cannot possibly indebt yourself to Puck any further. It is too dangerous. We are not even certain what kind of creature he is, nor what he will ask of you in return. You already owe him a debt for helping us escape Titania's court the first time."

"I don't see any other way," I said. "And I won't leave J.B."

"I wouldn't suggest it," Nathaniel said.

"He's all insightful now," Beezle said, looking at Nathaniel.

"J.B. went willingly against his mother and his court when Amarantha kidnapped Wade. I would not leave him to Titania, either," Jude said.

Nor would I, Samiel signed.

"It's like your insanity is infectious," Chloe grumbled.

"I like having her around," Beezle said. "It saves me the trouble of being the sensible one."

"There is no planet on which you would be considered sensible," I said.

"Compared to you, I'm a paragon of logical thinking," Beezle said.

"How will you contact Puck?" Chloe asked.

"He gave me a jewel," I said.

"That jewel brings him here," Nathaniel said.

"Yes, it does," I said. "And I'd better talk to him alone. I don't know how he'll respond to my call, and I don't want him to refuse just because he has an audience."

Plus, I wanted to keep Nathaniel out of his sight for as long as possible. I wasn't sure how Puck would respond if it did turn out that Nathaniel was his son and I'd revealed him—even if it was by accident. Nobody ever seemed to give me a pass for my accidents.

"I'll take the rest of the inmates downstairs," Beezle said.

They all looked reluctant except Chloe, who just appeared curious.

"I'm not certain you should be alone with him," Nathaniel said.

"He doesn't want to hurt me," I said. "He might refuse to help, but he won't hurt me."

I was pretty sure that if Puck was going to hurt me, it would be in service to his vendetta against Lucifer. And he did not appear quite ready for that yet. I didn't tell the others any of this, though.

After a few minutes they'd all cleared out, and I was alone in my apartment. I took a moment to breathe, and to appreciate the fact that a lot of tension went away when Nathaniel wasn't in the room. Whatever was between us, it wasn't healthy.

I realized I was in my pajamas and somewhat grubby, and detoured into the bathroom for a shower before I contacted Puck. If I was going to have a standoff with the faerie queen, then I wanted my hair to be clean.

I emerged from the shower several minutes later, wrapped a towel around my body and another around my hair, and padded in wet feet to my room.

I stopped in the doorway. On my bed was a pair of black leather pants that I knew did not belong to me. Next to the pants was a wine-colored sweater that looked like it left nothing to the imagination. There was also a scrap of black lace barely identifiable as underwear, and a matching bra. Next to all these things was a winking blue jewel—Puck's talisman.

"You little shit," I swore. I don't know how he knew I was going to call him, and not for the first time I wondered whether the talisman allowed him to eavesdrop on my life. I swept the clothes aside, intending to ignore his not-so-subtle directive.

But then I reconsidered. My own clothes were always getting ripped or torn or bloodstained, and I was never able to present myself very impressively to the faerie. Even though I could give a flying farthing about faerie protocol, I could appreciate that my chances of getting J.B. back were stronger if I made a good impression.

Not on Titania, of course. Nothing I did was going to make a good impression on her at this point. But the rest of the court could sway her if I presented my case well enough—and if I looked like I belonged.

I drew the line at wearing the underwear. There was something really creepy about Puck choosing underwear for me, like he expected to see me in it.

I put on my regular cotton undies and pulled on the pants and sweater. I glanced at myself in the mirror and almost changed my clothes. The pants and the sweater clung to every curve I had. I felt indecent, even though I was covered up from wrist to ankle.

The jewel winked at me, reflected in the mirror. I grabbed it and said his name. "Puck."

It grew warm to the touch. I sensed the air in the room change.

"Those pants look good," Puck said.

I spun around and found him lounging against the door-frame. He looked me up and down.

"Looks good from the front, too," Puck said.

"Will you quit ogling me? You're old enough to be Lucifer's brother," I said.

Puck gave me a half smile. "Not just old enough to be."

Well, it was certainly a week for revelations. "You're Lucifer's brother?"

"Why else would we hate each other so thoroughly?" Puck said. "Nobody knows how to swing the knife like family."

"And that means you're my great-great-great-whatever-uncle?"

Puck nodded, his eyes sparkling with mischief.

"Then that is even freaking ickier that you would buy me underwear."

"Don't worry. The blood relation is distant enough that it would not be unnatural for us to have sex."

"It would be unnatural in my *brain*," I said, shuddering.

"It would be like nothing you have ever experienced before, I promise," Puck said, winking at me.

"Stop talking, stop talking," I said. "Angels might have no compunction about screwing their relatives, but humans definitely do."

"You had sex with Lucifer's grandson," Puck said. "And you are also related to Lucifer."

"Yeah, but there are a lot of intervening generations between me and Lucifer . . ." I trailed off, because Puck was grinning at me knowingly. "It was different with Gabriel."

"How?"

"I'm not having sex with you, and that's final," I said.

"Too bad," Puck said. "In any case, I am not an angel."

"You said you were Lucifer's brother," I said.

"I am. But that doesn't make me an angel," he said.

"I know, you are the leaf on the wind or whatever," I said, remembering something he'd said the last time Puck was in my bedroom. "Why are you telling me all of this now?"

Puck shrugged. "Perhaps I would like you to call me Uncle. I thought you would like to know that we are family."

"Nobody swings the knife like family," I said, narrowing my eyes at him.

His blue eyes danced like the jewel I gripped in my hand. "So suspicious."

"I think I have earned the right to my suspicions. And you haven't asked why I called you here at all."

He tilted his head to one side. "I had presumed that you wanted your king back, and called me to assist you in that matter. Since brother dearest is out of touch again."

"He's not my king," I said. "J.B. is my friend. And where does Lucifer go when he disappears?"

Puck shook his head. "That is for him to tell."

"He'll never tell me," I said.

"He will. Soon enough," Puck said.

"Can you see the future, too?"

"Elements of it. Possibilities."

"Like Lucifer. In other words, nothing really useful."

"Would a crystal ball be a comfort to you?" Puck asked. "Would foreknowledge of your lover's death have made it easier to bear?"

"If I'd known about it, I could have tried to stop it," I said.

Puck tutted. "And you would have broken the rules. You know that once a death is foretold, it cannot be undone."

"Who sets these rules, anyway?" I said.

"Now, that is knowledge you are definitely not permitted to have," Puck said. He held out his hand to me. "Now, shall we go to fetch your king?"

"I can't go without the others," I said.

Puck frowned. "How many others?"

"Five," I said.

"Titania may take it amiss if you arrive with an entourage. She may interpret it as a hostile act," Puck warned.

"I've already interpreted her kidnapping of J.B. as a hostile act, so that will make us even," I said, and then asked the question I'd been afraid to ask. "How damaged is he?"

Puck considered. "He is alive. I cannot speak to the quality of that life."

"Why didn't you do anything?" I said. "You could stop her if you wanted to. You're more powerful than she is."

"I could, but it doesn't suit me to reveal my power to Titania at this time. And while one life may be essential to you, it is practically meaningless to me. I have witnessed more lives than you can number."

"And yet you came when I called," I said.

"So that you can rescue him," Puck said. "It is nothing for me to take you there. It is even a benefit to me. You will owe me another boon for this."

"I want it clear right up front that none of these favors I owe you will involve me getting naked," I said.

"I wouldn't waste such a powerful favor in such a manner," Puck said. "Besides, if I really wanted you naked, I'm sure I could convince you."

"No, thanks," I said, leaving the room as quickly as possible. "Why don't you go in the living room, and I'll get the others."

I went to the back door to call down to Samiel's apartment and found Nathaniel sitting on the landing with his sword slung across his knees.

"You didn't trust me?" I said.

Nathaniel got to his feet. "I did not trust him."

"Well, he said he would take us to the court," I said. I went out on the landing so I could yell down the stairs. "Hey! You can come back now."

I turned around to say something else to Nathaniel but he was already gone. In the living room I heard the sound of glass shattering.

"That can't be good," I said, sprinting down the hall.

Puck and Nathaniel stood like gunslingers in the dining room, face-to-face several feet apart and both stock-still. Puck's eyes blazed with light. At his feet were the shattered remains of a snow globe. The air in the room was thick with magic.

"What have you done to him?" Puck said, and his voice was not the merry lilt that he usually possessed. It sounded like the voice of the earth itself, and I was afraid.

"I didn't . . . I didn't mean to," I said, and didn't bother trying to pretend that I didn't know what he was talking about.

Footsteps sounded on the back stairs. Puck raised his hand and slammed the back door. I heard the others pounding on the wood, shouting my name.

"What is happening?" Nathaniel said. His hand went to his sword. Puck looked at Nathaniel's hand and it froze in place before it reached the hilt.

I tried not to breathe too hard or otherwise draw Puck's attention to me. I knew he was strong, but I'd had no idea how strong. He could stop my heart with a look.

"I'd hidden him so carefully, and you've undone that work in a moment," Puck said. "Worse, you left it at half, so that he cannot even defend himself from those who recognize him."

"I told you, I didn't mean to," I said. "It was an accident."

"What are you talking about?" Nathaniel said. "Tell me."

"Tell him," I said to Puck. "You owe him that."

"This is your fault," Puck said. "I should have known, daughter of Lucifer, that it was unsafe for him to be in your company."

"You cannot get angry with me for what I didn't know," I said. "If it's anyone's fault, it's yours. What did you hide him for, anyway? Why not claim him in the first place?"

"Tell me what is happening!" Nathaniel shouted, and the hot swirl of power in the room grew stronger. "Do not speak around me as if I were a child."

The glow in Puck's eyes receded a bit, and they seemed to soften. "But you *are* a child, Nathaniel. My child. My son."

I'd thought Puck would ease into it, that he would not say it so baldly. The words seemed to hang in the air between them.

"No," Nathaniel said, shaking his head. "I am the only son of Zerachiel."

I approached Nathaniel carefully, reached for his shoulder.

"I would not touch him right now," Puck said.

"I am the only son of Zerachiel," Nathaniel repeated.

"I had a feeling you'd take this hard," I murmured. So much of Nathaniel's self-worth related to his parentage.

"You knew of this?" Nathaniel said softly.

I eased around so that Nathaniel could see my face. "I didn't know before we kissed. But I suspected later."

"And why did you not mention your suspicions?" he said, equally softly.

It was as if Puck had ceased to exist, and there was only Nathaniel and me. I sensed I had to tread very carefully here.

"I wasn't sure. I didn't want to upset you if I was wrong," I said.

"You did not want to . . . upset me."

I'd miscalculated. "It wasn't my secret to tell."

"When would it have been your secret to tell?" Nathaniel said, and his eyes were like frozen winter. "After I fucked you? Would it have been *appropriate* for you to explain then?"

I felt sorry for Nathaniel, but it didn't mean that I had to stand there and take shit from him or his jackass dad.

"Listen, pal," I said angrily. "You need to redirect your animosity here. I'm not the one who showed up to your mother in the guise of Zerachiel and then kept your identity hidden from you for thousands of years."

"You could have prepared me for this possibility," Nathaniel said. "I am not stupid. I knew that something had changed after that spell."

"I will not be blamed for this," I said. "How was I to know that you weren't Zerachiel's son? Oh, and just to be clear, there was never any guarantee that you were going to wind up in my bed, so don't talk like it was a fait accompli."

"If I wanted to, I could have had you flat on your back and begging at any time," Nathaniel said.

I wanted to punch him. I really did. But he seemed kind of unstable at the moment, and I wasn't sure what would happen. I didn't want the whole building to blow up because I took offense at his attitude. But I would hit him later. I made a note of it.

"Off topic," I said through gritted teeth. "But we will continue this discussion later. In the meantime, why don't you ask *your father* why he never told you who you were?"

Nathaniel visibly made an effort to calm himself, to focus on Puck.

"If what you say is true, then why did you hide yourself from me?" Nathaniel said. "Why did you let me live so long believing I was someone else's son?"

I was vaguely aware of Samiel and Jude, Beezle and Chloe shouting outside. Whatever Puck had done, he'd effectively sealed us off from the rest of the building.

"I do not have to answer to you," Puck said, and he was so like Lucifer in that moment that I had no trouble believing they were siblings.

"Goddamned right you do," I said. "He knows he's your child now."

"Which is only due to your actions. I had no intention of revealing his origins yet."

I was angry. Really angry. I was tired of being pushed around, blamed and generally treated like I was responsible for every wrong ever perpetuated in the universe. And it's possible I was, as Nathaniel said, in the grip of my hormones.

Which is why I kind of lost my mind for a second, and stomped over to Puck, and clocked him.

I'm sure Puck could have stopped me from hitting him if he'd suspected that was what I was going to do. But he probably thought I had more self-preservation than that.

The sound of my fist hitting his flesh seemed to echo through the house.

There was a second where he was shocked, and staring, and then I was up against the wall with his forearm under my neck, and I was choking.

"How dare you," Puck said.

I kicked him in the balls and he dropped me. I haven't met a male of any species that could tolerate that. I landed more or less on my feet after a momentary stumble, and rubbed my throat.

"You didn't spend enough time researching me," I said hoarsely. "I dare whatever the hell I want. You will tell Nathaniel why you did what you did, and then you will take us to Titania's court."

"What makes you think I must comply with your demands? You are the one in debt to me," Puck said. We were only inches apart from each other. I wondered what kind of effect nightfire would have on him.

As it happened, I didn't have to find out. Nathaniel's sword came around his father's throat.

"You can do what Madeline says, or you can have your throat slit," Nathaniel said.

"I wouldn't do that if I were you," Puck said. "Did not Lucifer warn you about destroying ancient creatures?"

"I killed Azazel," I said. "I diminished Oberon. Maybe

you've noticed that I tend to do things without regard for the consequences."

"Oh, yes, you are Lucifer's child," Puck said bitterly. "Queen of all you survey. You have even taken my son in your thrall."

"Nathaniel is nobody's thrall," I said. "And I'm nobody's queen."

"You will be if Lucifer has his way," Puck said, then sighed tiredly. "Stand down, Nathaniel. I will tell you all."

Nathaniel looked at me for confirmation, and I nodded. He pulled the sword away from Puck's throat.

Puck looked at me speculatively. "Would you have let him kill me?"

I looked at him steadily, so he could see the truth in my eyes. "Maybe not over this. But if there ever comes a time when you are a threat to me and mine, I will eliminate you."

He shook his head in wonderment. "No wonder Lucifer has chosen you. Most creatures have more sense than to threaten me."

"Madeline fears nothing," Nathaniel said with a touch of pride.

That wasn't true. I was afraid of lots of things—more things than I could count, actually. But I didn't see any value in admitting that fear when everyone I encountered was a lot more strong and powerful than I was.

Puck wandered over to my bookshelf, scanning the titles. "You should know that Lucifer and I do not get along."

"I noticed that," I said. "Care to tell us why?"

"Lucifer believes that as the firstborn, he has the right to rule all. Our siblings and I disagree."

"There are more of you?" I asked, alarmed. That was all I needed—more frighteningly powerful relatives running around.

"Yes," Puck said. "There are four of us."

"And one of you is in the lake," Nathaniel said thoughtfully. "I could feel his presence."

"Why is your brother in my lake?" I said. I did not like this at all.

Puck shrugged. "Alerian settled there some time ago—perhaps three hundred years? He said that he was going to rest for a while. None of us questioned him at the time, as he has a habit of slumbering through decades. But . . ."

"But?" I asked.

"I wonder if he sensed this area would become geographically important," Puck said. "He is better than any of the rest of us at seeing the future. Alerian sees things more precisely."

"And now that the area *is* geographically important, he's waking up to do . . . what?"

"I imagine that he has intentions of some sort. I am not privy to them."

Awesome. Another immensely powerful being with *intentions*. "And your other sibling? Is that one hanging around here, too, hoping to take advantage?"

"We do not speak much of Daharan," Puck said. "He keeps to himself."

"Does he have plans for total world domination? Because if he does, I want to add him to the list."

"Very likely," Puck said, and it was not a kind smile. "None of us seem to be able to leave well enough alone."

Lucifer had three siblings. One of them had me in his debt, and one of them was rising from Lake Michigan for his own fell purpose. It seemed I had another crisis looming on the horizon, but first we had to sort out the Nathaniel/Puck issue. The clock was ticking—for J.B. and for the city.

"So you and Lucifer have some sibling rivalry issues," I said. "What does that have to do with Nathaniel?"

"Some time ago I considered that it would be wise to have a person well placed in Lucifer's court who was loyal to me."

"I can see the wisdom of such a thing," Nathaniel said. "But how does it benefit you when I did not know who you were or that I might be loyal to you?"

"When the time was correct I would have revealed myself, and your legacy, to you."

"And you thought that I would immediately swear allegiance to you?" Nathaniel said skeptically.

"You would have been unable to do otherwise. The time would have been right," Puck said.

"This plan seems like it has a lot of potential to backfire," I said. There was something bugging me, but I couldn't quite put my finger on it. "What, exactly, is 'the right time'? You let him believe he was Zerachiel's son for thousands of years."

"When I was prepared to move against Lucifer," Puck said vaguely.

Move against Lucifer, I thought. Why was he being so circumspect? If he wanted a loyal son who would help him overthrow Lucifer, then why not raise that child as his own . . . And then everything slid into place.

"You weren't saving your revelation so you could have a loyal person in Lucifer's court," I said. I could feel my anger rising again. "You were never going to tell Nathaniel in the first place. You were just going to flip the switch."

Nathaniel looked from me to Puck. Puck's expression was stony, revealing nothing.

"Madeline, what do you mean by 'flip the switch'?" Nathaniel said.

"He's made you a Manchurian candidate," I said. "He was never going to tell you he was your father. When the time came, and you were close enough, he was going to unleash you on Lucifer. You'd never know why you killed him, but it wouldn't matter because you'd probably die in the process anyway. I imagine that killing something as old as Lucifer would make a big explosion."

Puck nodded slightly.

Nathaniel looked horrified. "You would set me on Lord Lucifer as an assassin?"

Puck wandered around the room, picking up my things, inspecting them, putting them down again. "Whatever my intentions, they have been undone by this woman."

"This does not change the fact that your intentions sucked," I said. "Did you even care about him at all? Or was he nothing but a means to an end to you?"

"How did you do it?" Puck asked curiously. "I would have said no power but mine could release his legacy."

"I take it by your avoidance of my question that you did not give a care about Nathaniel at all."

"I take it by your avoidance of *my* question that whatever occurred likely involved physical intimacy, because you possess an annoyingly human sense of modesty."

"What happens now?" Nathaniel said, breaking into my verbal tennis match with Puck. I'd almost forgotten he was in the room. "My legacy has been revealed, at least partially. Am I in danger? When next I see Lord Lucifer, will I attempt to kill him?"

Puck gave Nathaniel a speculative look, like he was X-raying his son with his eyes. "The enchantment I laid on you seems to have changed. Really, Madeline. It is astounding that you managed to undo thousands of years of planning in a moment."

"Will I attempt to kill Lucifer?" Nathaniel asked urgently.

Puck shook his head, but he seemed resigned instead of especially angry. I did not trust that. Puck was a mystery to me, like Lucifer, and Lucifer liked to play the long game. If Puck was giving up on Nathaniel as Lucifer's killer, then he must be anticipating some other benefit from the situation.

"Guess you'll have to murder your brother yourself," I said.

"You don't seem especially grieved by the prospect, considering we are related to you," Puck said.

"If I'm lucky, the two of you will destroy each other and then I won't have to deal with either of you anymore," I said.

Puck gave a brief laugh. "If the two of us were gone, then Daharan and Alerian would remain. Don't think that either of them would permit you any peace. Any descendant of Lucifer's—or mine—would attract their attention."

"So what about Nathaniel, then? Are you just going to leave him like this, half-baked? What if your enemies recognize him? Will he be able to defend himself?"

"How do you know I have enemies?" Puck said.

"You're related to Lucifer. You have enemies."

"The question is not if I will leave him like this, but will *you*?"

"Why is this on me? It's your spell. It's your deal."

"Ah, but now that you have interfered in the magic, it's *your* deal, as you say. I no longer have the power to release it."

"How the hell am I supposed to do that?"

Puck's eyes twinkled. "I suspect that you need to do whatever you did in the first place, and just keep doing it until the spell is unleashed fully."

10

SOMETHING FLASHED IN MY BRAIN—NATHANIEL RIS-
ing above me, naked and straining. I could feel my face
turning red.

"There has to be another option," I said.

Nathaniel looked at me. "Would it be so terrible?"

"This is not a conversation I want to have with your
father looking on," I said through gritted teeth.

"He is in danger as long as the spell is incomplete," Puck
said, and he looked like he was enjoying this immensely.

"You are an incredibly powerful being of old," I said. "I
find it just a bit absurd that you can't wave your hand and
fix this."

"Even I have no control over the rules of magic," Puck
said. "You put the key in the lock. You must be the one to
turn it."

"Madeline," Nathaniel said, and he approached me with his hands out.

He reached for me, pulled me close, put his face to my ear. I was sure Puck could hear anything we said, but it was nice that Nathaniel was willing to establish the fiction that we were alone.

As soon as he touched me I felt the thrumming anticipation that had haunted me ever since we'd first kissed. It may have been the compulsion of the spell demanding that I finish what I started, but it felt like a sickness, like a disease. I didn't love Nathaniel like I'd loved Gabriel, but I wanted him more, and I hated that. I hated that I burned for him and there was no love between us.

"Madeline," Nathaniel said, his voice low in my ear. "If you do this for me, it will not mean that you have to choose."

"Nothing could make me choose before I was ready," I said.

"And it does not mean that we must . . . culminate our relationship," he said. "We need only to blend our powers together as we did before."

I shook my head at him. "You know and I know that we wouldn't be able to stop. And once we're done, who knows what will happen? What about my baby?"

"Your baby would not be harmed," Puck said loudly.

I looked around Nathaniel's shoulder. "Excuse me, this is a conversation between Nathaniel and I. You could at least pretend that you can't hear."

Puck held up his hands in surrender and went into the living room. He sat on the couch and flipped through a celebrity gossip magazine that Beezle had picked up somewhere.

"I do not trust Puck, but I don't believe that he would allow your child to come to harm," Nathaniel said.

"Because my baby is a bargaining chip with Lucifer," I said bitterly.

"Whatever the reason, your baby will be safe," Nathaniel said. He lifted my chin so I would look him in the eye. "I would not harm you, either."

If I didn't do this, then he could come to harm. Everything in me was straining toward him. It was probably inevitable, but . . .

"I can't do this now," I said. "Not with an audience. Not with J.B.'s life in the balance."

Nathaniel nodded, and he bent his head to mine. The kiss had a gentleness that I didn't know he possessed.

"When we bring J.B. safely home, then," he said. "We cannot wait much longer. And I would be a better ally to you against the vampires if my power was complete."

I knew he was trying to make me feel better, but it was difficult not to feel like I was being boxed in. If I slept with Nathaniel, I didn't want it to be for this reason. I wanted to choose, and like so many other things in my life I wasn't allowed.

I moved away from Nathaniel. Puck gave the appearance of someone very absorbed by the latest celebrity breakup.

"Can you let everyone else in the house?" I said. "I want to get this show on the road."

"As you wish, my niece," Puck said.

He waved his hand, and the back door opened. I heard it slam against the kitchen wall. Beezle flew in, followed by Chloe.

Beezle looked furious. "What in the name of the Morningstar is going on here?"

"Where are Jude and Samiel?" I asked.

"They're trying to break one of the windows from

outside," Beezle said. "I told them not to bother, but they were getting a little crazed when they couldn't open the door."

"Will you go and get them, please?" I asked.

"Why? They're probably hanging outside your bedroom window with a rock as we speak. And now that the spell is broken—"

As if on cue I heard the sound of glass shattering, and Jude's triumphant cry.

"You're going to fix that window," I said to Puck. "I am not sleeping in a room with duct tape over the window frame in the middle of January."

"Of course," Puck said.

"You're awfully compliant all of a sudden," I said.

From the bedroom came the further sounds of glass falling to the floor, and the thump of Jude's boots. Samiel grunted, and I imagine he was having a hard time squeezing his wings through the frame.

"You are going to have plenty to deal with when we arrive in Titania's kingdom," Puck said. "Our other issues can wait. If you survive."

"I am not going to be defeated by Titania, so don't worry. We'll have plenty of time to take up our *issues* later," I said.

Jude and Samiel came panting into the room. Both of them looked like they were loaded for bear.

"The crisis is over," Beezle announced.

His eyes darted between Nathaniel, Puck and me, and I could see him working things out. I gave him a look that warned him not to say anything.

Jude appeared slightly deflated by the news that he didn't need to hit anything. "Are you all right?"

"That's a complicated question," I muttered. "Yes, I'm unharmed."

What happened? Samiel signed.

"Puck wanted a private word," I said.

"Did he have to stop all of us from entering the apartment?" Jude growled. "We thought he was killing you in here."

"My apologies, Judas," Puck said.

Jude stiffened at the sound of his old name. He seemed to focus completely on Puck for the first time, his nostrils flared.

"I know you," he said, and sniffed the air. "I know you of old."

"Perhaps you do," Puck said.

Great. Now Puck had some kind of connection to Jude, too. It was starting to feel less like chance that we had all come together. Some fate was pulling all of us—me, Nathaniel, Samiel, Jude, maybe even Beezle and Chloe—to these ancient ones, to Lucifer and Puck and the animosity that was older than the earth.

"Can we talk about this later?" I said to Jude. "I want to get J.B. and get home so that I can take down Therion."

"If you will follow me," Puck said, and made a portal in the air. "You must all hold tight to one another. We are going through the old ways, and if any of you lets go, you could be lost forever."

Puck reached for my hand, and Nathaniel took the other. Jude reluctantly grabbed Nathaniel's hand, and Samiel's. Chloe made up the end of the chain.

"You guys look like one of those preschool walking buses," Beezle said. "All you need are the little waist leashes."

He flew toward me and stopped in midair. "Whoa. Where did you get the Catwoman pants?"

"You just noticed?" I said, my ears burning.

"Well, yeah, because there's no pocket for me to nap in," Beezle said, settling on my shoulder and digging in his claws.

"How about you try to stay awake during the rescue mission, just this once?" I said.

"Children," Puck said, and he entered the portal, pulling me with him.

This portal wasn't like the usual ones. Normally when I entered a portal I felt like I was being mashed in a blender. This was a pathway through the universe, a place that no human would ever see. Beneath our feet all the worlds looked like a necklace of jewels. We were draped in a veil of silence, and the stars spun around us.

Chloe and Jude both gasped. Chloe was the closest thing to a human that we had on our team. Even her work as an Agent had not prepared her for this.

"This is what's behind the Door," she whispered.

I felt a moment of panic. She now knew one of the secrets that the Agency tried to keep from the Agents. Would that put her on Sokolov's hit list, too?

Then I realized that just associating with me was enough to put her life in danger. It didn't really make me feel better.

"Hold tight," Puck said, and we were descending.

A few moments later we stood in a lush garden, surrounded by flowers so rare and beautiful that they could not have existed in my world. The air was scented and heavy and shimmering with gold dust.

"We just got dropped into a scene from *Legend*," Beezle said. "Where are the unicorns?"

Everyone had released hands except for Puck, who still determinedly clung to mine. I felt a current of magic strung between the two of us.

"What are you doing?" I said, tugging my hand.

"Giving you a boost. You will need it to find J.B.," Puck said. "You are blood of my blood, and that makes a connection between us. My power can help strengthen yours."

"Don't try any funny business," Jude growled.

"I would not think of it," Puck said, his eyes dancing.

"You're stronger than Titania is," I said softly. "Why do you stay here, pretending to be her subordinate?"

Puck let go of my hand and touched the tip of my nose with his finger. "Just because you are blood of my blood does not mean you get to know everything."

"What does he mean by 'blood of my blood'?" Jude said, looking from me to Puck.

"Later," I promised. "Take us to J.B."

"I cannot do that," Puck said.

"Why not?" I said. "What are we here for, then?"

"If you want him, you must find him," Puck said.

He was the mercurial Puck again, the court jester. I felt unsure of my ground with this Puck. His changeability made me feel that his loyalty was for sale. Perhaps it was, when he was here.

"I'm not here to play games," I said.

"Faeries love games," Puck said. "And so, a quest."

I narrowed my eyes. "What kind of quest?"

"Your prince is somewhere in the kingdom. To gain treasure, you must have the courage to seek it," Puck said.

"Is he in the castle?" Beezle asked. "Because I am going to be pissed if we go running all over the place and he was inside the whole time."

"He is not in the castle, although you are wise to ask," Puck said. "It is the sort of thing a faerie might do. No, he is outdoors. If you can overcome the obstacles in your path, you may return home with him."

"Is he alive?" I asked. If Titania had killed him, I would

take down this castle brick by brick and destroy everyone in it.

Puck considered. "Technically."

I didn't want to consider what kind of condition J.B. might be in. I didn't want to think about how badly Titania might have hurt him in order to hurt me.

"What did you do—beat him up and then throw him out there somewhere, broken?" I said angrily.

"I did not do anything," Puck said with a wounded air.

"You're no angel, either," I said.

As far as I was concerned the courts were just as complicit as their leaders. The courtiers who did nothing were more interested in keeping their own butts protected than in justice, even if some of them did object to Titania's choices. I'm sure Nathaniel—and even Jude—would have said I was naïve to expect otherwise. But I had been a part of Azazel's court, however briefly, and much to Azazel's consternation I had never bent to anyone's will except my own.

"No, I am certainly not an angel," Puck said, and he disappeared.

"Well, this is a fine thing," Chloe said. "He drops us here, tells us we have to find J.B. and gives us nothing to go on."

"Yeah," I said. "And Titania is probably watching us in her crystal ball, laughing her ass off."

"So what do we do?" Chloe asked.

"First, we find a way out of this garden," I said.

There was nothing to see except the high stone walls that surrounded the greenery, no hint of what might lay beyond.

"Find an exit," I said. "Spread out. Everyone look for a door."

"And then?" Beezle asked.

"Start looking for J.B.," I said. I looked at my palm, which still tingled from the magic Puck had given me. Would this "boost" make it easier for me to find J.B., or would it make it easier for Puck to track me, or use me, or otherwise do something I did not want? It had happened so quickly I didn't have a chance to object.

"That's your plan?" Beezle asked.

"Pretty much," I said. "I'm not sure what else to do right now."

"All I know is that you've been extremely lucky to have survived this long," Beezle said. "How long do you think your luck will last?"

"It better last long enough to get us home in one piece," I said, running my hand along the stone wall behind the foliage to check for an exit.

"Here," Jude called. He was in the far right corner of the garden, beckoning.

I trotted toward him as the others converged on his position. Jude silently lifted some protruding tree branches out of the way to reveal an arch cut in the stone, and a forest beyond.

"There are probably trolls in that forest," Beezle said as we hurried out of the shadow of the castle and toward the shelter of the trees.

"Yup," I replied.

"Giant spiders, witches, other things we'd rather not encounter," Beezle said.

"Yes," I said, drawing my sword as we reached the tree line. "Jude, you go in front. Then Chloe, then Samiel. Nathaniel and I will watch our backs."

Jude nodded and took the lead. We all kept tight in line as the forest closed in around us.

"We're probably going to be running for hours in fear for our lives," Beezle said.

"No, I'll be running. You'll be carried. Is there a point to all of this?" I asked.

"No, I'm just looking for something to complain about because I'm hungry," Beezle said.

"Well, knock it off," I whispered, because these woods seemed like a place where you talked quietly. There was menace in the air, a feeling of unfriendliness.

"I'm going to change," Jude said.

A moment later, his clothing fell to the ground and a wolf stood in his place. He trotted ahead of us, his nose pressed in the dirt.

We followed a rough trail through the trees. All around us was lush green foliage and moss. It looked a lot like the woods in every episode of *The X-Files*, that Pacific-Northwest-rains-all-the-time kind of woods.

It was very humid. The heavy moisture filled the air with the scents of bark and loam and green growing things. I could tell Jude was having a hard time getting a fix on any one scent because he was running all over the path.

"What's he trying to follow?" Chloe asked, pausing for a moment. She looked a little wilted. Her vivid purple hair was flattened by the heavy air and her face was pale and sweaty. She leaned on Samiel's shoulder and closed her eyes.

"I'm assuming he's looking for J.B.'s scent and can't get a fix on it. We can't stop," I said.

"I know," Chloe replied, her eyes still closed. "Aren't you beat? You're the one who's pregnant here."

"I think I'm getting used to running around while exhausted," I said. "And I slept for two days before we got here, so I'm a little perkier than usual."

"Well, I am definitely not accustomed to this much exertion," she said tiredly. "I sit at a desk most of the time."

"Stick with her long enough and it will seem normal to be chased by monsters while tired and starving," Beezle said.

"We've got to move," I said.

Chloe straightened with obvious reluctance and opened her eyes. "Hey ho, let's go."

I glanced down the path toward Jude. He wasn't there.

11

"JUDE'S GONE," I SAID.

Samiel raised his fists. Chloe pulled a dagger out of the small of her back. I had no idea she carried such a thing. A ball of nightfire appeared on Nathaniel's palm. Beezle flew off my shoulder.

"Where are you going?" I asked.

"Up to see what I can see," he said.

Without speaking we all turned around so our backs faced inward in a tight circle. And we waited. The others were looking all around the woods, but my eyes were skyward, waiting for my gargoyle to return.

For a few minutes nothing happened. Then I saw Beezle flying back to us as fast as his wings could carry him, his little face set in tense lines. Before Beezle could reach us, Jude burst out of the woods from our back trail, running flat out and barking. He sprinted ahead of us again, his yips and growls telling us that we needed to hurry.

"Whatever you do, don't fly," Beezle shouted, as he landed on my shoulder. "And run!"

None of us needed to be told twice. Something large was behind us. It crashed through the woods, making the ground shake. Chloe stumbled ahead of Samiel. He scooped her up easily and tossed her over his shoulder, running all the while. Samiel is exceptionally strong.

"Put me down, you idiot!" Chloe shouted. "I can walk!"

I'm sure Samiel could feel the vibrations of Chloe's shout in his chest even if he couldn't hear the words, but he chose to ignore them. He ran at a dead sprint, right at Jude's heels.

Nathaniel and I were several feet behind them. I was getting a good boost from terror and adrenaline, but I was starting to flag.

"Why can't we fly?" I panted to Beezle.

"There are things sleeping in the trees," Beezle said. "It's better if we don't wake them up."

"What could be worse than what's on the ground?" I asked.

The monster behind us roared. It sounded terrifyingly close. I didn't want to turn around and see what it was. It was enough to know that it was big, it was angry and it was chasing us.

Out of the corner of my eye I saw Nathaniel glance over his shoulder. His face paled.

"Beezle, what's following us?" I asked.

"A spriggan," he said. "Usually they're small, but this one has either eaten a lot of human children or it's swollen."

"Do I want to know what it will do to us if it catches us?" I asked, finding a whole new running gear as the spriggan's footsteps pounded closer.

"Do I need to paint you a picture?" Beezle said. "It's not going to offer you tea and biscuits; I'll tell you that much for free."

My lungs burned. My legs were slowing in spite of my desire to live. Even when faced with the possibility of death, I couldn't keep to an all-out sprint indefinitely.

Nathaniel grabbed my hand, pulling me along. "You must run."

"I know," I said.

"I can carry you."

"You can't carry me and fight at the same time," I said. "And I think we're going to have to fight."

"You're not fighting that spriggan," Beezle said. "They're barrow guards. Believe me, it's seen anything you can throw at it."

"I can't run much longer," I said.

Beezle looked behind us. "You have to. But I think it's slowing down."

The spriggan roared again, and it did sound like it was slightly farther away. Nathaniel gripped my hand hard, and I felt a little push of magical energy pass from him to me.

His magic burned through me, gave me the boost that I needed. My legs turned over faster and faster. Nathaniel kept pace with me, and after a minute or two we were right on Samiel's heels.

It seemed like the trees were thinning out, the underbrush growing sparser. The sounds of the spriggan's pursuit ceased abruptly. I risked a glance over my shoulder.

The spriggan was gone.

"Hold up," I shouted, coming to a halt.

I bent over, my hands on my knees, trying to catch my breath. Beezle flew off my shoulder, hovering beside me in the air. Sweat dripped over my face and onto the ground.

My fancy new leather pants stuck to my legs, and the sweater was sopping wet.

Jude and Samiel stopped and turned. When Samiel saw that we were no longer being pursued, he put Chloe back on her feet. She looked seasick. She sat on the ground, cross-legged, and breathed in through her nose.

"When I stop feeling like I'm going to puke, I'm going to punch you in the mouth," she said to Samiel.

Samiel shrugged. *I could have let that monster eat you.*

"I can run, you know," Chloe said.

Not fast enough.

"Don't argue with her, Samiel," I said. "She just wants to pick a fight because she knows you're right."

"How do you know that?" Chloe demanded.

"I live with Beezle," I said. "I recognize the symptoms."

I straightened up, wiping the sweat from my face with my sleeve. I looked at Nathaniel. "What do you think happened to the spriggan?"

"Either it was called off by Titania, or we got far enough away from its barrow that it decided we were no longer a threat to its treasure," he said. "But there will be more creatures like it in these lands."

"I know," I said. "We've got to figure out where we are in relation to everything else. And we need a more effective way of tracking J.B. than sniffing around for him. Sorry, Jude."

Jude barked once in acknowledgment.

"Weren't you here before?" Chloe asked.

"Yes, but the portion of the kingdom that we walked through was an illusion," I said. "I have no idea where we are in relation to the place where Lucifer brought us. And we might be walking through another illusion now. Faeries do like to maintain appearances."

"What was underneath the last illusion?" Chloe asked.

Nathaniel, Beezle and I looked at one another. "Umm, it was a kind of game board," I said.

Her eyes narrowed. "A game board."

"Yeah, and Oberon and Titania were watching us on the board . . . Never mind," I said, because Chloe looked like she might lose her temper. "Nathaniel, could we do a tracking spell to find J.B.?"

Nathaniel considered. "The tracking spell is usually used to find traces of magic. If J.B. has not used magic in this place, it would be very difficult to find him that way."

"We can't just walk around the forest banging into things and hoping we'll stumble onto him."

The next moment, Nathaniel shoved me to the ground. I hit the dirt hard and rolled over, ready to tell him off. But he stood where I had stood a moment before, an arrow in his hand. If he hadn't pushed me out of the way, I'd have that arrow in my heart. I don't know whether he could have caught it before his legacy from Puck had been revealed, and I took a moment to be thankful before standing again. Nathaniel pushed me behind him.

Jude tore into the woods, nothing but a furry blur. We heard someone cry out. Jude snarled and yelped, and Samiel ran into the trees after him. There was a flash of light, and the distinctive sulfur smell of nightfire.

Samiel came out of the woods lugging Bendith, Titania's son, under one arm. Jude trotted out behind him. The faerie queen's progeny was out cold, a nightfire burn on his shoulder. Jude had taken a good-sized chunk out of Bendith's leg, too. Samiel tossed him to the ground, a look of disgust on his face.

"Who is this guy?" Chloe asked, nudging Bendith's still form with her shoe.

"Titania's son," I said. "He doesn't like me."

"Do you think Titania sent him?" Beezle asked.

I shook my head, remembering the look on Bendith's face when last I was in Titania's court, when I had diminished Oberon in front of everyone. "He came on his own."

I'd neglected to consider the possibility of a son's desire for vengeance for his father. Well, Bendith *thought* Oberon was his father, and I was not going to be the one to disabuse him of that notion. Even though I couldn't believe that he didn't see the proof every time he looked in the mirror. His eyes were exactly like Puck's. I stared at Bendith, possibilities turning over in my mind.

"So now we've got the faerie queen's son," I said. "And that means we have something to trade."

"Bendith for J.B.?" Nathaniel said. "Are we going to return to the castle with a knife to his neck and demand Titania reveal J.B.'s location?"

"We could, if we had to," I said. "Or we could make Bendith tell us where J.B. is."

"If he knows," Beezle said.

"Well, we'd better wake him up and find out," I said.

"Shall I heal him?" Nathaniel asked.

"No," I said. "He tried to kill me. He's not getting courtesy from me."

"Dark side," Beezle murmured.

"I don't care," I said. "I don't want him healed. If we have to kill him, then that's a lot of energy wasted."

"Are you really going to kill Titania's son in cold blood?" Beezle asked. "I'm not sure I'm on board with this."

"Me, neither," said Chloe, who was eyeing me like she'd never seen me before. Even Samiel looked uncertain. It was hard to tell what Jude was thinking, as he was in wolf form. Nathaniel appeared unfazed. Nathaniel still thought like a member of the fallen, and that meant that whatever means were necessary were okay with him.

"Either I am in charge or I'm not," I said through my teeth. "If none of you like it, you can find your own way home."

There was an awkward silence that followed this.

"Wake him up," I repeated.

Samiel shook Bendith roughly. Titania's son groaned and opened his eyes.

"What . . . Where . . . ?" He sat up abruptly as he realized he was on the ground, surrounded by enemies.

"You missed," I said.

Bendith narrowed his eyes at me. "I will not miss again when next the opportunity arises."

"You're not getting any more opportunities," I said. "Get up. You can save me a lot of time and energy by taking me to J.B."

"And why should I assist my enemy?" Bendith sneered.

"Because if you don't, I will make you hurt like you never have before," I said.

"If you torture him, you're no better than Titania," Beezle said.

"She's the one who changed the rules," I said. "He doesn't have to suffer as long as I get what I want."

"No, I cannot allow this," Bendith said. "You must pay for what you have done to Father."

He pushed himself from the ground in a suicide strike, his hands outstretched, ready to strangle me. He moved faster than I thought he could have, given his injuries. My magic flared. But Nathaniel was already there.

Nathaniel grabbed Bendith's wrists, and then something strange happened.

Electricity arced between them, and they were surrounded by a blaze of white light. The light faded as quickly as it appeared. The two stared at each other, identical stunned expressions on their faces.

"Your eyes," Bendith said, and there was wonder in his voice. "Your eyes are like mine."

I shifted so I could see Nathaniel's face. It was true. The frozen blue had been replaced by the same sapphire as Bendith's—and Puck's.

I grabbed one of Nathaniel's hands and pulled. He released Bendith, but Titania's son took Nathaniel's other arm so that the angel stood between us like a tug-of-war rope.

"Wait," Bendith said, his eyes searching. "Who are you to me?"

I really didn't want to have this conversation. I had enough family drama of my own. But maybe I could get Bendith to help us if he knew the truth.

"He's your brother," I said. I half hoped Titania was watching us with her magic. I hoped she was gnashing her teeth as I revealed the truth to her son.

"My . . . brother?" He looked bewildered, his eyes like a lost puppy's.

Beezle shifted around on my shoulder so that he faced Nathaniel.

"I guess we know who you are now," he said to Nathaniel in a low voice. "Should I start calling you faerie child?"

"Nathaniel's a faerie now?" Chloe asked. She looked almost as confused as Bendith.

"Puck is no faerie," Nathaniel said. "You should know this, gargoyle. You can see the true nature of things."

Beezle muttered something so quietly that I could barely hear him, and he was perched right next to my ear.

"What was that?" I asked.

"I said, I can't get a clear reading on Puck." Beezle sounded disgruntled. "He's too changeable."

"That's interesting," I said.

I wondered how Puck was able to disguise himself so thoroughly. He had managed to live under Titania's nose for hundreds of years without her detection. And I still had yet to figure out why. He was playing a very long and deep game in the faerie court, and I hadn't yet determined how it benefited Puck to pretend to be Titania's subordinate.

"Are you saying that Puck is my father, and yours?" Bendith searched Nathaniel's face.

"You know the truth of this in your heart," Nathaniel said gently. "You have only chosen to believe otherwise."

Bendith closed his eyes, those orbs of brilliant blue that were exactly like Puck's. When he opened them, his face was relaxed.

"Yes," he said. "I have always known this to be true."

"Does that mean that you'll stop trying to kill me for diminishing Oberon?" I asked.

Bendith hardly seemed to notice me. He had eyes only for Nathaniel, starving eyes, the eyes of a child who has finally been given some longed-for desire. "I have always wished for a brother."

"Wish granted," Beezle said. "Now, can we get on with the quest so we can get out of here? I don't want to spend any more time in this forest than I have to."

"Would you aid us, Bendith?" Nathaniel asked.

He seemed so gentle in that moment. I was reminded of Gabriel and Samiel's first meeting, when they had discovered they were siblings. From the look on Samiel's face he was remembering, too. I turned my head to one side, taking a few deep breaths so that I would not weep. Sometimes it was hard for me to remember that I wasn't the only one who'd lost something when Gabriel had died.

"I will help you, but not because I am interested in your quest, or your quarrel with my mother," Bendith said. "I will help my brother. Because my mother betrayed the man I thought was my father, the father I have loved my whole life."

"Thank you," Nathaniel said.

Bendith nodded. "Follow me."

Nathaniel fell in beside him. I don't know whether Nathaniel wanted to spend some time with his brother or he wanted to be close enough to punch him if Bendith was tricking us, which was still a possibility.

He turned us off the main path through the woods. The foliage was thicker here, and it was harder to walk. I focused on putting one foot in front of the other and not tripping over anything.

Everyone was silent, lost in their own thoughts, except for Bendith and Nathaniel. The two of them spoke quietly, a conversation for their ears alone. I think Chloe, especially, had been disturbed by the prospect of torturing Bendith. She kept glancing warily at me when she thought I wasn't paying attention.

I was finding that I didn't much care about Chloe's opinion, or Beezle's, or Samiel's. I didn't see why our enemies got to do whatever they wanted but we had to follow some nebulous set of rules designed to appease human ideas of morality. As everyone was constantly reminding me, the creatures we dealt with were not human.

We walked for quite a while, long enough that I was starting to question whether or not Bendith was leading us into a trap. Then we emerged into another clearing, and J.B. was there.

He was lying upon a wide, flat stone, his eyes closed. I started toward him, but Nathaniel put his hand on my shoulder to hold me back.

"Is there a spell around the stone?" Nathaniel asked Bendith.

Titania's son shook his head. "No. It is safe for you to approach."

I pushed past Nathaniel so I could go to J.B., kneeling at his side. My merry band of misfits crowded around us.

"Gods above and below," I said.

J.B.'s face was covered in blood. His right cheekbone looked like it was broken. His chest was bare and covered in fist-sized bruises. His eyes were closed and his breathing shallow.

"J.B.?" I whispered. "J.B., can you hear me?"

"He's in too much pain to wake," Nathaniel said. "I can heal him."

He exchanged a look with Jude, and Jude nodded. The wolf took up the place at my back, and I realized they were worried about Bendith striking when I wasn't paying attention. Apparently Nathaniel didn't trust his brother completely.

It was a good thing I had them looking out for me, because Bendith could have stabbed me at that moment and I'd never have noticed. All I cared about was J.B., and that he had suffered this because of me.

Nathaniel gripped J.B.'s shoulders and closed his eyes. The air filled with magic, and I felt that pulsing awareness of Nathaniel again, like his power was seeking mine. I put my hands over Nathaniel's, and pushed through him and into J.B.

There was a lot of damage. Broken bones, torn muscles, and, most terrifyingly, I sensed a blood clot forming from the trauma. I carefully picked the clot apart cell by cell while Nathaniel healed J.B.'s other injuries.

After a while we had done all we could do, and I released Nathaniel's hands. He let go of J.B. and we looked at each other. J.B. still had not opened his eyes.

"He will likely need to rest for some time," Nathaniel said. "But he will be well now."

I touched J.B.'s cheek. "Where are his glasses?" I asked.

"I suspect they were broken," Nathaniel said.

"How will he see without his glasses?" I said. I felt tears forming in my throat and I swallowed them ruthlessly. It was a stupid thing to worry about, really. At least he was alive. I just hoped his brain was still intact when he woke up, that he was still J.B.

"Samiel?" I asked.

Samiel reached for J.B. and slung him over one shoulder.

"Now we have to get out of here," I said. "Bendith, you'd better get back to the castle before Titania finds out what you've been up to."

"I would like to stay with you," Bendith said to Nathaniel.

"No," I said, before Nathaniel could agree. "I'm grateful to you for your help, but you need to go home. I don't want to be responsible for anyone else's life."

"If I go home, when will I see you again?" Bendith asked Nathaniel.

"We will meet again," Nathaniel said.

"How are we going to get back home without Puck?" Chloe said.

"We need to get outside the borders of the kingdom. That's where we landed the last time we arrived here. Once we get there I'll try to contact Lucifer," I said.

"And what if Lucifer decides to leave us stranded here?" Chloe said. "Or you can't reach him?"

"One problem at a time," I said.

"If you return to the path through the woods, you will find what you seek," Bendith said. He seemed reluctant to leave.

"Until we meet again, brother," Nathaniel said.

"Until we meet again," Bendith repeated.

We started toward the path, leaving Bendith by the stone looking lost. I determinedly faced forward. I would not worry about what would happen to Bendith now that he knew the truth. Titania had made her own bed and now she could lie in it.

"There's going to be a reckoning for that," Beezle said, and I knew he was referring to the revelation of Bendith's parentage.

"Isn't there always?" I said sourly.

We walked until we came to the edge of the forest. Chloe sat down on a nearby log, dislodging several small insects as she did so. Ahead of us was an open field of grass, and beyond it, green foothills that led up to sharp mountains. The sky was blue; the sun was bright. Everywhere except . . .

"Hey, look there," I said, pointing to the topmost peak of the mountains ahead of us. At the very tip of the snow-capped mountain the bright blue sky was smudged with a patch of gray.

Chloe squinted. "What am I supposed to be looking at here?"

"The way out," Beezle said, clapping me on the shoulder with his little hand. "Not bad."

"How do you know that little dirty smudge is the way out and not another illusion?" she asked.

"Because when we arrived here the first time with

Lucifer, we were in a kind of no-man's-land, a place that was cold and gray," I said.

"But how do you know it's not an illusion?" Chloe persisted.

"I don't," I said. "I have to believe that it's not."

"I'm really amazed that you've survived as long as you have, with logic like that at work," she said.

"Everyone underestimates me," I replied. "I'm not offended."

"And besides," Beezle said. "I can tell that's not an illusion with my special gargoyle powers."

"I know you are tired," Nathaniel said, "but—"

"We should keep moving, I know," I said. I looked at J.B., sleeping on a tree root. "We're not going to be able to fly as long as J.B.'s knocked out. It would be hard for Samiel to carry Jude and J.B."

"I told you, you can't fly anyway," Beezle said.

"Won't it be safe to fly once we get away from the forest?" I asked.

He shook his head. "Absolutely not. They don't like anything in their territory. I was just lucky that I saw the nest before I got too high."

"What nest?" Chloe asked. "What's up there?"

"Harpies," Beezle said.

Nathaniel looked sharply upward. "Harpies. Are you sure?"

Beezle nodded. "I am definitely sure."

"How many?"

"I saw eggs," Beezle said.

"Then they're breeding," Nathaniel said. "There could be hundreds of them up there, and it would only take one or two to cause us considerable distress."

"Harpies are myths from the Greeks," Chloe said. "What are they doing in a faerie forest?"

"Titania must have made a deal with them," Nathaniel said. "And if the gargoyle is correct, then we most certainly cannot fly. If even one of the harpies sees or senses us in the air, then they will consider us fair game."

"Yay, harpies," Chloe said, standing up. "Let's walk now."

Samiel bent to pick up J.B. I went to his side for a moment, put my hand on J.B.'s head. He was cool to the touch.

"No fever," I said. "There's that, at least."

Nathaniel came up beside me, touched my shoulder. "His body simply needs time to recover."

I nodded, but I knew I wouldn't feel better until J.B. opened his eyes. Jude trotted silently ahead, and we all fell back into our positions.

The thing about mountains is that it's hard to tell how far away they are. I don't know how far or how long we walked with the sun beating down on us and no food or water. All I know is that after a while I started to feel woozy. And then a while after that everything went black.

I woke up with my head in Nathaniel's lap and a mouth full of dirt. I turned to one side and tried to spit, but my mouth was too dry, and I gagged. Beezle sat on my chest with a worried expression on his face. Jude sat beside my arm, still in wolf form, his tongue hanging out in deference to the heat. Samiel and Chloe were standing, leaning on each other for support. J.B. was on the ground beside me.

"This is taking too long," Beezle said. "You're not going to make it to those mountains."

"I can do it," I said through bone-dry lips.

"Yeah, and I'm an Australian supermodel," Beezle said. "Look, we're on a deadline with Therion as it is. Remember the vampire invasion of your hometown? We can't spend the whole three days messing around in the faerie kingdom. We have to get out of here so that you can get home and kick some vampire butt so that takeout can be restored."

He was right. I knew he was right. We just couldn't walk fast enough. Samiel was strong, but he couldn't carry J.B. indefinitely. Chloe was weakened from her ordeal in Azazel's mansion, and I was pregnant. Jude and Nathaniel could probably make it, but the rest of us wouldn't.

"What do you suggest we do, then?" I said.

Beezle looked grim.

"We're going to have to fly."

12

"WHAT ABOUT THE HARPIES?" I ASKED. "AND JUDE AND J.B.?"

"I can carry you and the wolf," Nathaniel said.

I shook my head. "That's silly. We'll need you to be able to fight if the harpies come after us."

"*When* the harpies come after us, you mean," Chloe said. "But I can carry Jude, anyway."

Samiel shook his head. *No, you can't. You aren't nearly strong enough.*

Chloe flexed her biceps. "I lift weights, you know."

"You can't carry a two-hundred-twenty-pound wolf through the air no matter how much you can bench-press," I said. "I can't, either, and I'm less human than you are."

"What if we wake up J.B.?" Beezle said.

"He's traumatized. And healing," I said, sitting up slowly

and trying to wipe the dirt out of my mouth. "How are we supposed to do that?"

"Well, we are in faerie land," Beezle said. "How are sleeping princes usually woken?"

I didn't have to see Nathaniel to know he was scowling. I stood up to put more distance between us.

"Look," I said, my face heating. "In stories it's the princess that's woken by love's first kiss. J.B. and I don't love each other."

"Yes, you do," Beezle said seriously. "Oh, there's a whole lot of human stupidity and some other stuff in the way, but at the core of it you love each other. If you didn't love him, you would have left him here and dealt with the vampires first."

"J.B. is my *friend*," I said. "I wouldn't leave any friend in Titania's hands."

"Keep telling yourself that," Beezle said.

Samiel tapped my shoulder so I would look at him. *It's worth a try. It doesn't mean you don't love Gabriel.*

Samiel's consent made me feel even more embarrassed and confused.

"I don't . . . I can't . . ." I said.

"We'll all give you some privacy if it makes you feel better," Beezle said. "But the only way we're going to get out of here is to fly. And the only way to fly is if J.B. can move under his own power."

"And what if this doesn't work, smarty-pants?" I asked.

"Then we'll try something else," Beezle said. "But I'm betting it will work. And you know I'm always right."

"I don't know how you fit such a huge ego in that tiny head," I said.

"The same way I can fit a pound of chicken wings in this tiny body," Beezle said. "Mad skillz."

"Okay, fine, I'll try it," I said. My cheeks were on fire, and I couldn't look directly at Nathaniel. I pointed toward the mountain. "Everyone just walk that way for a while."

"How far?" Beezle asked.

"Just keep walking until either I call you or we catch up," I said. "I am definitely not doing this with an audience."

"You know, Jude can hear everything for about a mile in any direction," Beezle said. "Privacy is really an illusion."

"Just go!" I said.

"All right, all right. No need to get huffy," Beezle said.

They all left except Nathaniel, who stood there for a moment while I determinedly stared at the ground.

"This doesn't mean I'm choosing," I said finally, looking up at him.

He looked back at me with Puck's eyes. It was disconcerting to see those eyes in Nathaniel's face.

He said nothing, just nodded and turned to follow the others.

J.B. lay still on the ground. His eyes were closed, his breath smooth and even. I'd been so focused on his injuries that I hadn't noticed his clothes. Now I realized that he was dressed for work in his favorite gray pants and a blue button-down. Both pieces were torn and liberally stained with blood, and his socks and shoes were gone.

He looked so unlike himself, lying there in the grass. J.B. was always moving, always shouting, always calculating the solution to the next problem. He wasn't a beaten thing, a broken toy that Titania had thrown away. He was J.B., and Beezle was right. I did love him.

I just didn't know what kind of love it was, and Gabriel's shadow was still with me. It was too soon to make any kind of decision. It felt like circumstance was forcing me to move on, to choose. I didn't want to choose. I wanted to do things in my own time and in my own way, the same way I did everything else.

Nathaniel or J.B. J.B. or Nathaniel. Part of me just wanted to not have to choose at all, to have Gabriel back.

I knelt beside J.B., brushed my hand over his forehead. I didn't have to decide now. I just needed to wake him up, to get us all home safely.

I bent closer, until I could feel his slow exhalations on my mouth. This had to work.

"Wake up, J.B.," I said, and I kissed him.

His lips were warm but yielding, and it seemed like it wasn't going to happen. And if I kissed J.B. for nothing, then I was going to hide all the popcorn from Beezle for the next month.

J.B. groaned, and shifted in the dirt. I pulled away, grabbing his shoulders.

"J.B.?" I said, shaking him a little.

He opened his eyes. They were bleary, and it took a second for him to focus.

"Maddy?" he said. "Were you kissing me?"

"Yes," I said.

"*Now* you kiss me? While I'm unconscious?"

"Beezle said it was the only way to wake you up."

"I'm going to buy that gargoyle all the popcorn he can eat," J.B. said.

His arms wrapped around my waist, pulled me on top of him and rolled us over until I was underneath him. He did this so fast that I didn't really have time to process what was happening.

"Um, J.B.?" I said.

"Shh," he said. "I was asleep for the last one."

And then he kissed me. The sun shone down on us, warm and comforting. The grass rustled in the wind. All that was between us was breath and air, and I felt a sweet peace, one I hadn't felt in a long time.

There was no madness of magic and desire like there was when I was with Nathaniel. J.B. didn't push me. He didn't ask for more than I could give.

He kissed me one last time, and then lifted his head. I opened my eyes to look at him. He brushed his hand through my hair.

"Your hair grew back," he said. "How long was I gone?"

"Only a day," I said, and pressed his shoulders so that he would get off me.

"I imagine there's an interesting story about why your hair is back, then," he said.

"Yeah, interesting," I said. *And I have no intention of ever telling it to you.*

He rolled to the side and then to his feet. He shielded his eyes from the sun, squinting in the direction the others had gone.

"Is that Chloe?" he asked. "I can see a purple blob kind of floating above the grass."

"Yeah, and Jude and Samiel and Nathaniel and Beezle," I said, standing up and brushing dirt from my pants.

"Where did you get those pants? I never pegged you for the leather type. Although I like them," he said, wiggling his eyebrows suggestively and peeking around me. "They make your backside look good."

I punched him in the shoulder. "Just because I kissed you does not mean you get to be a lech."

"Well, what does it mean?" he said.

"Right now, not much. This isn't the time for a heart-to-heart," I said. "We took you from Titania but we've got no way of leaving this place until we can get to the borders of her lands and call for Lucifer's help. We can't walk there without killing a lot of time, and time is something we don't have much of."

I told him about Therion's message and what was happening in Chicago. Then I told him about the harpies.

"Are you out of your mind?" J.B. asked. "If the harpies detect us, they will rip us limb from limb and eat us, and not in that order."

"We're pretty much out of options," I said. "If we stay here, Titania will rip us limb from limb and then feed us to one of her pets."

He rubbed his forehead. "Why is it your plans are always insane?"

"Maybe because we're always in insane circumstances," I said. I saw the others approaching us. "Listen, J.B. Titania punished you because of me."

"Yeah, I know," he said. "Don't worry about it."

"No," I said. "I can never make it up to you."

He looked down at himself. "You seem to have already, since my previously broken parts are no longer broken."

"J.B., she tortured you," I said. "That doesn't just go away."

"Don't worry about me, Black. I've got a sturdy constitution," he said.

Beezle landed on my shoulder. "Told you it would work."

"Are you going to be insufferable now?" I said. I was a little annoyed that J.B. wasn't taking his trauma and my guilt about it very seriously.

"No more than usual," Beezle said. "So, how are we going to do this, then?"

"I will carry Madeline," Nathaniel said. "And Samiel can carry Jude."

"I can carry Maddy," J.B. said.

"You were just unconscious a second ago," I said. "And you can hardly see without your glasses."

"I'm fine," he said in that tone that men get when you imply that their manliness might be less than optimal.

"We are not going to argue about this," I said. "You're still recovering. All I want you to do is get yourself safely to the top of that mountain."

He screwed up his face. I knew he couldn't see the point that I was referring to, and there was no way in hell he would admit that.

Chloe and J.B. pushed out their wings. I watched them with no small amount of jealousy. Nathaniel and J.B. tried to prove who was the better man by carting me around, but I would have preferred to be able to fly without assistance from either of them.

Nathaniel scooped me into his arms and Beezle shifted from my shoulder to J.B.'s. Samiel slung Jude over his shoulders.

"Fly as fast as you can," I said to all of them. I looked at Chloe. "Stay close to J.B."

She nodded. J.B. looked insulted, but he was half-blind at the moment and I didn't want him veering off course.

Nathaniel shifted me in his arms. It was going to be difficult for us to defend ourselves from the harpies with me in this position.

"How do you kill a harpy?" I asked curiously.

I didn't know much about them except that they were half-bird, half-woman and that there was one in the film *The Last Unicorn*. That harpy had scared the bejeezus out of me as a kid.

"Play to your strengths," Beezle said.

"You want me to set them on fire?"

"It's probably the most efficient way of getting rid of them," J.B. agreed. "And you're the only one here who can throw fire."

"Nothing like the fate of the whole party resting on your shoulders. You'd all better fly ahead of us, then, so you don't get caught in the cross fire," I said. "All right, let's go."

We waited for the others to take off first. I looked at him.

"I'm not going to get much done if you carry me like a baby," I said.

"If you shift to the position you were in when the Agents chased us, I could hold you steady while you fired behind me," he said.

"Yeah," I said, and climbed up, wrapping my legs around his waist. Nathaniel put one hand under my butt and the other around my waist. I could see over Nathaniel's shoulder in this position, and both of my hands were free. *Please, don't let J.B. look back.*

I felt that same electricity between us again, that crazy burning lust that had settled just under the surface of my skin. Nathaniel felt it, too. It was there in the flare of his eyes, but he didn't say anything and neither did I.

Nathaniel spread his wings wide and lifted from the ground. I focused intently on the sky behind us, watching the trees in the forest that we had left hours ago. There was no sound, no movement.

"How quickly could the harpies catch up with us?" I shouted to Nathaniel.

"Very quickly," he said. His hand shifted, pressing me tighter against him.

I was getting breathless, and not from the stress of watching for harpies. "Nathaniel, now is not the time."

"I know," he said.

It was like we were in the grip of insanity, both of us

knowing that our lives were in danger, that we had friends depending on us to keep them safe. And even with all of this I still could think of nothing but him, his heat, his skin.

Then there was a terrible cry floating on the wind, from far and away across the field, and that sound was finally enough to break the spell of lust.

I saw black shapes rising from the trees, and the harpies came screaming for us.

Their cries permeated my blood, danced over my nerve endings. It was the most horrible sound I have ever heard. It was the sound of death on wings, death without mercy.

"How far away are the others?" I asked Nathaniel.

"They are ahead of us, but not far enough."

I couldn't risk turning around to see. The harpies were moving fast, much faster than I would have thought they could, and I needed to be ready. They were still far enough away for their faces to be indistinct, but they were no longer formless blobs. I could distinguish their heads from their bodies and their wings.

My magic had flared high when Nathaniel had lifted me against him, and I was still riding that surge of power. I felt more than prepared to take out some harpies.

"They are only a little ahead of us," Nathaniel said. "We are over the foothills of the mountain now."

That was what flying could do for you over walking. It had taken us hours to get halfway across the field on foot, and in a few short moments in the air we had covered the remainder of the distance.

The harpies screamed as they came closer. I could see their faces now, and I wished I couldn't. They were the faces of beautiful women, but contorted by a hate so fierce that it made them horrible to look upon.

I let loose the fire that blazed in my blood.

The vanguard fell screaming and smoking to the earth. Their sisters took up the cry with twice the ferocity, and I thought my eardrums might burst. I let the flame pour from my hands, and harpies plummeted to earth. The air was filled with stench of burning flesh and the howls of burning women. But still there were more, and more. There was a stream of harpies flowing from our wake back to the forest, and it seemed to have no end.

"How much farther?" I said, still loosing flame, still burning harpies with all the power I could muster.

"It's farther away than it looks," Nathaniel said.

"There are so many of them," I said, and I wondered whether we would make it in time.

"Madeline," Nathaniel said, and he put his lips on my neck.

I felt his magic flow from the place where his mouth touched, felt his power twining around mine again. And as it did, there was a blaze, as there was the first time our powers had touched. Heat blasted from my hands, uncontrolled, and then everything seemed to explode.

We were blinded by white light, and for a moment I was afraid Nathaniel would drop me. But he held me close, and my arms wound around his neck, my power spent. We hovered in the air, our eyes closed against the light.

When the light seemed to recede I opened my eyes and looked over Nathaniel's shoulder toward the harpies.

The harpies were gone. So was the field, and a good portion of the forest. The path we had walked was a blackened husk.

"What about the others?" I asked, panicking. "Were they caught in the spell?"

"No, you maniac," Beezle said beside me. "Although it

was a near thing. You should have mentioned that you were going to set off a nuclear bomb."

"You told me to play to my strengths," I said, nudging Nathaniel so he would shift me back to our original carrying position. Jude, Samiel, Chloe and J.B. were floating in the air several feet ahead of us, and they all looked a little shocked. And smoke-smudged.

"So I should have expected you to reduce all animal and plant life for miles around to ash?"

"Yes, you should have," I said. "That's pretty much my M.O."

"Titania's going to be really mad at you now," Beezle said as we started forward to join everyone else.

"Like she wasn't mad before?"

"These faerie queens seem to take it amiss when you burn down their forest and their creatures," Beezle said. "Remember when you killed Amarantha's Cthulhu-thing and her giant spider?"

"Barely," I said. "I've burned so many things it's kind of all blurring together. And Amarantha was ready to be pissed at me before that, just as Titania is."

"Then stop antagonizing her," Beezle said.

"Maybe she should stop antagonizing me," I said. "Before I wipe out her whole kingdom."

"Dark side," Beezle said.

"I am not going dark side," I said impatiently as we flew along toward the top of the mountain.

"If you're not going dark side, then you've definitely decided to adopt a scorched-earth policy for dealing with your enemies," Beezle said.

"And why shouldn't she?" J.B. said.

We all stared at him in surprise. J.B. was pretty much a

rule follower. He was usually one of the first to chastise me when I killed someone or burned something to the ground. Of course, that may have been because he'd have to file paperwork about the incident when I was an Agent. Now that I was no longer an Agent, paperwork didn't apply.

"She shouldn't because she's getting a reputation for being ruthless. No one will want to ally themselves with her if they think she might go crazy and blow them up at a moment's notice," Beezle said.

"I have never done that," I said. "I only blow up people who are mean to me first."

"If Madeline is not ruthless, she will never survive, gargoyle," Nathaniel said. "Her enemies have no mercy, and neither should she."

"Well, then, if you want to be a monster like everyone else," Beezle said.

"I don't," I said. "But I don't want anyone thinking they can have a go at me—or my friends—without consequences."

The air was getting colder, and as we got closer to the peak, snow began to blow. Nathaniel did not seem even remotely bothered by the weather, but after a few moments I was shivering. I was wearing nothing but the stupid leather pants and the flimsy sweater that Puck had given me. Even Nathaniel's body heat wasn't helping.

After a while the snowflakes became a blizzard, and we could barely see a few feet in front of us.

"Stay close!" I shouted to the others. I didn't want to lose anyone in this mess.

Everyone clumped up so tight that it was difficult to fly. Wings tangled together; people bumped and snarled. Beezle climbed into my lap and huddled there with his wings over his head.

"There's the top," Nathaniel said.

I don't know how he could see anything at all except snow, but since his hearing had been enhanced by the discovery of his legacy, it wasn't that far-fetched to think his vision would be as well. At least we knew we were still heading in the right direction.

Samiel was a little ahead of the rest of us. Jude was a snow-covered length of fur on his shoulders. The snow swirled for a moment, and we could all see the gray wasteland that was the end of Titania's kingdom a few feet in front of us.

Then Samiel seemed to smash into an invisible wall in midair, and fell to the ground. Luckily, the ground wasn't very far away.

"Samiel!" Chloe and I both cried.

Nathaniel and the others flew down to the place where Samiel and Jude had landed in a snowbank beside a large cave opening. Jude shook the snow off his fur. Samiel sat up, rubbing his head. Chloe ran to his side.

"How many fingers?" she asked, holding up her hand.

Two, Samiel signed, looking sheepish, as we crowded around him. *What happened?*

Nathaniel placed me on my feet. Beezle climbed up to my shoulder and settled in. Nathaniel walked toward the sharp edge where the snow ended and the wasteland began. He reached toward the space, palm out. And was stopped.

"There is a wall here," Nathaniel said.

"There, see, you aren't a klutz," Chloe soothed Samiel. "There was a wall there. What's a wall doing there?"

"This is a faerie kingdom," J.B. said. "You didn't think it would be easy for us to leave, did you?"

"We were chased by a spriggan and a horde of harpies. You call that easy?" Chloe asked.

"Easy is a relative concept," I said, thinking of the Maze and the Hob and all of the other horrible faerie things I'd encountered.

I joined Nathaniel by the wall, and J.B. followed me, standing on my other side.

"What do you think?" I asked. "Could we take it down with magic?"

"You could, I'm sure," Beezle said. "Just make with the explodey-thing."

"Possibly," J.B. said. "But it would likely be difficult and draining, and there's a very good chance that the wall will make sure that anyone who tries to destroy it will pay the price."

"Maddy might just blast the whole thing into oblivion, including any booby traps," Beezle said.

"And us, too?" J.B. said. "If she unleashes that much power at such a close range, it's unlikely to be good for any of us. And there's still no guarantee it would work."

"What can we do, then?" I said, looking through to the wastes on the other side. They were so frustratingly close. "Tunnel under?"

Nathaniel shook his head. "It will be like this world is encased in a snow globe. If you tunnel under, you will still find the same barrier."

"Well, there's got to be a way out," I said.

"Not necessarily," J.B. said. "Usually when creatures come and go from this land, they have the power to transport themselves across dimensions, or are at the very least accompanied by someone who does."

"I refuse to believe that we are going to be stuck in this godforsaken place because of a piece of glass," I said.

I stared at the barrier, trying to will it to come down,

and that was when I noticed it. There was a cave on the other side of the wall. I glanced back at the cave that was beside the place where Samiel had landed, and then to the other side again. The two openings were mirror images of each other.

"That's the way out," I said, pointing at the cave on the wasteland side.

J.B. followed my gaze, and then looked over at the cave on our side. He nodded. "You're probably right. It's got the feeling of a faerie solution."

"That means that the cavern will be some kind of obstacle course or proving ground," Nathaniel said.

"Of course," I said. "Nothing is easy, especially when faeries are involved."

"Hey," J.B. said mildly.

"You're only half-faerie," I said. *And nothing is ever easy with you, either,* I thought, but I didn't say it aloud.

We walked back to the others and explained what I had found.

I'm willing to try it, Samiel said.

"Sure, why not?" Chloe said. "It's not like I'm claustrophobic or anything."

"You're claustrophobic and you work in that little room every day?" I asked.

"I have all the light I want in there," Chloe said, her breath visible in the cold air. "That's not going to be the case in here."

We all paused at the mouth of the cave. A current of warmth came from the interior. It should have felt comforting, especially in the bitter cold, but it didn't. It felt like standing near the mouth of a dragon that's about to make you his dinner.

"This could be a trap," J.B. said.

"I've already considered the possibility," I said. "The only other option is to go back, and we know there's nothing for us in that direction."

"Heigh-ho, then," Beezle said. "No time like the present."

I stepped into the darkness.

13

AS SOON AS I STEPPED INSIDE I FELT SOMETHING inside me go black, like it was being smothered, and I realized it was my magic.

"Wait!" I said to the others, but they were already beside me. "Am I the only one who can't access their powers?"

"No," Nathaniel said, his voice grim.

His answer was echoed all around, Jude included.

"I've turned back into a human," he growled.

The darkness was absolute, and the sounds of the wind howling outside had ceased as soon as we entered the cave. I could hear a drip of water, and the harsh breath of everyone else.

"Okay," I said, thinking hard. "I've got my sword, and so does Nathaniel. Does anyone else have a weapon?"

"I've got the little knife, and some bobby pins in my pocket. Somewhere," Chloe said.

"I'll take that as a no," I said. "We can't make nightfire to see. And I bet we can't get out of the cave now that we've gone in."

"No," Jude said. "I already checked."

"So we've got to go forward," I said.

Part of me had expected something like this. Faeries loved their games, and they didn't like you to have advantages. It was more fun for them if you lost.

"I don't want to lose anyone in the dark," I said. "So everyone chain up. I'll go in front, and Nathaniel in the back since we're the only ones with weapons."

"I will go in front," Nathaniel said.

"Don't try to be a man," I said. "I can swing a sword just as easily as you can."

"I'd prefer if Nathaniel went in front, too," Beezle said. "I don't want to be the first in line when some slavering monster appears out of the darkness."

"Then go sit on Samiel's shoulder," I said. "Because I'm going first."

"I would, if I could find Samiel," Beezle said.

There was no way in hell I was letting anyone else take the fall. That had happened twice now. First Gabriel had taken the sword that was probably meant for me. And then J.B. had taken Titania's abuse. No one was standing in front of me anymore, no matter how much it hurt their masculine pride.

"Madeline," Nathaniel began.

"No," I said. "You will trust me."

"There's no reason for . . ."

"There's every reason," I said, and my tone said that we were done discussing the matter.

I groped in the darkness for the hand of the person nearest me, and Jude was there.

"I'm right next to you, Agent," he said to Chloe.

There was a rustling as everyone formed in a line. I drew my sword carefully and found that the darkness was not absolute. There was a very faint silver gleam as the blade was revealed.

"It would be helpful if you would light up like you did in the Maze," I said to the sword.

Nothing. Not even an answering wiggle from the snake tattoo on my palm.

"Who are you talking to?" Jude asked.

"My sword," I said.

"Don't ask," Beezle said. "You'll just get an answer you don't want to hear."

I slid forward as quietly as I could, my hand slick with sweat in Jude's grip. The others followed.

There is nothing quite like moving in the dark. Your eye creates shadows and movement where there is none. Your mind fills in the black space with nightmares. And all around you, the darkness is like a living thing, pressing on you, making you fear, making you doubt.

I'd spent more than my fair share of time in darkness lately. Maybe one day I'd go to the Caribbean and lie in the sun until all of the dark was burned away.

Do you think Lucifer will ever let you do that? I thought. *Do you think he'll let you go now that he has you so close to his grasp?*

I already knew the answer to that. The darkness would be with me forever, and no amount of sunshine would ever light those shadowed places again. That was Lucifer's gift to me—the power of the stars and the universe, cloaked in the black emptiness of space.

We had been walking for some time without incident when I heard Chloe. Her breath had been coming faster and louder gradually, and now she sounded like she was hyperventilating. Samiel must have tried to comfort her because she said, "Not helping. Not helping at all."

"What's the matter?" I said.

"I can't breathe," she said, sounding strained. "I can't get enough air in here."

"You can," I said, trying to cut through her panic by being firm. "There's plenty of air."

"There's not," she moaned. "I can't breathe. I can't breathe!"

"She's having a panic attack," J.B. said, and there was the sound of a struggle.

Jude let go of my hand.

"Hey, don't let go," I said.

"I have to get out of here, I have to get out, I have to," Chloe said.

"Hold her still!" J.B. said.

Sheathing my sword so I wouldn't accidentally stab anyone in the dark, I turned on the spot and reached out in front of me, trying to find the others by sound.

"Get ahold of yourself, girl," Jude growled.

Jude, J.B., Nathaniel, Samiel and Chloe were nothing but shadows moving in the dark, formless, indistinct. My hand touched someone's shoulder, but before I could figure out whose it was, I was decked in the face by Chloe's flailing arms. I staggered backward, hearing J.B. grunt as Chloe hit him, too.

Chloe seemed to lose more control as the moments passed. Her words ceased to have meaning and instead turned into a low keening noise. None of the men was able to get hold of her. A second later, she bolted.

I felt and heard her go by rather than saw. Her boots crunched in the dirt of the cave floor, and her moan trailed behind her as she ran.

"Chloe!" I shouted, and scrambled after her.

"Don't go haring off after her, idiot!" Beezle said.

Samiel shot past me, nothing more than a sense of a body moving in space. I knew it was him because he didn't call her name. I ran behind both of them, deeper into the black.

"Maddy, wait!" J.B. cried.

I should have waited. That was the whole point of the chain, so that we would not lose one another in the darkness. But all I could think was that Chloe was panicking, and Samiel couldn't call us if he needed help.

Then Chloe screamed, and my blood ran cold.

"Chloe!" I called, running harder. Beezle dug his claws into my shoulder so he wouldn't fall off.

She screamed again, and it sounded farther away—much farther than she should have been able to run.

"It sounds like something's carrying her away," Beezle said.

"I know," I said.

The rest of the guys were running behind me and soon caught up. We were sprinting together like a pack, me in the center, J.B. and Nathaniel on each side, and Jude behind. The cave tilted downward, and there was a faint illumination ahead.

"Chloe! Samiel!" I called.

"Samiel can't answer you," Beezle said.

"I'm hoping he'll come back to us," I said.

"He won't come back if his woman is in danger," Jude said.

"What's that ahead?" J.B. asked. "I can see some kind of halo."

"The walls of the cave are lit," Nathaniel said.

The cave was gradually getting brighter, the walls shot

through with twinkling veins of luminescence. It was a tremendous relief to be out of the suffocating dark.

It was less of a relief when we came to the place where the cave was split.

"Great," I said, looking at the two identical paths. "How are we supposed to know which way they went?"

Jude sniffed the air. His nose wasn't quite as good when he was in human form, but it was still better than an ordinary person's.

"Samiel went this way," he said, pointing toward the right-hand cave. He then pointed to the other tunnel. "Chloe and some kind of reptile-mammalian thing went that way."

"Reptile-mammalian thing?" Beezle said.

"I don't know what it is, but that's what it smells like," Jude said.

"I don't want to meet anything that fell off two branches of the evolutionary tree," Beezle said. "Let's go away from the multispecies monster."

I was less worried about the reptile-mammalian thing than I was about the fact that Samiel and Chloe had entered different passages.

"We have two choices," I said. "We can all stay together and go after Chloe, then come back here to try and find Samiel after we retrieve her."

"And the second option is that we divide forces," Nathaniel said. "The answer is no."

"I second that," J.B. said.

"It's impractical for us to move like one big amoeba and leave Samiel alone," I said.

"I'll go after Samiel," Jude said. "And then I'll find you. I can follow your scent easily enough."

"Thank you," I said, keeping my eyes firmly on his face. His clothes were somewhere in the woods. "I'm going after

Chloe. You can go with him or go with me," I said to the other two, and I started jogging down the tunnel on the left side.

"I don't think it's good for you to be friends with Jude," Beezle said. "He enables your bad decisions."

"No," I said. "Jude trusts me, which is more than I can say for anyone else."

"I trust you," J.B said, running up on my left.

"You just don't think I can do anything without you there to keep me safe. And that's what Nathaniel thinks, too," I said, as the angel silently joined us. He ignored my jibe. "Nothing to say?"

"A wise man knows when to keep his own counsel," Nathaniel said.

"And you know that nothing you say will stop her, anyway," Beezle said. "Wait—I just realized we went down the tunnel of the freaky combination animal thing. I don't want to go down this tunnel. I want to go with Jude."

"Too late," I said with a lightness I did not feel. The monster could be eating Chloe right now. "Look at it this way. You'll be able to see something very few have ever seen."

"That's because they're not alive to tell us about it," Beezle muttered. "You know, I'm not much of a let's-make-discoveries-for-science gargoyle. I'm more of a watching-science-on-TV-while-eating-pan-fried-noodles gargoyle."

The cave was lit by the same trails of light that were in the main passage. After a while I noticed that the walls were also covered in some kind of white fluid, and that my boots were no longer crunching over rock. The ground was covered in the same goop.

Beezle noticed it the same time I did. "Once you start seeing viscous liquid, it's time to turn around before you get put inside a cocoon and eaten at a later date."

"Should we leave Chloe inside a cocoon to be eaten at a

later date?" I asked. I slowed my steps, moving more cautiously now that there were obvious signs of the creature.

Beezle muttered something that sounded like, "Better her than me, and she eats all the pancakes, anyway."

"All the more reason to get her back," I said. "She's the only person who can give you a run for your money at the dining room table. And Samiel would be heartbroken if anything happened to her."

"Fine," Beezle said. "But when we're encased in goo, I'm definitely saying I told you so."

Nathaniel stopped, holding up his hand. "Shh."

He tilted his head slightly, listening. "We are nearly upon it," he said softly. "I can hear it moving."

"Chloe?" I asked, afraid to hope.

"She is still alive," he said. "I cannot vouch for her condition."

"I can't hear anything," J.B. said.

"Nathaniel can," I said, moving as carefully and quietly as I could. Even when trying to be silent I sounded like a lumbering bear next to the other two. Nathaniel's footfalls were so light I had to check to make sure he wasn't floating above the ground.

"When did he get bat ears?" J.B. asked.

"It's a long story," I said.

J.B. looked between me and Nathaniel. "Yeah, I bet."

The tunnel appeared to continue on straight ahead of us for hundreds of feet.

"Where is it?" I asked.

Nathaniel shook his head. "It is nearby. With every step we take, its movements become louder."

We walked a little farther. Nathaniel was very insistent that he could hear the creature, but there were no corridors or rooms off the main passage.

I stopped in the middle of the cave, looking all around. "Something isn't right here."

"You mean besides the fact that I'm hungry and there's no food to be found?" Beezle said.

"Yes," I said. "Nathaniel can hear the creature, but we can't see it, and there's nothing ahead of us but more tunnel. So there's got to be some kind of entrance to another room or cavern that we can't see. Beezle, did you lose your abilities when we entered the cave, too?"

"Yup," Beezle said. "I'm just like a regular person now, no special gargoyle X-ray powers."

"You'll never be just like a regular person," J.B. said.

"That doesn't sound like a compliment," Beezle said.

"I wouldn't take it as such," J.B. said.

I ignored their byplay and reached toward the wall. I had a suspicion and I wanted to see whether it was valid. Nathaniel grabbed my wrist.

"Do not touch that," he said. "You do not know what kind of effect it may have on a human."

I shook my head at him. "I'm not sure it's there at all."

Nathaniel narrowed his eyes at the substance coating the cave. "You think it's an illusion?"

I nodded, and shook off his hand. I placed my palm on the wall of the cavern.

For a moment it seemed that my hand would become trapped in the fluid, which had the substance of craft glue. Then I put some will and some force behind it, and my hand passed easily through the wall, and the rest of me with it.

Nathaniel grabbed my other hand before I disappeared, and J.B. lunged for Nathaniel. All four of us slipped easily through the wall, which wasn't really there at all.

I wished we had stayed put.

"So that's a reptile-mammalian thing," Beezle said. "It's certainly . . . large."

We were in a massive cavern, similar to the one where the nephilim had been imprisoned in the Forbidden Lands. At the far end of the cavern, blessedly away from us, was a gigantic creature coiled in a ball, sleeping. It had roughly the body shape of a lizard, the diamond-shaped head of a snake, and its body was covered in shaggy fur like a woolly mammoth.

Between us and the monster were piles of bones. Piles and piles and piles of bones, stacked higher than I would have thought possible.

"How long has that thing been here?" I breathed.

"It must have eaten everything that's ever come through the passage for thousands of years," Beezle said.

"Where's Chloe?" J.B. said, squinting. "Are those bones?"

"I'm going to be so happy when you get your glasses back," I said.

"There," Nathaniel said, pointing toward the ceiling.

Three human-shaped cocoons hung there, suspended by thin strands of webbing. All three cocoons were wiggling, indicating that the person inside was still alive and trying to get out.

"I told you that once there was viscous fluid, there would be a cocoon," Beezle said triumphantly. "Although I'll tell you that I don't want to know where it gets the thread for the cocoons from. That thing is already weird enough as it is."

"Where did the other two come from?" I asked.

"It's Jude and Samiel," Nathaniel said. "Can't you hear Jude?"

Now that he mentioned it, I could. The wolf's voice was muffled by the webbing, but it was definitely him.

Chloe, Samiel and Jude were directly above the sleeping

whatever-it-was. The monster didn't seem to have been disturbed by our presence or our whispers, but that couldn't possibly last.

"Well, at least we're all together again," I said. "I think the only option is for the two of you to fly up and cut them down. Then bring them back here and I'll cut the cocoon off so we can get out of here."

They nodded, and I bit my lip as I watched them fly away from me. I wanted my wings back. I was tired of watching everyone else do things I ought to be doing. I was tired of being carted around like a child when I could have been flying.

J.B. and Nathaniel had a quick, quiet conference as they reached the cocoons. Beneath them, the monster shifted in its sleep, grunting and snorting, and we all went still.

The creature didn't seem like it was waking, so J.B. positioned himself next to one of the cocoons. Nathaniel cut the thread with his sword and J.B. caught the person easily. I saw his mouth move, reassuring whoever it was, and he flew toward me.

Nathaniel was right behind him. He stopped only for a moment to whisper something to the person who remained.

J.B. landed just ahead of Nathaniel. "It's Samiel," he said, laying my cocooned brother-in-law on the ground. Samiel was contorting inside the web.

Nathaniel put another person next to him. "Jude," he said briefly, and went back for Chloe.

I bent close to Samiel. "Samiel, you have to lie still for a minute. I'm going to cut you out, and I don't want to cut you."

He stopped moving. I placed the blade at his shoulder and carefully used the tip to lift away the tightly wound thread. Then I sliced through on a diagonal from his shoulder to his hip, and hoped I missed all the major arteries.

Once I'd loosened the thread, Samiel burst out of
the cocoon like the Hulk bursting out of his clothing. He
looked wildly around, and J.B. grabbed Samiel before he
could go tearing through the cavern. He made Samiel look
at his face.

"Nathaniel's getting Chloe," J.B. said.

I repeated the procedure with Jude, who looked very
annoyed once he emerged.

"Never even heard it coming," Jude said. "I think it only
makes noise if it wants to."

"Uh, yeah, I think so," Beezle said, and pointed.

We all turned. Nathaniel was hanging in midair, his wings
flapping just enough to keep him there. He held Chloe in his
arms, and she was deathly still. Very likely she had fainted
inside the cocoon, which was a mercy given her intense
claustrophobia.

The reptile-mammal thing had silently risen from its
sleep and drawn its head level with Nathaniel. It watched
the angel and his cargo with orange-yellow eyes, the pupils
slit like a snake's. Its mouth hung open, full of shiny fangs.
Those fangs were only a few feet away from Nathaniel and
Chloe. The monster and Nathaniel were both frozen in
space, staring each other down. It was almost as if they
were silently communicating.

"Get out," I said to the others.

"Don't have to tell me twice," Beezle said, lifting off
from my shoulder.

"No," J.B. said, his voice strained as he struggled to
hold Samiel in place. Samiel had gone wild as soon as he'd
seen Nathaniel and Chloe so close to the monster's head.
"We all stay together."

"Yeah," Jude said. "Whatever you do, we're in for it, too."

"I was going to distract the monster so that Nathaniel

and Chloe could get away, and then I was going to run down the passage," I said.

"We're not trying to kill it?" Beezle asked, hovering in the air next to me.

"I'm not going to try to kill anything that big or that old without magic," I said. "Besides, I don't need it to be dead. I just need for us to get away."

"Hey!" I shouted. "Hey, over here!"

Jude and J.B. shouted as well. Jude even picked up a heavy bone that looked like a human femur and tossed it in the direction of the creature.

Neither the monster nor Nathaniel moved. I was again struck by the sense that they were somehow communicating. Or that Nathaniel was being . . .

"Hypnotized," I said.

"Non sequitur," Beezle said. "We're trying to distract the monster here."

"We can't distract it, because the monster is trying to hypnotize Nathaniel," I said.

Samiel broke free of J.B.'s grasp, which was inevitable. Samiel was amazingly strong, stronger than most supernaturals.

However, Jude was amazingly fast and grabbed Samiel's ankle, pulling him back to the ground as Samiel tried to fly to Chloe.

Jude punched him in the face.

"Quit it," Jude growled. "Do you want to get her back, or do you want her to be eaten?"

I want her back, Samiel said, and then he swung at Jude. The wolf was more than prepared, and grabbed Samiel's fist.

"Then stop and think," Jude said. "Or at least do what Maddy thinks."

What the hell does she know? Samiel signed. *She makes it up as she goes along, and the person she loved got stabbed to death. I don't think Maddy is the best person to decide how to save Chloe.*

I turned away from them. I didn't want to see what else Samiel might say, what other truths he might reveal in the heat of anger. It wasn't the time for hurt feelings. But it did hurt. I'd always thought Samiel loved me unconditionally, that he didn't blame me for Gabriel's death. I guess it just proved that, as everyone kept telling me, I needed to stop taking people at face value. I was the only person I knew who wasn't any good at deception.

While all this was happening Nathaniel and the monster remained locked in their silent communion.

"Why is it taking so long?" I wondered aloud.

"Nathaniel's resisting," Beezle said. "That's pretty impressive, considering he's got no magic right now."

"How can you tell?"

"If he wasn't resisting, then it would be over by now. And since the monster wasn't responding to us, it must be unable to get out of the spell until its victim is hypnotized," Beezle said.

I looked at the monster, then at Nathaniel and Chloe, and I had an idea. "Are you willing to bet my life on that theory?"

Beezle looked uncertain, an expression I'd hardly ever seen on his face. "Why? What are you going to do?"

"J.B.," I said. "Can you put me on top of the monster's head?"

14

"NO, I CANNOT," J.B. SAID.

"Cannot or will not?"

"It's the same damn thing," he said. "You're crazy if you think I'm going to let you do whatever you're thinking of doing."

"I want you to fly me up to the top of the monster's head and drop me there, and then I'll stab it through the eye," I said.

"And now that I know your plan, I am definitely not helping," J.B. said.

"I thought you weren't going to kill it," Beezle said.

"That was when I thought it was distractible," I said. "It's not, so I'm going to kill it. Or at least injure it horribly enough that it won't be able to chase after us. And if you don't fly me up there, Jacob Benjamin Bennett, I will climb up to the top of the monster's head from its tail, and you can stand there and watch me."

"She threw down the middle name," Beezle said.

"You'd do it, too, just to piss me off," J.B. said.

"No one else has a better idea. You've got the wings; I've got the sword."

"It's a goddamned freaking miracle you've survived this long," J.B. said, and he scooped me up.

"Keep Samiel here," I said to Jude.

"No problem," he said. He had wrapped his arms around Samiel's and was holding the furious angel still.

"I think I'll just stay here and keep score," Beezle said.

"You do that," I said. "Everyone be ready to run."

J.B. held me close to him as we flew. I was tense in his arms, preparing for the moment when he dropped me. I wasn't completely convinced that the monster would be able to ignore my presence once I landed on its head, and I wanted to be able to stab it and get out of there as quickly as possible.

"Once you drop me, circle around and wait close to the ceiling," I said.

"Like I'm going to leave you there alone," J.B. said. "Don't be stupid."

"You don't have a sword," I said. "What are you going to do?"

"Make sure you don't get tossed into a wall when the creature goes berserk after you stab it," J.B. said. "I agreed to this insane plan, but I am not leaving you alone there, so forget it."

We were above the monster long before I was ready. It hadn't seemed to notice us flying directly toward it. As Beezle had noted, all of the creature's energy was focused on Nathaniel.

The angel hadn't registered our presence, either. His face was red from the exertion of trying to resist the creature's spell, but he *was* resisting. Now that we were close, I could see the spark of fury in his eyes.

J.B. straightened so that it looked like we were standing in the air, and very gently lowered us toward the monster's head. The creature's fur was matted and filthy, and it smelled like it had been rolling in meat for the last hundred years.

I have a sensitive stomach, and pregnancy did not help. My first deep breath of the monster made me gag.

"If you puke on me, I'm going to drop you on the monster and leave you there," J.B. said.

"Your shirt already has blood on it," I said, breathing shallowly and trying to suppress the urge to vomit. "What's the difference?"

"Blood is cool and manly. Puke just makes you look like a loser," J.B. said.

It was astounding that we were this close to the creature's head and that it wasn't trying to swat us away. Or wrap us up in silk. Or gobble us in midair. It was really that absorbed with Nathaniel.

My boots touched the monster's head. J.B. stayed aloft, his hands under my shoulders ready to lift me away if the monster made any indication that it noticed I was there.

It didn't move.

"Just stay right there," I whispered to J.B.

"I told you, I'm staying with you," he said.

"Then don't put your feet down," I said. "Just fly close to me so you can scoop me up if anything goes wrong."

J.B. had placed me on the broadest part of the creature's diamond-shaped head. Its eyes were set on each side, close to its snout and under a prominent brow ridge like a snake's.

To sink the sword deep enough, I'd have to kneel close on the ridge and stick the sword into the eye with my arms over the edge.

I proceeded carefully across toward the creature's right eye. J.B.'s wings made a little current of air behind me.

I knelt above the reptile-mammalian thing's eye and drew my sword. I lowered it until the tip hovered above the slit pupil.

Still the monster did not move.

I plunged the sword into its eye with all the strength I had.

Several things happened at once. The monster howled, thrashing its head, its cries so deep and strong that the cavern rumbled. Rock cracked and fell from the ceiling.

Nathaniel shot toward the exit with Chloe in his arms.

I held on tight to the hilt of the sword as the creature shook its head back and forth. My grip on the handle was the only thing keeping me from getting tossed into a wall as J.B had predicted.

I pushed harder with the sword, trying to do as much damage as I could. Fluid gushed out of the monster's eye and over my hands.

And then I started to scream. And scream. And scream. The stuff that was pouring from the monster's eye was burning my skin, burning through it, into the muscle and bone beneath.

J.B. grabbed me, pulled me away. My hands were bound to the sword now, the acid melding my palms to the hilt. I couldn't let it go even if I wanted to.

The creature bellowed as the blade slid out of its eye, tearing nerves as it went. J.B. was forced to carry me in front of him, the sword still before me like I'd just drawn it from Arthur's mystical stone.

Nathaniel had deposited Chloe with Samiel and Jude and flown back to help J.B. The angel grabbed my legs and the two of them carried me through the air like I was on a stretcher. I barely registered Nathaniel's presence or the screeching of the monster. The reptile-mammalian thing was now knocking over piles of bones as it tossed its head and lashed its tail.

The crash of bones was tremendous, like a rock slide, and I had just enough sense left to realize that the bones were just as much of a danger.

"Get everyone out of here," I said through gritted teeth.

"They are already moving down the passage," Nathaniel said.

"We will be right behind them."

Somehow the two of them got us out of the cave without being crushed by rocks, bones, or reptile-mammalian thrashing. The cries of the monster receded as they hurried down the passage to catch up to the others.

My eyes were blurred with pain. The burning was going right down inside me, deeper and deeper, scorching every cell it touched. Nothing had ever hurt so much. I whimpered.

"Gods above and below," Beezle said, but his voice sounded like it was very far away. "What did you do to yourself now?"

"I have no way of healing her until we get out of this thrice-forsaken cavern," Nathaniel said.

Chloe said something then, and Jude, but it was watery in my ears. They were conferring, trying to determine the best way to get out.

"Just keep going forward," I slurred, but none of them seemed to hear me.

And then everything was quiet, and black.

I woke to the feeling of cold rock beneath my cheek. I was curled like a baby on a wide flat stone, and the wind whipped my hair into my face. My sword was gone, and my hands no longer burned. I sat up and looked around.

I was alone, and a vast expanse of white sand stretched in every direction. There was nothing for the eye to see except that unbreaking, unyielding ocean of white.

"What now? Another trick?" I said. "J.B.? Nathaniel?"

"You won't find them here," a voice said behind me.

I scrambled to my feet and spun around, wishing to all the gods that ever were or would be that I had my powers at that moment, because Evangeline stood there.

Evangeline, my many-greats-grandmother, the consort of Lucifer, also known as the crazy bitch who'd possessed me and tried to use me as the instrument of her revenge.

"What are you doing here?" I asked warily.

"I should ask you that question," Evangeline said, and her smile was crafty. Her black hair danced in the wind like contorting snakes. She wore a simple gown of gray, and she looked young and fresh again, the way she had when Lucifer had first fallen in love with her.

"Death agrees with you," I said, avoiding her leading comment.

I quickly realized that I was not in Titania's realm anymore. Or maybe my body was, but my mind and spirit had taken a walk. I wasn't about to give Evangeline the advantage by letting her know that I had no idea how or where I was.

"Yes, it does," Evangeline said. "You could probably be improved by death."

"Death doesn't seem to stick that well on me," I said. "You should have thought of that before you let Ramuell tear out my heart."

"Like your grandfather," she said. "Always thinking the rules don't apply to you."

"So far, they don't," I said. "You seem to have suffered the fate of the ordinary, though."

Evangeline narrowed her green eyes at me. "I have never been ordinary to Lucifer. He has defied space and time for me, the most sacred laws of the universe."

I remembered something Puck had said when Lucifer and Puck had encountered each other on my front lawn. *He's been going someplace he shouldn't. He's been a naughty, naughty boy.*

"Lucifer's been coming here, to see you," I said. "This is where he's been going when he's out of touch."

"Yes," Evangeline said. "That is how much I meant to him, that he has spurned death to be with me."

"But he's not supposed to," I said. "Death is final. Death is forever. I met Gabriel by accident, in a dream, and the Agency wanted my head for it. Lucifer can't come here. He's breaking the rules."

"As are you, by being here now," Evangeline said.

"I didn't come here on purpose. I would rather eat a basket of wriggling spiders than spend five seconds with you," I said. "Lucifer can't keep doing this. He has to know that there will be a price to pay. There always is when you bend the laws of magic."

"Lucifer would gladly pay any price the universe asked of him, especially now," she said, and she stroked her hand over her belly.

I could see the taut roundness under her gown, the first budding of her pregnancy.

"Are you kidding me?" I said. "Not only has Lucifer somehow found a way to cross into the land of the dead, but he's managed to knock you up?"

"Are you frightened, little granddaughter? Scared that you will no longer be Lucifer's first and most precious once my son is born?" Evangeline sneered.

"I'm scared, but not for the reasons you think," I said, staring at her belly in horror. "You've got a child conceived in death growing inside you. How do you know it won't be some abomination unleashed on the world?"

Evangeline smiled, and my blood turned to ice.

"I'm counting on it."

Then I woke again, to biting cold and to searing pain. My head was in J.B.'s lap and Nathaniel's face was over mine. He knelt beside me, his hands on my hands, and the light of the sun was healing the burns. It hurt almost as much getting damaged in the first place. I screamed again and again, tears running down my face. J.B.'s hands on my shoulders held me in place.

Lucifer's sword was still in my grasp. Jude, Samiel and Chloe crowded around. Beezle was on the ground next to my head, peering at me like I was something under a microscope.

After a while Nathaniel finished, his face drawn and sweating. "I did the best I could, but they will always look a little damaged."

He pried my fingers off the sword one by one. "You can let it go now, Madeline."

I waited for the waves of pain to recede so that I could think. Then I held my hands up to my face. I expected to see ridges of deep scars, like the victim of a fire. Instead there was a fine webbing of shadows running from the tips of my fingers up to my wrists in all the places where the creature's blood had touched.

The result was like a faded tattoo. Well, it wasn't any worse than the scars on my face from the Hob, or the mess on my neck from the pix demon. All things considered, it was pretty good, actually. I still had all my digits in working order, and in my book that was a win.

"Where are we?" I croaked.

"In the wastelands," Nathaniel said. "I would not have been able to heal you otherwise."

"How did we get out?"

"Unbelievably, your advice was sound," Beezle said. "We just kept going forward. I guess Titania figured she didn't need any more tricks with that monster in there."

"The quantity of bones would suggest that the monster had been a sufficient deterrent in the past," Nathaniel said dryly.

I sat up, rubbing my eyes. "Well, we escaped the faerie kingdom."

"For now," Beezle said ominously. "But we're still stuck in this netherworld until you can get your granddaddy on the line."

"And Titania can and will certainly send someone after you now that you've managed to get away again," J.B. said.

I touched my stomach, felt the reassuring flutter of little wings. This was going to be one hardy kid when he was finally born—if his mother survived that long.

"That's the least of my worries," I said grimly, thinking of Lucifer and Evangeline. I didn't say anything about my vision, though. I wanted to have a little talk with Lucifer first.

The snake tattoo on my palm wriggled, as if it knew I was thinking about Lucifer.

"Tell him I want to see him," I said to my hand.

"You know, you look insane when you do that," Beezle said.

My palm tingled, and then I felt Lucifer drawing near.

"He's coming," I said, getting to my feet with J.B.'s assistance.

"You should be quoting *Macbeth*, you know," said Lucifer's voice behind us. "I always liked that scene with the three witches."

"Nobody here needs reminding that you're something wicked," I said, turning around calmly to face him while everyone else jumped in surprise.

Lucifer started to speak, caught sight of Nathaniel, and paused. His eyes narrowed as he stalked past me until he was face-to-face with Nathaniel. Nathaniel stared back at Lucifer with his brand-new eyes.

"That little fuck," Lucifer said.

"I think you mean Puck," Beezle said.

"No, I meant what I said," Lucifer replied, and there was a low current of anger mixed with amusement in his voice. "What did he intend? For you to kill me at the most opportune time?"

Nathaniel nodded briefly. "But I was revealed too soon, he says, and the spell no longer will work correctly."

"I should kill you now, you know," Lucifer said conversationally. "Eliminate the possibility that the spell might go off anyway."

"No, you really shouldn't kill him now," I said meaningfully. "Not until you and I have had a chat about a few things. In private."

Lucifer turned to me, raised one eyebrow. Everyone else looked at me in curiosity and astonishment, as if a private conversation was an exotic concept from a foreign country.

"Very well," Lucifer said. "I presume you called me here to get you home since Puck has neglected you."

I nodded.

"Everyone hold hands, then," Lucifer said. He watched carefully as both Nathaniel and J.B. lunged for me, and then he smiled like some private suspicion of his had been confirmed.

Beezle settled in on my shoulder. "You need your coat back. This sexy-clubgoer look lacks comfortable pockets."

"Try not to fall off into another dimension while we're crossing the universe," I said.

Everyone else linked up, Lucifer nudging J.B. aside to take my hand. "Grandfather's privilege," he said.

J.B. crossly joined the end of the line, and then we were off. The wonders of the galaxy seemed a lot less wondrous to me this time around. Maybe I was getting jaded. Maybe I was too preoccupied with the new horror of Evangeline's baby, the vampire invasion of Chicago, the threat of Lucifer's brother rising from Lake Michigan, and the very high probability that Titania or Bendith or both was going to try to kill me in my sleep sometime soon.

That didn't even begin to cover the complexity of my relationship problems with Nathaniel and J.B., or the fact that Samiel had apparently been harboring a lot of unkind thoughts about me. All in all, I had more than enough to keep my mind busy as we passed through space and time.

We were back in Chicago and standing on my front lawn before I knew it. The sky was gray and swirling, and lightning crackled to the east, above the lake.

Lucifer stared in the direction of the lightning, his face revealing nothing.

"Let's take a walk," I said to him.

Everyone protested in their predictable ways, but I silenced them with a look. Nathaniel and J.B. led the parade inside the house, and Lucifer and I were left alone in the snow. I led him onto the sidewalk, still unshoveled.

The snow had been tamped down in a slippery path by dozens of feet. I wondered whether escaping humans had passed by here, or whether the path had been cut by Therion's roaming vampire brigades.

"Is Alerian causing the storm?" I asked.

Lucifer seemed unsurprised that I knew about his brother. "What else did Puck tell you?"

"More than I wanted to know, really," I said. I watched his face for a reaction. "And so did Evangeline."

There was a tiny spark there in his endless eyes, nothing I would have noticed if I hadn't been looking for it. And then it was gone.

"I'm glad you brought up Evangeline, because I have a task for you," Lucifer said.

"I'm not interested in your tasks," I said. "I want you to help me get rid of the vampires in Chicago."

"If you would ask a boon of me, then it is churlish to refuse one that I would ask of you," Lucifer said.

"You're going to ask me to do something that's disturbing, wrong and probably illegal," I said. "You always do."

"Human laws don't apply to me," he said.

"Magical ones do," I said.

"Which is why I need your assistance," he said smoothly. "You can do that which I cannot."

"First help me get rid of the vampires," I said. "You have the power to wipe them all out with one fell swoop."

"Yes, but I am not permitted to do such a thing. I can't interfere in the doings of humans in such an obvious way," Lucifer said.

"You are not permitted to cross into the land of the dead and impregnate your dead lover, either," I said angrily, stopping and turning toward him. "You don't mind breaking the rules when it suits you to do so."

"I don't break them, exactly. Just bend," he said. "What did you do to Nathaniel that revealed Puck's spell so soon?"

"How do you know I had anything to do with it? And don't change the damned subject," I said, my face coloring.

"Ah," Lucifer said. "And my grandson hardly cold in his grave."

"It's not like that," I said.

"What's it like, then?" he asked, his eyes dancing.

"I don't have the time or the inclination to explain it to you," I said. I could hardly explain it to myself. "And you're hardly in a position of moral authority."

"I had thought you would seek comfort from Amarantha's son," Lucifer mused. "You didn't seem to like it very much when I sent Nathaniel to you as your bodyguard."

"I didn't," I said, feeling I was losing ground here. I'd meant to stand my ground until Lucifer agreed to help me, not become embroiled in a conversation about my not-a-romance with Nathaniel.

"Still, this could be useful," Lucifer said. "He obviously has affection for you, and Puck's revelation could hardly have been welcome. It would certainly be handy to have Puck's son on my side."

"I'm not going to help you manipulate Nathaniel so you can piss off Puck," I said. "I don't want to get in the middle of your sibling rivalry."

"My dear, you are already in the middle of it," Lucifer said.

I shook my head. "No. I've got enough to do. Now, if you won't help me by blasting all the vampires into oblivion, will you at least tell me what I have to do to get rid of them, short of raising my own army?"

Lucifer stroked his chin thoughtfully. "You did not completely unleash Nathaniel's power, did you?"

"I told you, I don't want . . ."

"This is relevant," Lucifer cut in. "You want to know how to defeat the vampires, yes?"

"Yes," I said cautiously.

"You need to finish what you began with Nathaniel, and the solution will be revealed," Lucifer said.

"I'm not going to bang Nathaniel for your amusement," I said.

"Nobody said anything about 'banging,'" Lucifer said. "But if that's your preferred method, then who am I to argue?"

"I'm not discussing this with you anymore," I muttered. "Are you saying that once Nathaniel comes fully into his power, he will be able to get rid of the vampires?"

"No. I am saying the solution will be revealed to you," Lucifer said.

"Why can you not just help me?" I shouted in frustration.

"If I did, then my enemies would descend on you like ravening wolves," Lucifer said seriously. "You need to demonstrate that you are capable and strong, that you do not require my assistance."

"Haven't I done that already, over and over and over again?" I said, my anger draining away and leaving exhaustion behind. "When do I get something out of this relationship besides misery?"

"I have offered numerous times to make you my heir and you have refused," Lucifer said.

"Yeah, that doesn't really seem like a gift to me," I said.

"But it is," Lucifer said. "If you were my heir, you would also have the benefit of my protection. Those who seek to destroy you or your child would be subject to my retribution."

"So you're saying that this blood relation confers all the disadvantages and none of the benefits unless I am recognized officially?" I said.

"In a manner of speaking, yes."

It was tempting. Oh, so tempting. It would be a blessing to throw off the weight of responsibility, to live a day without feeling hunted. But on further examination, that apple Lucifer held out to me looked a lot more like a cage. Temptation was his first and best skill.

"Thanks, but no thanks."

"I can wait," Lucifer said easily. "I think my offer will appeal to you sooner or later."

"Keep dreaming."

Lucifer smiled in a way that made me nervous. "Now that we have answered your question, it is time for my request."

"You don't make requests," I said. "And I'm not feeling inclined to help you."

"Too bad you do not have a choice," Lucifer said, and he didn't sound as though it was too bad for me at all. He sounded like he was quite enjoying himself. "You can either carry out my task under your own power, or you can do it under the compulsion of the Hound of the Hunt. And believe me, you will not be able to resist that compulsion. If I order you, then you must obey."

Lucifer looked triumphant. He'd boxed me in again. A part of me had been expecting this ever since Lucifer had made me the Hound.

"What is it that you want me to do?" I asked, knowing the answer, dreading the words.

"I want you to fetch Evangeline and my son from the land of the dead and return them to me, of course."

15

"NO," I SAID AUTOMATICALLY. "NO, I WON'T DO THAT."

"I told you, you haven't a choice," Lucifer said silkily.

"I don't even know how to get to the land of the dead," I said desperately.

"You're an Agent of Death," Lucifer said. "The ways are within you, even if you are not aware of them."

"I'm not an Agent anymore," I said.

"Once an Agent, always an Agent," Lucifer said. "The Agency can give nothing to you nor take anything. It is all within you."

"I don't even have wings," I said. "Why don't you do it?"

"I am not permitted," Lucifer said.

"I'm not, either. The Retrievers will come for me for sure," I said.

"You have more flexibility than I," Lucifer said. "The one rule that neither I nor my brothers will break is this."

"But you are breaking it. You're just sending me to do your dirty work."

"The letter of the law will be honored," Lucifer said. "I will not leave my son in that dead place."

"You should have thought of that before you got busy with Evangeline," I said. "You're putting my child, *Gabriel's* child, at risk."

"I will allow you the time you need to deal with the vampires," Lucifer said. "And then you will go."

"No," I said.

"You will go, by my word or your own," he said. "And I know you well enough that I think you would prefer not to be under the compulsion of the Hound."

"I hate you," I said.

"Of course you do," he replied, and then he disappeared.

I stood there on the empty street, fighting back tears, trying to pull myself together. There was no way I could tell anyone else about this.

J.B. would never let me defy the Agency so openly. Despite everything that had happened between the Agency and myself, he still had a strong belief in the system. He still believed that there was an order to the universe that could not be undone. I had seen enough of Lucifer's machinations to know that this wasn't true.

I sucked in a heaving breath and wiped my cheeks dry. Crying wasn't going to solve my problems. I walked slowly back toward the house, dreading the moment when I'd have to explain to everyone else that I had no idea how we were going to get rid of the vampire infestation.

"Madeline Black!"

I turned around, surprised to hear someone calling my name. In the middle of the street were three teenage boys that I hadn't noticed earlier. Had they been there while I was talking to Lucifer? They were all skinny and had scraggly pubescent beards. The boys carried a variety of weapons that looked like they might be handy for killing vampires—swords and crossbows and stakes. Where had they gotten all those things from?

"Yeah?" I said.

The boy in the center leveled a crossbow at me. He had a red bandanna tied around his head like he was a refugee from an '80s action film. "You're coming with us."

I couldn't help it. I laughed.

All three boys scowled at me.

"We're taking you to the Vampire Authority station," Red Bandanna said. "Don't make us hurt you."

I'd completely forgotten about Therion's stupid message. Now these boys had somehow managed to find me and were intent on collecting the bounty on my head.

"Listen, kid, you can't take me anywhere I don't want to go," I said, trying not to be angry.

They were just humans. Little humans who lived in a city that I had nearly killed myself trying to protect. If the ungrateful little shits knew what I had done for them, to protect them and their families and others like them, they wouldn't be standing there threatening my life.

One of the other boys also raised his crossbow in a menacing fashion. "You have three seconds to agree or else we shoot. One . . ."

I blasted nightfire at his crossbow and the weapon burst into blue flames. The kid screamed and dropped the bow, holding on to his hand. The skin on his palm was blackened and peeling. I'd never seen the effects of nightfire on a human before. Was I really prepared to kill some boys whose only sin was stupidity? Maybe Beezle was right. Maybe I was going dark side.

My anger drained out of me suddenly, leaving me exhausted. "Get out of here before I get mad," I said.

The other two stared at me with mouths agape while the third boy turned and ran.

"Go," I repeated.

The other two followed, dropping their weapons on the ground in their haste to escape.

I dragged myself down the street, up the stairs and into my apartment, anticipating the expectant glances of my friends.

Instead, no one was there except Nathaniel. He looked grim. He held a piece of paper in one hand and he stared at it as if he hoped his gaze would set it on fire. He had removed his coat and shoes and rolled up his sleeves.

"Where's everyone else?" I said, putting my sword on the side table and taking off my wet boots.

"Beezle, Samiel and Chloe are downstairs. I believe Samiel and Chloe are . . . reuniting," Nathaniel said delicately. "The gargoyle said something about a video game. J.B. and Jude have gone to the Agency."

"To the Agency? Why? J.B. shouldn't be going to the Agency. He should be recovering," I said.

"He went to deal with this," Nathaniel said, thrusting the paper at me.

It was an ordinary piece of printer paper with the Agency's seal at the top. The message below was brief.

Dear Ms. Black,

It has come to our attention that at 2:29 pm today you passed beyond the Door. This is your second offense.

*As a former Agent, you are well aware of the conse-
quences should you continue to defy the Agency.*
    This is your final warning.

                          Sokolov

I was so angry I could hardly see. I ripped the paper into a bunch of tiny pieces, threw them on the floor, jumped on them several times, picked up the pieces again, smashed them in a ball and then set them on fire in the palm of my hand. The paper went up in a whoosh of smoke and ash.

"Madeline, calm yourself," Nathaniel said.

"Don't *tell* me to calm down. There are people dying all over this city. Soon they'll be dying all over the country. And all they care about is a violation of their precious *rules*," I spat. "Sokolov doesn't care that we're in the middle of the goddamned apocalypse."

Deprived of the proxy of the Agency's letter, I went to the hutch in the dining room and pulled out a wineglass. I threw it at the wall with all the force I could muster. It shattered into a very satisfying kajillion pieces, but I still didn't feel better. I wanted to find Sokolov and pound his smug little face until his features were unrecognizable.

I stomped away from the hutch, looking for something else to break. Nathaniel stepped in front of me.

"Madeline, stop. Think," Nathaniel said. "A temper tantrum is not productive."

"This is not a tantrum," I said furiously.

"It looks like one," he said.

I clenched my fists. I had so much anger inside, months of it, months of frustration and pain and fear mixing with fury until I felt like I would burst. I needed somewhere to put that anger. Either I could vent it on Sokolov, or I could take it out on whatever was closest.

"You'll do," I said, and pulled Nathaniel's head down to mine.

I was truly in the grip of madness now. I sent my power and my anger coursing into him, pushing up against his magic. His own power met mine and we crashed against each other in a furious storm.

He pulled my sweater off, tore the fastening of my bra. His hands replaced it, then his mouth. And then his mouth went lower, and my pants disappeared. I writhed under him, the power and the anger and the lust stretching my skin, making me burn.

His mouth touched the core of me. I arched under him and the magic inside me surged as I peaked. I found the heart of his power, the true heart, the one that Puck had kept hidden from him his whole life, and I lit it on fire. When I did that, the secret source of my own magic was revealed, and I suddenly understood everything Lucifer had told me.

I had never seen, never known, the depths of my magic. I could do anything. I could find the hidden paths of the universe. I could defy death. And no one would be able to stop me.

Nathaniel reared back and away from me, his hands on his face, in the grip of the revelation of his legacy. He was surrounded by a halo of blue, and his hair was darkening, turning black before my eyes.

The skin of my back tore away, and I screamed as my wings formed anew. I rolled to my stomach, panting, feeling the muscles stretching, the brush of feathers against my skin. Fine particles of silver floated in the air. The mad surge receded, leaving me spent. I put my head in my hands and covered my body with my wings.

Nathaniel cried out once. I felt the pulse of magic in the air as it brushed over me. Then he was silent except for the sound of his breath, harsh in the silence of the room.

Now that the insanity was over I felt embarrassed. Maybe we hadn't officially done the deed but we'd come pretty damn close, and I was naked. But I couldn't lie with my head in my hands forever. Sooner or later I would have to turn around and face him.

I sat up, coiling my wings around me to keep my nudity covered. Nathaniel watched me in wonder.

"Your wings," he said, and reached out to touch the feathers. "They're just as I saw in my dream."

I realized then that it was not my black Agent's wings that had returned. The feathers were silver, and glittered even in the weak rays of the ceiling lightbulb.

"You can destroy the vampires," Nathaniel said. "I felt the strength inside you, at the end."

"Nathaniel," I said, and took a deep breath. I needed to get this out quickly before mortification set in. "I'm sorry I did that. I'm sorry I used you."

"Sweet Madeline," he said, and bent to kiss me again, gently, just for a moment. "Do not apologize. You have given me a gift. I know who I am now. My power is no longer hidden from me."

"It's no gift to find out that you're related to Lucifer, believe me," I said. "Your hair has turned black. You look more like Puck than ever."

Nathaniel stood and looked at himself in the small mirror that hung over the side table. I saw him touch his hair in curiosity, and then his face.

"It's strange, is it not?" he said. "My face is still my own. It is only my coloring that mimics him now."

"You're wearing his colors," I said. "Literally. Everyone will know to whose house you belong."

"My father will be heartbroken," Nathaniel murmured, and I saw a shadow cross his expression at the thought of Zerachiel. "I was his only son, his pride. Even when all believed I had participated in the rebellion against Lucifer, my father did not lose faith in me. Now he will know that I am not a son to him, that he has nothing, that he has been a cuckold."

"I wouldn't go anywhere near the Grigori, if I were you," I said. "You heard Puck. He and Lucifer don't get along. If you showed up in court, or even went to see Zerachiel, Lucifer will probably find some excuse to have you killed."

I stood up awkwardly. "I'll be back in a minute."

I went into the bedroom to get dressed, and tried not to imagine that Nathaniel was watching my naked butt as I walked away.

I put on some underwear and a pair of jeans, then took out a new bra and T-shirt. I soon discovered that it was a lot more difficult to get dressed when your wings didn't recede into your back at will.

"How the hell do I put this on?" I said.

"You'll need to cut slashes to accommodate your wings in all of your clothing," Nathaniel said. "And then they will furl up small enough for you to dress. Once you have your top on, you can uncoil them again."

I turned around, holding the shirt to my bare chest. Nathaniel smiled.

"Madeline, I have already seen it all," he said. "There is no need for shame."

"Oh, yes, there is," I said.

Nathaniel approached me, pulled the shirt away from my fingers. I sucked in my breath. I guess I'd thought the electricity between us would go away once his power was revealed, but it felt like nothing had changed.

His hands went to my breasts, and I closed my eyes.

"I know you have not chosen," Nathaniel said. "But don't think you can pretend it did not happen. *I* will not let you forget that it happened."

I put my hands on his wrists so he would stop, so I could think again. "Help me get dressed," I said raggedly.

He chuckled, and went to get a pair of scissors.

Once we had fixed up my shirt and my favorite sweater, I sat down on the bed to coil my hair into a braid. It had grown about another three inches during our interlude on the dining room floor.

"If we keep this up, you can start calling me Rapunzel," I said.

"I don't think any interactions we might have in the future will have the same effect," Nathaniel said. "You have come fully into your power, and so have I."

Yeah, but we haven't had a complete "interaction" yet, I thought. What if the full power of Puck and Lucifer were combined within us?

It was a little scary to contemplate. I wrapped a rubber band around the bottom of my braid and stood up.

"Time to get rid of this vampire problem," I said.

"Shall I gather our forces, then?"

"No," I said, going into the dining room and slinging my sword across my body. "Leave them be. You and I can handle this."

Plus I didn't feel like having a conference in which I was a) grilled about the sudden appearance of silver wings, and

b) questioned about every decision I might make. There was something to be said for traveling light.

We didn't even bother going downstairs. I didn't want the others to hear us on the stairs and come outside. I opened the kitchen window and flew out, Nathaniel following.

I'd been without wings for only a short time, but I'd almost forgotten the wonderful feeling of freedom that came from flying. I wished I had time to enjoy it, to swoop and twirl and revel in the joy for a few moments.

I couldn't remember the last time I'd felt happy like that, happiness untempered by responsibility and fear and guilt and confusion. Even when I was with Gabriel there had always been a sense that our time was limited, that the bliss we felt couldn't last.

I hardly remembered being a child, much less a carefree one, although I suppose there must have been a time when I turned cartwheels and collected dandelions like other little girls.

All my life, death had been a constant companion. Death was the reason my mother was never at home, the reason why my father was gone. After my mother died, death was my profession.

And once I met Lucifer and Azazel, death become the instrument by which I exerted my will. There was a trail of bodies behind me, and my hands were soaked in blood. I should have been more troubled by this, but I wasn't. Every choice I had made had been in defense of me and mine.

The gray clouds over Lake Michigan were still swirling, and I could see a poison green fog rising above the surface.

"Alerian rises," Nathaniel said. "Can you not feel it?"

I could feel it. I hadn't been able to before my new wings and new powers had emerged, but now I sensed Alerian's presence the same way I could sense Lucifer's. He was still muted, though, like he hadn't fully awoken yet.

"Let's worry about Alerian later," I said. "I've got a checklist I'm working from here."

"Where should we go?" Nathaniel said.

"We want all of the vampires to gather in one place," I said. "So we need a place that will accommodate them, and then we need to call them to us."

"And can you do that now?" Nathaniel said.

"Oh, yeah," I said. "I realized a few things about Azazel's formula that can work to our advantage."

"Which are?"

"First, Azazel used the blood of Agents. Lucifer and Puck both told me, 'Once an Agent, always an Agent.' I realize now that they were both trying to help me in their usual back-handed way. I am an Agent still, even if I've chosen not to be affiliated with them. They can't take that away from me. The power was always there inside me. I just didn't realize it."

"And how will this help you to draw the vampires to you?"

"I have an affinity with the Agents' blood that's in the formula. In addition, I was the daughter of the maker of that formula. I'm pretty sure that Azazel put a little of himself inside that serum, too. Remember how the vampires behaved when we found them at Azazel's mansion?"

Realization dawned on Nathaniel's face. "Like zombies. Like they were under some kind of compulsion."

I nodded. "How much do you want to bet that Azazel made sure there was some kind of fail-safe in the serum? If Therion tried defying Azazel, then dear old Dad would be able to bring all of the vamps that had taken the formula under his control."

"If you exert your will, the vampires that have taken the

serum will not be able to resist you, just as they would not have been able to resist Azazel," Nathaniel said.

"That's what I'm counting on," I said.

I pointed to the giant bowl that protruded from the top of Soldier Field. "What do you think? Can we fit all of the vampires in there?"

"Even if they cannot all fit inside the building, they will gather near it if your ability to call them to you works," Nathaniel said. "But I think it will be sufficient."

"I hope it will," I said, and we flew toward the Chicago Bears home field.

If there were more vampires than could fit inside a giant football stadium, then our troubles were bigger than I thought. Despite my newfound power and my expressed confidence to Nathaniel, I wasn't as certain as I seemed. When we'd flown over the city as the invasion started, it seemed that there were millions of vampires, but that couldn't be. There was nowhere for all of them to hide. Except . . .

"Nathaniel, where did all those vampires come from in the first place?" I said. "I can't believe we never thought about this before."

Nathaniel frowned. "I presumed that Therion and Azazel gathered vampires from other regions to them. The courts in Chicago were certainly not that big."

"But where was Therion keeping them all?" I asked, remembering the vampires that had poured into Daley Plaza. "They had to have somewhere to gather."

"They seemed to be coming from the underground," Nathaniel said.

I nodded. "There could be thousands more down there, in the pedways and the freight tunnels."

"If any of them have taken the serum, then you should still be able to call them to you," Nathaniel said.

"What if not all of them have taken it?" I asked.

"As you say, let us worry about it at another time," he said. "The majority of the vampires that we saw were strolling under the sun, and you know that you can reach them. Once we have wiped out the majority, then we can deal with the stragglers of this infestation."

"Okay," I said, trying not to worry. "Okay."

We approached the museum campus and Soldier Field from the north, almost perfectly retracing the path we had walked just a few days before. The surface of Lake Michigan was covered in Alerian's fog for as far as the eye could see. Beneath the fog there were dark shadows moving.

"No one is ever going to come back to this city," I said, my heart breaking a little. "And if anyone does, they'll never truly feel safe here again."

Nathaniel followed my gaze, saw the shadows shifting. "You do not know that Alerian intends harm to the people of the city," he said, but he didn't sound very certain.

"He doesn't have to intend harm in order for people to get caught in the cross fire," I said.

We flew over the top of the large bowl that perched on top of the original structure of Soldier Field. I lowered down to the center of the field, right on the fifty-yard line.

"I don't know what's going to happen when I try to do this," I warned Nathaniel. "You might want to be ready to run."

He looked insulted. "I would not leave you any more than you would leave me. Shall I help you? I can boost your power, as we did before."

"I don't think that's a good idea," I said. We'd end up naked and rolling in the grass instead of wiping out the vampires. "Just make sure nothing attacks me while I try to draw the vamps here, okay?"

Nathaniel nodded. "Very well."

I closed my eyes and drew deep within myself, searching for the spark of magic that came from Azazel. It was buried deep. I hadn't acknowledged my relationship with Azazel for some time, but blood didn't lie. He was inside me, whether I wanted him to be there or not.

When I found the source of Azazel's power I drew it forth so that it was at the forefront of my magic. Underneath that stream I layered my Agent's strength. Finally, I took both abilities, wound them together, and used the power of the Morningstar to push the call forth. The call of blood. It poured out of me, seeking blood that had the same qualities as mine.

My magic quested all over the city, long tentacles brushing up against living things in search of what it wanted. I felt the presence of other creatures, other things that lay in wait should the vampires fail. Some of those creatures felt me, too, and the wise ones fled.

I would take care of the stupid ones later.

My power touched the humans that remained in Chicago, whether imprisoned by Therion or hiding in their own warrens, little rabbits trembling with fear as they felt me pass by.

The Agents hunched over their desks or collecting souls paused. They felt something, but they couldn't figure out what. The call of the Agent's blood had tugged on them for a moment, but since they didn't also possess the blood of Azazel, it passed them by.

Only two looked up and knew it was me, and they stood facing each other across a desk.

"Maddy?" J.B. said, looking into thin air.

"Black," Sokolov growled.

I kept going until I found a vampire that had been

infected by the serum. I lit the fire of compulsion inside it, and then I found that I did not have to draw each vampire to me individually. Azazel had made the formula so that when one was compelled, all would have to follow. I pulled them toward me, made it impossible for them to resist.

I could feel them in my head, all of them, thousands upon thousands of vampires. They emerged from buildings and sewers. They abandoned their posts at the human encampment, released victims they had been in the midst of torturing. They surged toward me, like a great, black wave.

There was one I searched for among the many, one that I did not feel.

Therion. He was smart enough to have realized that any gift from a fallen angel came with a price. He hadn't taken the serum.

A moment later, I did feel his presence. But not the way I thought I would.

Therion's power snaked along the mindless rows of marching vampires, making them pause, making them turn back to their master.

"No," I said, and drew them toward me again, pushing more power into my spell.

Therion tugged back, trying to re-exert his influence over the horde. I sensed some of them waking up from my compulsion, turning back to him.

"No," I snarled, and this time I really put some force into it. I sent a pulse of magic through the original spell, and shot it inside Therion's.

The vampire king faltered, choking on my magic. I sensed him drawing away. His minions continued on to-ward me.

I smiled as the vampires marched as one body, without mind, toward me, toward their doom.

16

I OPENED MY EYES AS THE FIRST OF THE VAMPIRES came within reach of Soldier Field. I used my power to open all of the gates. The vampires spilled inside, moving inexorably toward me.

They entered the stadium and filed into the seats in an orderly fashion, first filling up the bottom rows and gradually moving toward the top.

"Are you making them do that?" Nathaniel asked.

"Yes," I said. I couldn't have a long conversation at the moment. It was taking a lot of effort to hold on to so many vampires.

"I cannot believe you have such a fine measure of control over them," Nathaniel said. "You could make them do anything you wanted. You could make them your own army."

I didn't care for the speculative tone in his voice, which sounded a little too much like the old Nathaniel for my liking.

"I don't want my own army," I said. "And it's not easy to do this, you know. It would be exhausting to keep them all under this kind of control forever."

"Mmm," he said.

I didn't know whether to interpret his "mmm" as an "I understand, just a thought" kind of noise or an "I still think having a vampire army is a good idea and we'll revisit this later" kind of noise. No matter what it meant, I wasn't going to change my mind. Nothing on this earth would let me allow these vampires to live after what they had done to my city.

I don't know how long we stood there. The tide of vampires swelled, then trickled, and finally stopped.

All of the vampires sat or stood inside Soldier Field. They had crowded into the aisles and spilled over onto the field. They had pushed within ten yards of where Nathaniel and I stood. Now they all waited, standing eerily still and watching me without blinking.

It should have been noisy in my head, with so many minds connected to mine, but it wasn't. In this state the vampires had no thoughts of their own. It was like being bound to thousands of empty balloons.

"Let's go up," I said to Nathaniel.

We rose above the field, and as we did the sun broke through the storm clouds for a moment. My wings were illuminated by the sun. All of the vampires followed me with their eyes, their heads tilting back in perfect unison.

"Therion," I called, feeling along the line of energy between us for the remnants of his magic.

I gathered all my power to me. It felt endless, a vast

reservoir that had always been there without my being able to access it. Until now.

I sensed Therion turning toward me, his cautious attention.

"You'd better run," I said.

I let the light of every sun in the universe shine through me. No serum of Azazel's could withstand that kind of power.

The vampires didn't even throw up their arms to protect themselves. They just stood there, thousands and thousands of monsters of the night, entranced by the blaze of light that poured from me. Then they were gone. Just gone. No flaking bodies, no ash, not even a smudge of black where they had stood.

They were gone. Forever. And Therion was afraid.

"I'm coming for you next, rat," I said.

"Madeline," Nathaniel said urgently.

"What?" I said, lowering the blaze.

I looked at the spot where Nathaniel was pointing. Several news helicopters hung in the air just past the Field Museum, far enough away to avoid getting blasted but close enough to have gotten quite the eyeful. I hadn't even heard the sound of the rotors. I'd been so focused on maintaining control of the vampires that I hadn't seen or heard anything except them.

For a second, a very brief second, I considered just blasting the helicopters out of the air. That would take care of that problem.

Then I remembered that I was not Lucifer or Puck or Therion. I did not swipe at humans just because they annoyed me. And it was very likely that the newscast had been a live feed anyway. So blowing up the helicopters wouldn't solve anything. The video of me destroying the vampires would be all over the place anyway, no matter how much I would have preferred anonymity.

And I wasn't a monster. I wasn't.

"What do you think?" I said to Nathaniel. "Should we just make a run for it, or should I fly up and ask if they want an interview?"

"They will probably try to knock you out of the sky with one of the helicopters if you approach them," Nathaniel said.

"Veil up, then," I said, and winked out of sight.

Nathaniel followed suit. Interestingly, I could now see a faint outline of him when he was under the veil. Handy. It meant that I wouldn't lose him, even when we were both invisible. However, to the humans in the news copters it would seem as if we had disappeared in midair.

He tilted his head to the side. "I can see you."

"Like a ghost, right? Sort of see-through?" I said. "I can see you, too."

"What is next on your checklist?" Nathaniel said as we glided over Columbus Drive and then continued north.

"Therion," I said. "I want to know who is working with him now."

I sent out a thread of power, looking for Therion's signature. I noticed several creatures fleeing through the streets of Chicago as we flew over. Word got out fast when there was a bigger player in town.

"Those are demons, right?" I said to Nathaniel.

Nathaniel looked down. "Yes."

"Is there any such thing as a good demon?" I asked.

"I have never met one," Nathaniel said. "Why?"

"I've got a lot of excess rage to get rid of," I said, blasting one of the demons. It went up in flames in the middle of Michigan Avenue, right in front of the Art Institute. "It was a little anticlimactic, scorching all of the vampires in one shot."

The other demons tried scuttling out of sight, but they were too slow. A moment later they were ablaze.

"Madeline," Nathaniel said, grabbing my wrist before I set anything else on fire. "Stop. This is not like you. You do not burn ants with a magnifying glass."

"Why not?" I said. "I have the powers of a god, and nothing good has ever come from a demon. You said so yourself. I'm just saving myself the trouble of having to hunt them down at a later date."

"They were leaving Chicago," Nathaniel said.

"So that they can go and harm someone else in some other city," I said fiercely, yanking my hand away. "When does it end, Nathaniel? When is it okay for us to take the fight to them? Why do we always have to be on the defensive, waiting for them to kill somebody, or hundreds of somebodies, first before we'll do something about it?"

"Do not start crossing those lines unless you want to live in Lucifer's kingdom," Nathaniel said.

I heard Gabriel's voice in my ear, from long ago and far away, saying, *Lord Lucifer has a way of making choices seem gray.*

And I heard Beezle, too, saying, *Dark side.*

Was I crossing the line by taking out a few demons just because they'd never done anything to me directly? Or was I just ridding the world of some vermin?

"I thought you wanted to find Therion," Nathaniel said.

"I do," I said.

"The longer you spend toying with these creatures, the more likely it is that he will escape, and then you will never discover the identity of his cohort," Nathaniel said.

"Fine," I said. I felt like a chastised child, and I sulked

as we flew along. I was still tracing the signature of Therion's power through the city.

As we passed over Daley Plaza I felt the tug of my trace pulling me downward. I should have known he would be here, where it had all started.

I landed in front of the Picasso statue. The plaza looked like the war zone it had been a few days earlier. Everywhere I turned there were coffee cups, sandwich wrappers, coiled scarves and lost mittens, open briefcases. Blood. Lots and lots of blood.

I stood still for a moment, sending my senses outward, looking for the source of the signature I had traced.

"There," I said, pointing toward the Washington Blue Line stop. "He's underground, and moving fast. He's using the subway tunnels."

Nathaniel looked at my shiny new wings. "Those won't be of much used to us belowground. And fire in a close space is a dangerous prospect."

"I know," I said, drawing my sword. "Don't worry. I know how to behead a vampire."

We approached the stairs that led into the station. I sent out a little pulse to make sure that nothing waited for us at the bottom of the steps.

There was nothing there. I stepped onto the first stair. Nathaniel tried to object, as usual.

"Madeline, let me . . ."

"I just barbecued a stadium full of vampires and you're still trying to make me walk behind you? What's next, foot binding?" I said, and jogged down the stairs before he could do anything about it.

I heard him muttering something about chivalry and modern women but I didn't ask for clarification.

We entered the station. The vending box for fare cards

had been knocked to the floor, and two of the turnstiles had been torn out.

The splattered brains of the former attendant had dried on the window of the CTA personnel's box.

I moved cautiously through the station to the stairs that led down to the platform. I sent another pulse of power out, and this time I didn't detect Therion at all.

"He's cloaking himself," I murmured. "Even a vampire couldn't have gotten out of range so quickly."

Nathaniel held his hand up so he could listen.

"There are several creatures moving in the tunnel below," he said.

"They could be rats," I said. "The regular Chicago kind."

"The 'Chicago kind' are far from regular," Nathaniel said. "I have seen the size of those rodents, and there is nothing ordinary about them. However, I can tell the difference between a rat and a vampire."

"Can you tell how far away they are?" I asked.

Nathaniel listened again. "Not precisely. The tunnel makes strange echoes."

"Yeah, it does," I said, thinking of the way that the El sometimes sounded like it was coming from the south when it was actually coming from the north. "Let's go down."

"No fire," Nathaniel said. "Even if you are startled."

"I am not a pyromaniac," I said. "I only set things on fire because it's expedient."

Nathaniel gave me a look.

"I already agreed, all right?" I waved my sword around. "I'll only kill them with the pointy stick."

The steps to the platform were wide enough to walk side by side, so of course Nathaniel made sure we were joined at the hip. I fully expected to find a platoon of vamps waiting to leap upon us as soon as we got to the bottom of the stairs, and was a little disappointed to find the platform empty.

I indicated to Nathaniel that he should walk down one side while I took the other, so that we could see—or hear—whether there were any signs of which tunnel they might have taken.

Nathaniel took the northbound side, and I the southbound. The platform stretched between the tracks, so Nathaniel and I were within sight of each other at all times. There was nothing between us except some empty customer benches.

We walked slowly and carefully from the Dearborn end of the platform. Halfway down, Nathaniel waved his arm at me. I joined him and he pointed south.

He hopped down to the tracks, holding his arms up for me. I let him swing me down.

"Stay away from the third rail," I whispered. "We don't know if the electricity to the subway has been shut off."

He nodded, and we stared into the tunnel. Ahead of us there were no lights except the occasional service lamp for CTA workers. I could have lit a ball of nightfire, but that would have advertised our presence for miles. Once we went in there, the vampires would have the advantage. My new superpowers didn't seem to have come with the ability to see in the dark.

"Can you see in there?" I asked softly.

Nathaniel shook his head. "Now would be a good time to have the werewolf with us."

Despite the fact that I had just burned thousands of vampires with one spell, I didn't want to go into the tunnel. In the tunnel I would be a trapped rat, just like them. I could sense Nathaniel's reluctance as well. We had so recently been in the pitch black of Titania's cave, and I hadn't forgotten how helpless I'd felt there. Gabriel had told me once that angels were born of the sun. Creatures of the sun do not like to scurry in the darkness.

But our quarry was scurrying away, and I wasn't going to let him escape.

I stepped into the tunnel, and Nathaniel kept pace with me. The air felt close and damp. I focused on breathing steadily—and quietly. The scrape of our boots on the tracks sounded like gunfire in the silence.

We crept along for a while, trying to be crafty, both of us tense. And as we crept along I started getting annoyed. And I went from annoyed to angry to insanely furious with no stops in between.

"Why are we tiptoeing around in here?" I said loudly. "What freaking difference does it make?"

"Madeline, shh," Nathaniel said.

"No, I will not be quiet," I said. "They can see in the dark. They can hear better than we can. Why should we play by their rules?"

I raised a ball of nightfire and launched it up so it would float ahead of us. "If they're going to run, then they'll run whether or not we're scuttling in the dark. If they're going to fight, then we should be able to see them as well as they can see us."

"Madeline, stop. Do not be impulsive," Nathaniel said.

"Who's being impulsive?" I said as the ball of nightfire lit up the tunnel. "THERION!"

Nathaniel stared at me like I'd lost my mind.

"THERION! You COWARD!" I roared.

There was no answer.

"They are gone," Nathaniel said angrily. "They were ahead of us. I could hear them, and now they are gone. As soon as you began yelling they disappeared."

This news just made me even angrier. Therion had escaped, and I wanted him to pay. Still, I wasn't going to play the vampire king's game.

"Fine," I said. "Let's go home."

Nathaniel's eyebrows went up to his hairline. "You are giving up?"

"Hell, no," I said. "I'm going to track him down and take out his intestines through his nostrils. But I'm not going to chase him through miles of tunnel to do it. I'll find him later. I have something else I need to do, anyway."

"Deal with Alerian?" Nathaniel asked.

"Alerian's not even awake yct," I said, trudging back in the direction of the Washington stop. We hadn't really walked that far. I could see the lights over the platform a short distance away. "I have something I need to do for Lucifer."

"Then I will accompany you," Nathaniel said.

"No," I said shortly. "This is not optional. You're staying home, and so is everyone else. This is for me to do."

"Have I not proven that I am trustworthy?" Nathaniel asked, an edge in his voice.

"This isn't about whether or not you are trustworthy," I said. "This is about me and Lucifer and my duties as the Hound of the Hunt."

"What has he asked of you?" Nathaniel said.

"I can't tell you," I said. "You may assume that the task sucks and that there are about ten million things I would rather do."

"Let me help you," Nathaniel persisted as we reached the platform and clambered up from the track level.

"Nathaniel, I am the Hound of the Hunt. Where I go, you cannot follow," I said. "Besides, I need you to stay in Chicago. You're the only one here who can deal with Alerian if he does rise. Or at least, you're the only one who can contact Puck to come and deal with his brother."

We climbed the stairs back up to the station. Everything looked the same. When we reached the street I half expected Therion to be waiting there with another army of vampires to take me down, but he wasn't. I guess the vampire king really was a coward, and the nightmare was over. For the moment.

There were a few people on the streets, wandering in a daze, blinking at the sky like they'd never seen it before. News helicopters soared overhead. Nathaniel and I quickly cloaked ourselves and then took off flying. I wasn't interested in being attacked by an angry mob just because I looked different, and I'd already had enough television exposure to last a lifetime.

As we flew home I noticed that the clouds had stopped swirling over Lake Michigan, and much of the green fog had dissipated. I pointed toward the lake.

"What's that all about?" I said to Nathaniel.

"Perhaps he has decided to go back to sleep."

"That would be a load off my mind," I said. "It would be nice if all the people who fled the city could come back."

We returned to my house and flew back into the kitchen. Beezle was sitting on the counter eating a bag of pretzels.

"Saw your light show on the news," he said conversationally, but I could tell he was pissed off. "I see you've got some spanking new wings. And Nathaniel's had his hair colored. There was a lot of banging around going on up here earlier. Anything you want to tell me?"

"Not right now," I said. "I've got to run an errand for Lucifer."

"Oh, you're running errands for Lucifer now? Haven't we come up in the world?" he said.

"Don't start, Beezle," I said. "You were standing right there when he made me the Hound of the Hunt. Oh, wait—maybe you were napping, as you tend to do when there's actual work to be done."

Nathaniel was edging his way around me and out of the kitchen.

"Don't you go anywhere," Beezle said, pointing a claw at Nathaniel. "You're in this, too. I know what the two of you have been doing when no one's looking."

"I do not answer to you, gargoyle," Nathaniel said.

"And I don't answer to you, either," I said. "You're not my father, and I'm tired of being second-guessed."

"Someone needs to rein you in before you become exactly what Lucifer wants," Beezle said.

"Do you think that I don't know what he wants?" I shouted. "He wants me in a cage and my baby bouncing on his knee. I am not stupid, whatever you might think."

"Do you know that most of the people who saw you on the news are scared of you, even though you saved this damned city from the vampires?" Beezle said. "The news anchors were discussing you like you were a monster. People were calling in, saying you needed to be exterminated. No one is going to thank you for what you did."

"I don't care," I said. "I only did what was right. I've only *ever* done what I thought was right. I don't need a bouquet of flowers from the mayor."

"You don't understand," Beezle said. "Because of Therion's message, everyone knows who you are. They know that you are Madeline Black. How long do you think it will take for people to track you down here? How long do you think it will take before there are police outside breaking down the door? Or worse?"

"What's worse than being chased from my own home?" I asked.

"The curiosity seekers. The people who will want you to use your powers to help them with their petty problems. You're in danger now, and so is anyone who stays here with you," Beezle said.

"How is that any different from before?" I said. "There have been creatures hunting me since the day Ramuell returned, and all of you have been willing to take the risk."

"Everyone is willing to fight supernatural monsters, but they aren't willing to have their identities exposed to humans," Beezle said. "Samiel and Chloe have already gone."

"Gone where?" I said, stung. I couldn't believe Samiel had left without a word. I'd taken him into my home, made him a part of my family.

"To Chloe's. They both think it's safer there. Neither of them wants to be here when the news vans roll up. And they will, sooner or later," Beezle said. "I'm sure Jude will want to return to his pack now, too."

"Well, that's the best place for him," I said, trying not to be hurt by all of this, and failing. "Werewolves belong with their packs. It's not healthy for him to be away for so long."

"It's not healthy for anyone to be near you right now, either," Beezle said.

"And you?" I asked. Something was breaking inside me, something that might never mend.

Beezle looked grim. "I promised your mother I would stay with you."

"But?" I said. I wouldn't cry. I would *not* cry.

"I'm not sure I know the person you're becoming. And I'm not sure that I *want* to know that person."

I wanted to scream, to shout, to argue. I wanted to kick things and throw things and protest that it was unfair. I'd never asked to be an Agent, or to be the daughter of a fallen angel. I'd never asked to be the last direct descendant of Evangeline and Lucifer's union. I'd never asked to have the power of the universe within me. I'd never asked for a life shrouded by death.

All I'd wanted—all I had ever wanted—was to be plain Maddy Black. I would have liked to have gone on dates and stayed out past curfew. I would have liked to have gone to college and gotten a job. I would have liked to have met a man who was no good for me and had a torrid affair, and then met a man who was really good for me and gotten married and had a bunch of kids. I would have liked to have worried about taxes and the next election instead of the latest monster or the pending apocalypse. I would have liked to have been normal.

Sure, I never would have been able to fly. But I would have been able to live without a lot of heartache, too.

But I'd had no choice. I was never given any choice. And now, for this, everyone was leaving me. Even Beezle.

"Go, then," I said, my voice hard. "Go with Samiel. He's your favorite person anyway."

"I didn't say . . ." Beezle began.

"Go!" I said, and I grabbed the nearest thing at hand and threw it at him. It was a coffee cup, and it smashed into the counter a few inches from Beezle. The handle broke off.

I stared at it, stricken. Not because I'd just thrown a coffee mug at Beezle, although that was bad enough. But because I'd thrown the last coffee mug that Gabriel had used. The mug that had sat, untouched, in the dish drain since the morning he'd died. I'd almost bitten Samiel's head off once when he tried to put it back in the cupboard.

Beezle said nothing. I couldn't read the expression on his face.

Fight for me, I thought. It was a little girl's voice in my head, the little girl who'd always wanted to be first to her mother but always came in second. The little girl who'd dreamed of a daddy to love her, a daddy who never arrived. *Show me I matter. Show me you care enough to stay.*

But he didn't. He pushed the half-eaten bag of pretzels to one side, made a great show of dusting crumbs off his claws, and flew out the kitchen window without another word.

17

NATHANIEL STOOD IN THE CORNER OF THE KITCHEN, near the hall. He hadn't said a word, hadn't tried to intervene.

I didn't look at him. My throat was tight. I thought that if he gave me one kind word at that moment, I would crumple to the floor and never get up again.

"I would comfort you," Nathaniel said carefully, "but I sense that is precisely what you do not want."

"You sense correctly," I said. I was proud of the fact that my voice wobbled only a little. "You know, you don't have to stay, either. All the other rats are leaving the sinking ship. You should get out while you still can."

"Madeline. I would not leave you. Now more than ever we are two of a kind. Could any of the others understand your magic, your burdens, as well as I?"

"No," I admitted. "But that doesn't put you under any obligation to me."

"It is my choice."

It was astounding that the last person I'd ever expected to stand by me was the only person left with me now that my life was going to hell in a handbasket.

When I'd first met Nathaniel I thought he would protect himself at any cost. I thought if he had a chance to keep out of personal danger, he would take it. I thought he would never be the kind of man who stood in front of me, sword raised, ready to keep me from harm.

Yet Beezle was gone. Samiel was gone. Gabriel was dead. And Nathaniel was still here. He was *choosing* to be here.

"Thank you," I said. I didn't say the other thing I was thinking. *I could love you. Maybe. Someday.* "I'll see you when I get back."

I didn't embrace him, or give him one last longing look. I flew out the window, because I needed to forget about those things that tethered me to life. I was going to a place of the dead, and if I longed too much for life, then I wouldn't be able to do it.

I flew up and up and up, soaring above the city, into the place where the atmosphere became thin. The lack of oxygen might have bothered me before, but not today. My body seemed to adjust as needed, without direction from me.

I kept going, past the clouds, past where the blue sky touched the dark of space. Still I went up, and beyond, and I passed into a place on the edge of starlight. There, time moved at a different speed.

I could see all of the worlds beneath me, all the worlds that had ever been and ever were and ever would be. I did not have to search for the correct place. Evangeline's spirit called me, a flare of red like a homing beacon. I sensed her in my head, drawing me to her just as I had drawn the vampires to me.

Beneath me was the land of the dead—or one of them, anyway. My newfound knowledge told me that all of the dead of history were scattered throughout many worlds. It was the choice of those worlds that a soul was given when it passed through the Door.

My descent began, past the blazing sun of this world, through the empty air. The landscape was as stark as it had been in my dreams. Everywhere I looked there was white sand, bleached bone, gray rock.

I alighted on the same flat stone and looked around, shielding my eyes from the sun's glare. One moment she wasn't there. The next moment she was.

She stood before me in the same gray gown she had worn in my vision. The small round bulge of her belly was just visible when the wind brushed her dress against her body. Her hair fluttered in the wind, black corkscrew curls, and I had the disturbing realization that my hair was exactly like hers.

"I knew he would send you for me," Evangeline said with a self-satisfied expression.

"You know, you had the choice of all the worlds," I said, ignoring her jibe. "Why did you pick this barren shithole?"

The smirk dropped from her face. "This land is very like the place where I was raised."

"Oh, you mean the nuclear wasteland," I said, rolling my eyes. "What, you missed the radiation poisoning?"

"Your judgment means nothing," Evangeline spat. "I will leave this land soon, in any case. Lucifer is defying the universe for me, for our child, just as I knew he would."

"Except that he's not defying anything," I said. "Lucifer isn't here. I am."

"So?" she challenged.

"He doesn't love you for your brains, does he? Obviously, he isn't here because you are not vital enough for him to risk his own precious self, even with that monster in your belly," I said.

Her face fell for a moment; then she visibly gathered herself. "Lucifer is far too important to endanger his physical being. I understand why he sent you in his stead. If he were destroyed, the very fabric of the universe would come undone. You, however, are expendable."

"Keep telling yourself that."

"You are in no position to sneer at me, as you are present, acting upon his orders," she said.

"I am here," I admitted. "But it's not a done deal. I could leave you."

Evangeline stared at me. "You cannot. You must do as Lucifer bids."

"No, I must not. I'm human. We've got this thing called free will."

"If you do not take me willingly, then Lucifer will command you to as Hound of the Hunt," she said triumphantly.

"I could still drop you somewhere along the way," I said casually.

Her eyes widened. Apparently my reputation as a loose cannon was potent enough that she took my threat seriously.

"Lucifer would kill you if you caused the death of his child," she said.

"And he'll kill you if you cause the death of mine," I said, finally coming around to the point. I wanted to make sure that she knew I was not to be trifled with. "I don't see you as a threat. But you obviously see me as one. So don't get any ideas about trying to take me or my kid out just so you can be number one with Lucifer."

"No one except my child will be Lucifer's heir," Evangeline hissed.

"That's not up to you," I said. "But I'll tell you this—I've already killed two of Lucifer's children, and I'm still up and walking around. Don't think I'll hesitate to take out your little monster if I have to. If you try to harm my child, then you will not live to see another dawn."

We stood there, face-to-face under the blazing sun in a desert of white sand, and took each other's measure. Evangeline blinked first.

"You will not threaten me," she said haughtily, drawing her bravado around her like a cloak. "I will be Lucifer's queen."

"Remember what I said."

"You—"

"Remember what I said," I repeated.

Maybe I was going a little dark side.

"Now, get walking," I said, and pointed west, toward the horizon.

Evangeline's lips parted. "Walk?"

I nodded. "You don't think we can just fly out of here, do you? We've got to earn it. I'm taking a soul from the other side of the Door."

"Surely you have the ability to . . ."

"Do you want to stay? Because that will make my life a lot less complicated, and I'm very big on anything that will make my life easier right now," I said.

"I cannot believe that you expect me to pay the price for our return," she muttered.

"I'm not paying it," I said. "You want to live again, you pony up. I'm just the delivery girl."

It was helpful to consider myself that way, to think that I was simply doing the same duty I had always done as an

Agent, except in reverse. It was easier than thinking about the fact that I was doing something that undid the order of the universe just so Lucifer could exert his will.

When I thought about it that way, my bitterness was like chalk in my mouth. Of course I'd never had a real option to leave Evangeline behind, no matter what I'd said. If I'd come home without her, Lucifer would have simply ordered me back as Hound, and I would have been unable to resist. I'd thought it would be better to do it of my own free will, but it was almost worse. I couldn't fall back on the excuse that I'd been nothing but a puppet for Lucifer.

Evangeline reluctantly trudged forward. She looked like a pouty child who was told that she couldn't have a lollipop.

There was something of the child about Evangeline still, I mused. She had been very young when she'd fallen in love with Lucifer, and she had destroyed her whole village and anyone who crossed her in order to get to him. She had been taken from Lucifer by a rival faction of fallen angels, and then been rescued by Michael and hidden away.

In a sense she had never really grown up. And I knew from experience that when Evangeline wanted something, she would lay waste to anything in her path to get it. When she'd wanted her vengeance on Ariell, the angel who had stolen her from Lucifer, she had possessed me. She'd lost her mind completely when I'd refused to let her work her will through my body, and then she'd been killed by Ramuell and ended up here.

I was pretty sure that she was right on the edge of insanity. I was also sure that whatever plans Lucifer had for the future did not include having a mad queen on the throne beside him.

He wanted the baby. Just as he wanted my baby.

My son gave a little flutter underneath my belly button.

I wished I could be as other mothers were, the ones who lay on their sofas and dreamed of their child's face, their child's future. When I looked into my child's future I saw a life of turmoil and pain.

And love, a little voice whispered from the back of my head, and it sounded a lot like Beezle.

Yes, I would love this baby. I already did, with a fury and a power I had not expected. I would do anything for my son.

And so would Evangeline. I glanced at her as she padded along in the sand in bare feet, her hair waving about in wild Medusa springs. She was nuts. She would kill me in an instant if she thought she could get away with it, because it was pretty clear that she was jealous of my standing with Lucifer. I'd like to tell her she was welcome to him if she would just keep him away from me, but I didn't think she would believe me.

Still, she was a mother, too. And that made me feel a little sorry for her. Her first two children had been taken by duty and Death, made to serve as soul collectors in Lucifer's stead.

I don't know whether I could bear it if my child were taken from me. Her instability was easier to understand in that light.

We walked on, two mothers-to-be, without food or water or shade or shelter. The horizon looked farther away with every step.

"How much more?" she asked through parched lips.

"We'll know," I said. I had long since abandoned my favorite sweater and rolled my shirtsleeves to my shoulders. I was getting a sunburn.

Something shimmered in front of us. I stopped, squinted at the thing that must be an illusion.

"Do you see that?" I asked.

Evangeline shaded her eyes. "Something silver? Water?"

"Something silver," I breathed. "Not water. A portal."

We walked faster. I stumbled over my own feet in the sand. Evangeline went ahead of me, her gown flowing behind her. Her crazy cackle trailed in the wind as she laughed and laughed harder the closer she got to the portal.

I ran, trying to catch up with her, but I was wearing heavy boots and lugging a sword that kept banging around. I would have flown, but ever since I'd landed I'd felt the air pressing on me in a way that told me flying would be impossible here.

I think that she thought she would be able to dive through the portal and close it on the other side, leaving me there. She found out soon enough that wouldn't happen.

She launched herself at the portal and bounced off it as if it were a brick wall. She staggered backward, her hands thrown wide.

"What is this?" she screeched. "Why have I crossed this desert if not to escape?"

"Chill," I said, coming up behind her, panting. "Keep the lid on the crazy for a second, will you?"

"I swear by all the gods, granddaughter, if you have made me suffer for no reason . . ."

"You'll what?" I said. "Talk me to death? You have no power, Evangeline. Here you are nothing more than a spirit, and you cannot pass through that portal without me. And without paying the price."

She narrowed her eyes. "I thought I just paid the price."

"You thought a walk through the desert was the price?" I asked. "No way. You're asking to be restored to the living. The only way you pay is in blood."

Evangeline covered her belly protectively. "You will not take my child from me."

"I am not taking anything," I said impatiently, although it was a possibility I had already considered. The universe might let Evangeline through that portal—if she gave her baby's life in return. "It's not up to me."

I held out my hand to her. She gazed at it fearfully, as if I were a snake about to strike.

"If you want to return, you have to come with me. And you have to agree to the price that is asked of you," I said. "Otherwise, you stay."

After a long pause, she took my hand. Her fingers were cold, and I was seized by the sudden impulse to comfort her.

Then I remembered that she had laughed like a maniac when Ramuell had torn my heart out, and the impulse passed.

We approached the portal, which looked like a long silver mirror hanging without wall or wire above the sand. I stretched my other hand toward it, and I passed through. Evangeline flowed in behind me.

Unlike every other portal I'd experienced, this one did not immediately suck us into a vacuum and send us hurtling through space and time. Instead we were floating in a kind of misty netherworld, surrounded by streams of white smoke.

One of the puffs of smoke curled into a face and gazed at me with empty eyes. I realized that what I thought was smoke were ghosts, the ghosts of all those who had tried to pass through here and been unable or unwilling to pay the price.

The ghosts wound around us. They seemed fairly harmless to me, like kittens. But Evangeline started to struggle, to try to shake them off her.

"Quit it," I said. "If you keep that up, I'll lose you."

"Make them leave," she said, her voice trembling. "They want my baby."

I frowned at her. "I don't think so. They're just curious."

"They want me to pay," she said. "Can't you hear them whispering?"

I shook my head. "No. I can't."

"They are in my head," she said, her green eyes wide with terror. "They are telling me of all the sins I have done."

It was like Evangeline was trapped in her own personal Maze while I was drifting along in a stream of cotton candy. There was nothing I could do now. I had fulfilled Lucifer's charge to me, and fetched Evangeline from the dead. Now it was up to her whether she would pass into the land of the living again.

She began to thrash, and it was harder for me to hold on to her. I knew if I released her now, she would end up in the netherworld forever. That wasn't really a problem for me, but Lucifer might think I'd left her there on purpose.

I grabbed onto her other shoulder with my left hand while keeping a good grip on her fingers with my right. She couldn't even see me now. Her gaze was somewhere else, far inward.

Then she nodded. And then she screamed, and we were falling, rushing through the air like we'd been dropped from the top of the tallest building in the world. There was no chance for me to slow us down. Her shoulder slipped out of my grasp, and there was something wet and sticky on my fingers. I white-knuckled her hand, and hoped that we would make it. There wasn't much else I could do.

The ground appeared out of nowhere, and all the breath

left my body. Evangeline's hand was still in mine, and it was colder than death. I sat up slowly, realizing I was in my own backyard, and that it was night. I don't know how long I had been gone, but all of the snow had melted.

"Thanks, universe," I muttered. I didn't really want to have to stash Evangeline until Lucifer felt like coming to pick her up.

I looked over at Evangeline. Her eyes were closed. Now I knew why I'd lost my grip on her shoulder, and why my fingers were all sticky.

Evangeline's right arm was gone, cut as cleanly as if by an ax, and she was bleeding to death on my lawn.

"Gods above and below," I swore.

The back door slammed open. Nathaniel stood silhouetted in the doorway.

"Madeline," he said, his voice full of relief. "You have been gone for three days. I thought you would never return."

"Never mind that," I said urgently. "I need you to help me with Evangeline. She's bleeding to death."

I have to give Nathaniel credit. He didn't stand around asking about the whys and wherefores. He rushed to my side, and seemed to know what I wanted immediately.

His fingers twined around mine, and we each put our other hand over the gaping hole where Evangeline's arm used to be.

Our magic, Nathaniel's and mine, lit up the night like a searchlight. It took a long time to close the wound. There was a lot of damage.

After a while it was done. Evangeline was still breathing, although it didn't sound like she was restful. I lifted her right eyelid to check her pupils and gasped.

"What?" Nathaniel said.

"Look," I said.

There was no eye underneath, just a black hole where the orb used to be. Nathaniel checked the other socket. I watched expectantly.

"Empty," he said.

I put my hand over Evangeline's belly, wondering whether her child had survived the passage. Beneath my hand there was movement, but it wasn't natural. It felt like she was carrying a litter of snakes. I yanked my palm away, rubbing it on my pants leg.

"Both her eyes and her arm," I said.

"It seems a small price to pay for returning from the dead," Nathaniel said.

"And still, I wonder how happy she'll be about paying it once she wakes up and realizes she can't see," I said.

Nathaniel lay down in the grass. He pulled me to him so I could rest my head on his chest.

"It's done," I said. Evangeline's happiness with her choice was not of any concern to me. My eyes closed. I felt an almost overwhelming urge to sleep right there. "Lucifer, she's here."

I drifted into a doze, woke when I felt him beside her, kneeling in the grass, lifting her away. His voice was nothing but a whisper on the wind—*Thank you, granddaughter.*

Nathaniel and I both slept right there in the yard. When I opened my eyes again all that remained of Evangeline was a bloodstain in the grass. It was still very dark out, not even close to the dawn yet.

I sat up, rubbing my eyes, and stretched. I was stiff all over. I wanted a proper sleep in a proper bed after a very hot shower with lots of soap. There was sand in my eyes, sand in my clothes, sand in my socks. I still had Evangeline's blood on my hands.

Nathaniel opened his eyes. They glittered in the starlight, the deep blue of the sapphires. He was beautiful to me in that moment, a creature of another world, black-haired and white-winged, bathed in the night.

I lowered my head to kiss him, drawn by a force I could not resist.

He smiled, and I realized at the last second that it was not his smile. Something was wrong.

His hands latched on my neck and he pushed me to the ground, his weight on top of me, suffocating me.

I tried to say his name, to pry his hands from my neck. I put my hands over his, fought for consciousness, pushed power through the connection between us.

I didn't find Nathaniel's magic welcoming me as I had before. There was someone else inside him, someone else at the controls.

My life was fading fast. My baby beat its wings against my belly. I found the spark of the Morningstar inside me, and gave one tremendous heave, pushing all of that power into Nathaniel. The source of his power, that gift from Puck, rose up to meet me. Together we chased the thing that was inside Nathaniel out.

There was an audible *pop*, and then Nathaniel released my neck. I coughed, breathing great lungfuls of air. Nathaniel looked horrified.

"Madeline, I am so—"

"Don't apologize," I said, and jerked my thumb at the silvery apparition floating in the air. "It was her fault. You're some piece of work—you know that?"

Amarantha smirked at me. "I may have failed in this instance, but you will never know when I will strike again."

I stood up, rubbing my throat. "Whose magic did you steal to be able to do that?"

"I stole nothing," Amarantha said, miffed. "Your useless brother left his cupboard of toys behind when he was beheaded. There are many useful things in there."

Greenwitch's magic. She'd been an exceptional witch, and since Antares had no magic of his own she had bequeathed him a collection of magical objects to help him. I'd noticed the cupboard in the cave in the Forbidden Lands where I'd killed Antares, but once the mountain came down on the cavern I'd assumed nothing could survive.

Somehow Amarantha had ferreted out Antares' goodies. Before, she'd just been an annoying ghost. A closetful of magic suddenly made her a lot more dangerous. That meant I would have to find her stash and destroy it before she could do any more damage to me and mine.

Amarantha smiled like she knew what I was thinking. "You will never discover it, Agent. You will be forever looking over your shoulder for me."

She rose up, her tinkling-bell laugh just as irritating in death as it had been in life. She threw her arms wide. "But first, a gift for you."

The vampires came slithering over the fence from the alley, dozens of them. Behind them clambered humans with blank eyes, and I realized that Amarantha had somehow ensnared these humans with other ghosts, just as she had possessed Nathaniel. It was a crafty move, since she knew that I wouldn't deliberately harm a bunch of innocents. And because it severely limited my brand of blast-and-burn magic.

"I guess we know who was working with Therion," I muttered, drawing my sword. Nathaniel and I moved so that we were back-to-back. "Don't hurt the humans. They're not responsible for what they do."

The vampires surrounded us, snarling. They descended on us, and so commenced the hacking and the slashing.

The vampires were hopelessly outmatched. I'm not sure why they bothered, really. The hardest part for me was making sure that I didn't accidentally behead any humans in the close quarters.

"Why are we bothering to engage them?" Nathaniel said as he sent a blast of nightfire directly into the chest of nearby vamp. "There is no need. We could fly away."

"Yeah, but then the vampires would eat the neighbors," I said. "And I think they just got home after the last vampire crisis."

The vampires were dispatched fairly quickly. The humans were another problem. They surrounded us with their blank and staring eyes, their hands outstretched.

"This is a lot like being in a George Romero movie," I said. "Except that I don't have a shotgun."

We both lifted off from the ground at the same time, floating above the yard. The possessed humans milled around for a minute, confused.

"Now, where did that bitch Amarantha go?" I said.

"Here," J.B.'s voice said behind me.

18

AMARANTHA GLARED AT ME THROUGH J.B.'S EYES. SHE pointed her finger at me and shot a blast of red light at me. I dodged it narrowly and pointed my sword at her.

"Let him go," I said. "Hasn't he suffered enough abuse at your hands?"

"You won't hurt this body," Amarantha said confidently. It was disturbing to hear her speaking with J.B.'s voice. "I can do whatever I like with you and you cannot defend yourself."

She blasted at me again. I was lucky her aim was crappy, because otherwise that blast would have hit me square in the chest.

"We have to get her out of J.B.," I said to Nathaniel.

"Yes," he said. "But we have another problem."

He pointed toward the east. A vanguard of Agents was flying toward us, led by Bryson, and carrying weapons.

Apparently Bryson just wasn't scared enough by my little performance on the bridge a few days before.

"Oh, you've got to be kidding me," I said, exasperated. Amarantha tried knocking me out of the sky again, and I avoided it once more. "Sokolov really has a lot of time on his hands."

"I will take care of the Agents," Nathaniel said.

"Don't kill them," I warned.

"Bryson would kill you in an instant," Nathaniel said.

"Don't kill them," I said. "They're following orders."

I turned my attention on Amarantha. I was pretty sure I could get her out of J.B.'s body if I could just get ahold of her. But she was right. I wouldn't willingly hurt him, so I couldn't just blast her out.

I flew toward her, building up speed. Her eyes widened. I don't think she expected me to charge her.

But she acted exactly as I hoped she would. She ran. Amarantha had never been one to stand and fight on her own. She hid behind monsters, behind underlings, behind protocol and politics. She had never engaged me in battle, although legend had it that she led an army once. If so, there was nothing left of that woman when I met her. Amarantha was not a warrior.

J.B.'s wings carried her over the rooftops, away from the sounds of battle and gunfire that were now coming from the air above my yard. I hoped that Nathaniel would be all right. I hoped that he would not have to kill any of the Agents and thus give Sokolov yet another excuse to come for me.

She headed toward the lake. The surface of the water churned, mysterious and dark, and I felt the presence of Alerian once more.

I sped up, grabbing J.B.'s ankle. Amarantha tried to

shake me off, to blast me in the face with her magic. I turned J.B.'s body upside down and shook it, and several tokens fell from his pockets to the beach below.

"No!" she shrieked. I knew then that she couldn't access J.B.'s own magic inside his body. She needed Greenwitch's charms to perform a spell. I lowered to the sand, dropping J.B. somewhat unceremoniously.

I saw the charms a few feet away, scattered on the ground, visible in the light from the streetlamps that lit the lakefront path. Amarantha scrambled for them, but I did what I did best.

I set them on fire.

There was a small explosion, a puff of red smoke as the spells dissipated into the air.

Amarantha fell to her knees, pulling on J.B.'s hair. I walked up behind her, clapped my hands on his face, and sent my power inside him. I chased her screaming through his blood, all the way to his heart.

She paused there, and squeezed. I could sense her smile.

J.B. coughed, his hand going to his chest.

"Enough," I said, and sent more power inside his body. I needed to be careful. I could blast J.B. apart with the force of my magic, even as I was trying to save him.

Amarantha was a black shade on his heart, wrapping herself around and around him, smothering him.

I heard J.B. gasping. Brute force wasn't working. I couldn't blast my way out of this one.

I tried to think. Amarantha was a ghost. What could destroy a ghost?

Nothing, I thought hopelessly. You cannot, by definition, kill something that is already dead.

But perhaps I didn't need to. *Once an Agent, always an Agent.*

Instead of blasting Amarantha out of J.B.'s body, I called her name.

Amarantha.

I put the force of my will behind it, like I did when I was separating a soul from its body with my Agent's magic.

Come to me, I said, and she uncoiled like a reptile, releasing J.B.'s heart. I was the charmer and she the snake. I kept my focus on her, drawing her on, drawing her out.

A silver mist rose from J.B.'s skin, and Amarantha emerged, spellbound.

J.B. fell forward in the sand. I let Amarantha go.

I came to my knees beside him, turned him over. "J.B.? J.B.?"

He lay so still.

"J.B.!" I shouted, shaking him.

He coughed once, twice, and opened his eyes. "I liked the way you woke me up the last time better."

I laughed and wiped my eyes.

"Are you crying?" he asked, reaching up to stroke my cheek.

"Nah," I said. "I got sand in my eyes."

I didn't say that when Amarantha was squeezing his heart, I'd felt my own heart about to burst from grief. I didn't say that for a moment I thought I'd lost him, too, like I'd lost Gabriel.

I looked around, realized Amarantha had escaped.

"Dammit," I said. "I wanted to follow her and find out where she's keeping her hidey-hole. She's been working with Therion. She's probably the one who enspelled the hospital for the vampires. She found Antares' stash of magical stuff from his mother."

J.B. sat up, rubbing his head. "That explains a lot. She

gave me one hell of a headache. Hey, you have wings again. Fancy shiny ones. How did you get those."

"It's a long story," I said. One I would never tell. You do not tell a man who has proposed to you that you got brand-spanking-new powers by being intimate with another man on your dining room floor.

I helped J.B. to his feet. "Do you remember anything from when she possessed you? Maybe the location of her secret base?"

He shook his head, wincing. "No. The last thing I remember I was in my office, reading a memo from Sokolov about you . . ."

He trailed off, staring at me. "A memo that said you had taken a soul from the other side of the Door and returned it to the living."

"Don't lecture me," I said. "I didn't have any choice."

"You know, I seem to recall Nathaniel saying something similar about his role in the rebellion. And you were very adamant that there's always a choice. So I'm sure that you could have made a better one," J.B. said angrily.

"Not if you're Lucifer's Hound of the Hunt," I said. "You were standing right there when he gave me the second-crappiest job I've ever had in my life. This was my choice—I could either fetch Evangeline and their unborn child under my own power, or I could wait for him to compel me to do it."

It was hard to tell in the streetlight, but I think all the blood drained out of J.B.'s face. "Evangeline? You restored Evangeline?"

"Yes," I said. "And yes, she's pregnant."

"I know she's pregnant," J.B. said. "We've been keeping tabs on Lucifer's activities. You don't think a conception beyond the Door would go unnoticed by the Agency, do you?"

Now it was my turn to be angry. "If you were keeping tabs on him, then why didn't you say anything? Why didn't you stop him? I got a letter of warning just for accidentally straying into the land of the dead during a dream. Lucifer's been doing a lot worse for months."

"Do you really think the Agency is going to send Lucifer a letter of warning? They don't want to attract his attention, and rightly so. He might decide to destroy the whole Agency on a whim."

"But why didn't you say anything to me about it?" I asked. "Don't you think that information would have been useful to me, given that he is my grandfather?"

"We didn't see any reason to say anything about it."

"Who is 'we'?" I said. "You and Sokolov? Are you guys buddies now?"

"No," J.B. said. "There are other managers and executives besides Sokolov, you know. And he's not very well liked generally, but he's got powerful connections with the people who matter."

"So why didn't you tell me about Lucifer and Evangeline?" I persisted.

"The consensus was that nobody needed to worry about it as long as Evangeline stayed put. We didn't think that even Lucifer would try to remove her."

"He didn't," I said. "I did."

"And that was something we didn't anticipate," he said, running his hands through his hair. "But now that you have . . . Maddy, you have to leave."

"Leave where? Chicago?"

"This universe," J.B. said. "If you can travel to the land of the dead, then you can cross to another world. You've got to get away before Sokolov discovers what you've done."

"I'm not going to be a fugitive for the rest of my life," I said. "If he wants to come for me, let him."

I'd relish the opportunity to take Sokolov out. He'd tortured J.B., and for that I could never forgive him.

"It's not Sokolov that will come for you. It's the Retrievers," J.B. said.

As he said the name of those creatures, it seemed that the wind echoed him—*Retrievers, Retrievers, Retrievers.*

"I'm not scared of the Retrievers," I said. "You don't even know what kind of shit I've seen. Or what kind of power I have now."

"It doesn't matter," J.B. said. "The Retrievers are the final resort. Nobody is immune."

"Then why didn't you send the Retrievers after Lucifer once he started sneaking past the Door?" I said.

"I think what it comes down to is that upper management doesn't want to tangle with Lucifer," J.B. said. "They're still smarting from the attack by Ramuell and Antares. They know Lucifer is more powerful than either of those creatures were."

"But it's okay to tangle with me?" I said suspiciously. "You seem to know a lot about Lucifer all of a sudden. More than I do, actually. And I'm wondering why you never told me any of this before."

"It was need-to-know," J.B. said.

"Don't give me that Agency line," I said. "I thought we were past that. I thought that we were friends."

J.B. was silent, and in that silence I figured out why he'd never told me any of this.

"You don't trust me," I said.

"I do," J.B. protested. "But upper management doesn't."

"No," I said, hurt beyond reason. "You don't trust me, not really. Because if you did, you would have told me all of this no matter what upper management said."

"Maddy . . ."

"No," I said, cutting him off. "You stood in front of me less than two weeks ago and said that you loved me. If you love me, then you trust me. And it's obvious you don't."

"Don't try telling me about love," J.B. said angrily. "Your husband died less than a month ago and you've been climbing all over Nathaniel ever since."

The urge to slap him in the face was strong, but I resisted. "I don't owe you anything. If anything, you owe me. I've saved your life more times than I can count in the last week."

"Keeping score, like your grandfather?" J.B. said. "You're becoming more like Lucifer every day."

I couldn't believe it had come to this, that we were standing on the beach in the middle of January cutting each other to ribbons. I was losing him, too. Maybe I'd already lost him. But the gulf between us seemed too wide to cross.

"I am nothing like Lucifer," I said through my teeth.

"Could have fooled me," J.B. said.

"Then go," I said, pointing to the sky. "Get your own damned self home. I hope you can avoid being kidnapped by faeries or possessed by your mother without someone to watch you."

J.B.'s face was purple with anger now. "Someday, someone is going to give you your comeuppance. I just hope I'm there to see it."

And then he was gone. Like everyone else. Everyone except Nathaniel.

I crossed my arms and turned toward the lake. The wind was cold. I was abruptly aware that my sleeves were still rolled up from my trek through the desert with Evangeline, and that I wore nothing except a T-shirt and jeans. My hair had come out of its braid somewhere along the way and it whipped and curled in the breeze. Just like Evangeline's.

I let myself have a cry. I deserved it. Everyone I'd thought would stand by me was gone. And now that I was alone, I started to doubt myself. Could I have made different choices? Could I have avoided becoming further embroiled in Lucifer's machinations?

No matter how I replayed the last four months, it seemed that the only choices I could have made were the ones that I did. From the moment Ramuell had killed Patrick to the moment that led me here, there wasn't anything else I could have done. At least, I didn't see how.

Nathaniel landed on the beach beside me. I jumped about four feet in the air.

"Are you crazy?" I said. "What's with the ninja act?"

"I am sorry," he said, smiling a little. "I did not think to announce my presence."

"Next time bring a bullhorn," I said. "I could have taken your head off."

"You were not even holding your sword," Nathaniel said. "What has become of J.B. and Amarantha?"

I gave him an edited version of events, leaving out the details of my argument with J.B. Nathaniel seemed to read between the lines, though he didn't say anything.

"What happened at the house? You didn't kill Bryson, did you?" I said.

"No," Nathaniel said. "All of the Agents were safely returned to the Agency. They are not happy, but they are not harmed."

"What did you do?"

"I took away their weapons, tied them up and then

deposited them on the Agency's front step," Nathaniel said. "Then I followed you here."

"How did you find me?" I asked.

Nathaniel caressed my cheek. "I would be able to find you even if you crossed all the worlds, Madeline. The spell we performed, the one that bound our powers—it bound us together. Can you not feel it?"

I could, but I'd thought it was nothing more than lust. Now I knew it was more than that, that Nathaniel and I were connected on a deeper level than I realized. He would always be with me, and I with him.

He bent his head to mine, kissed me, and as our passion surged so did our power. A pulse of magic emitted from our entwined bodies.

And a pulse answered us.

We broke apart, staring at the lake. Far out, beyond the breakers, the water was bubbling and surging. Something big was rising up.

"Alerian," I breathed.

I took a step backward, and so did Nathaniel. He grabbed my hand and held it tight. The water was rising up into a column, and there was a sense that something of impossible size was beneath the water. Green mist rose from the surface of the lake once more, except this time it poured off in a continual fog.

That fog didn't stay confined to the lake but drifted out to the sand, onto the path, onto Lake Shore Drive and beyond. The drive was silent, the cars still abandoned. The city had not even begun to rebuild itself yet, and here was another monster.

A huge tentacle emerged from the column of water. It lashed the breakers, smashing the rock into a million tiny pieces. The creature surged forward, emerging from the column and moving toward the shore. Everywhere I looked there were arms, huge squid-like arms. The rest of his body was still submerged, and I sincerely hoped it stayed that way. If I saw all of him, I might start gibbering.

"That's Alerian?" I said faintly.

"Bit of a show-off, isn't he?" said Lucifer from behind my shoulder. "I'd say he read Lovecraft once and never got over it, but he went to sleep eons before Lovecraft was born."

"How did he manage to hide in the lake without anyone ever discovering him?" I said. "He's enormous."

"He doesn't have to stay that size," Puck said from the other side of Nathaniel. "As my dear brother says, Alerian is a show-off. He's displaying his true form for no other reason than he can."

I looked askance at Puck. "Are you saying that you and Lucifer have forms other than these?"

Puck winked at me. "That's for me to know and you to find out."

"I don't really want to know," I said.

"I'll thank you not to wink at my granddaughter," Lucifer said.

Puck leaned around Nathaniel so he could get a good look at Lucifer. I swear I could see the two of them bristling like cats, their tails getting puffy and indignant.

"She's my niece," Puck said. "And Alerian's."

"As Nathaniel is my nephew," Lucifer said silkily.

"Stay away from my son," Puck said.

"Stay away from my granddaughter," Lucifer replied.

"Shut *up*, the two of you," I said. "He's coming out of the water."

"You know he's only rising because of you," Puck said to Lucifer. "If you had stayed out of the dead world, then he probably would have slept forever."

"How do you know it's not your fault?" Lucifer said. "The awakening of Nathaniel's power would have been just as noticeable as anything I did."

"I noticed Madeline has some lovely new wings," Puck said.

"Stop trying to pin this on me," Lucifer said. "We'll both have to deal with him now, whoever is responsible."

The first enormous tentacle slapped onto the shore. Nathaniel and I scooted back a little farther, until our feet scraped the surface of the bike path.

Puck and Lucifer walked forward, although they were both careful to keep a sufficient amount of distance between them. The only sibling hatred that I knew of to rival theirs was Antares' hatred of me. I was sure the only thing that stopped the two of them from actively trying to kill each other was some arcane law of the universe that bound them.

A second tentacle followed the first. The majority of Alerian's body was still far from shore. That's how big he was. His tentacles were slapping up on the beach and most of him was still submerged several feet out in the deeper water. He stopped moving as Lucifer and Puck approached.

Nathaniel and I moved forward again, cautiously.

Then two things happened at once.

Therion came flying out of the darkness, fangs bared, obviously intent on me.

Alerian coiled one huge tentacle around the vampire king and squeezed. There was a sickening *pop* as Therion was crushed into two pieces. Alerian threw Therion onto the beach. The upper half of Therion tried to turn over and crawl away.

"He's a vampire, you idiot," Puck said. "You've got to behead him or set him on fire."

In response, Alerian grabbed Therion around the neck with one tentacle and around the remains of his waist with the other and pulled the vampire king's head off like a cork.

"Ah," I said, feeling sick to my stomach. "That takes care of that problem, then."

The tentacles receded into the water, and the fog dissipated. For a moment I hoped that Alerian would go back to sleep, having woken just long enough to save me from the belated vengeance of the vampire king.

But my luck didn't run that way.

A moment after the giant squid arms disappeared, a third figure stood on the beach with Lucifer and Puck.

I dropped Nathaniel's hand, moving closer so I could see Alerian clearly.

He had blue-green hair, like seaweed, drawn back in a long queue. His eyes were the same color. His face was handsome, and he wore a suit that looked as though it had been tailored for him. There was none of Puck's impishness about him, nor of Lucifer's smooth control. Even with the trappings of civilization on him, Alerian seemed wilder than the other two. More untamed. More dangerous.

And according to Puck, Daharan was worse than all of them put together. I definitely did not want to meet Daharan. Ever.

"Brothers," Alerian said formally. The ancient siblings stood on the sand like three points of a triangle, a precise amount of distance maintained.

"Alerian," Lucifer said. "You have decided to wake from your long sleep."

"What my brother wants to know is *why* you have chosen to wake," Puck corrected. "And I want to know that, too."

"What I would like to know," Alerian said, looking at

Nathaniel and me standing just outside the circle of their conference, "is what the two of you have been doing while I have been asleep."

"There's so much to tell," Lucifer said. "We should adjourn to my court where we can discuss it."

"He's not going with you so you can poison his mind with your serpent's tongue," Puck said.

"Too bad you do not have a court to offer," Lucifer said. "Pretending to be Titania's servant does have its disadvantages."

"I do not wish to go with either of you, anywhere," Alerian said. "I wish to know what you have been doing. And then I wish to spend some time with my kin."

Alerian waved his hand in the direction of Nathaniel and me.

"Um," I said. I couldn't imagine putting Alerian on the futon in the living room.

"Come forward, my niece," Alerian said imperiously. He held out his hand to me.

I didn't want this. I definitely did not want to be on the radar of another of Lucifer's relatives/enemies.

But Alerian had just saved my life. And everyone was watching me, waiting to see what I would do.

I lifted my chin. I wasn't afraid of anyone, not even a giant squid—sea god—thing. I took his hand.

He drew me close to him, stared deep into my eyes, and I was drowning.

I could taste the salt of the ocean, feel the freedom of the water, the pressure of its depths. The waves crashed against me, crashed against the shore.

Someone was pulling me, tugging me out of the water.

I stumbled backward, Nathaniel's hands on my shoulders, gasping for breath.

Alerian stared at Nathaniel. His face was impassive. I couldn't tell whether he was shocked or impressed that Nathaniel had pulled me away. Puck and Lucifer both appeared stunned.

"Yes," Alerian said finally. "I will be spending some time with the two of you. But for now, I must speak with my brothers."

We were dismissed. I can't say that I was sorry to go. I wasn't sure what had happened there with Alerian, but it was as if I were being drawn inside him, smothered by the sea.

Nathaniel was quiet as we flew home. I wasn't feeling particularly chatty myself. We had been through a lot in the last few days, even for people who were accustomed to being in constant mortal peril.

We landed on the front lawn. I looked at him, and he at me.

"Now what?" I said.

"Now we eat pancakes," Nathaniel said.

"You can cook pancakes?" I said as we walked inside. There was no noise from Samiel's apartment.

"Who said anything about cooking them?" he said.

I gave a short laugh as we climbed the stairs. "That's not usually the way you ask a woman to cook for you."

He stopped me with a tug on my arm. His eyes were full of heat. "I could convince you, I am sure."

"I'm sure you could," I said breathlessly. "But if you do that, I'm not sure how much cooking would get done."

"Oh, there would still be pancakes," Nathaniel said. "Eventually."

I tried not to be sad, not to think about Gabriel, not to think about the fact that Nathaniel didn't smell like Gabriel, that cinnamon sweetness that was always in the air around him. Couldn't I forget for a little while? Wouldn't that be all right, for me to stop hurting every second of the day?

I pulled Nathaniel up with me, almost broke down the door trying to open it. We had just stepped inside when the phone rang.

"Let it go," Nathaniel murmured.

"It might be . . ." *Samiel. Beezle.* I didn't need to say it.

Nathaniel nodded, and I went to the side table to pick up the phone.

"Maddy," J.B. said. He was breathless. He sounded like he was running.

"What do you want?" I said.

"You have to get out of the house—now," he said.

"Why?"

I was facing the front window, the portable phone tucked under my ear. A strange black shadow slid across the surface of the glass, like an oil slick.

"Sokolov has sent the Retrievers after you," J.B. said. "You have to go. You have to go now."

The side window in the living room was drenched in the same shadow. So were the ones in the dining room. I ran through the house, looking for an escape, but there was none. The things looked like nothing more than black liquid, but I could feel their hate. They wanted me, and they would not leave without me.

"It's too late," I said, backing into the dining room. I felt Nathaniel's arms close around me.

"They're already here."

What good is an Agent of death
when the dead won't leave?

FROM AUTHOR
CHRISTINA HENRY

BLACK
HOWL

A BLACK WINGS NOVEL

Something is wrong with the souls of Chicago's dead.
Ghosts are walking the streets, and Agent of death Madeline Black's boss wants her to figure out why. And while
work is bad enough, Maddy has a plethora of personal
problems, too. Now that Gabriel has been assigned as her
thrall, their relationship has hit an impasse. At least her
sleazy ex-fiancé, Nathaniel, is out of the picture—or so
she thinks . . .

"A gutsy heroine."
—Nancy Holzner

christinahenry.net
facebook.com/ProjectParanormalBooks
penguin.com

M1138T0712

An Agent of death
should know when her time is up.

FROM
CHRISTINA HENRY

BLACK
NIGHT

A BLACK WINGS NOVEL

If obstinate dead people were all that Maddy had to worry about, life would be much easier. But the best-laid plans of Agents and fallen angels often go awry. Deaths are occurring contrary to the natural order, Maddy's being stalked by foes inside and outside of her family, and her two loves—her bodyguard, Gabriel, and her doughnut-loving gargoyle, Beezle—have disappeared. But because Maddy is Lucifer's granddaughter, things are expected of her, things like delicate diplomatic missions to other realms.

penguin.com
facebook.com/ProjectParanormalBooks